The Mudlark Murders

A Victorian Historical Murder Mystery

Book 2 of
The Field & Greystone Series

Lana Williams

USA Today Bestselling Author

Copyright © 2024 by Lana Williams

Ebook: 979-8-9914769-2-8
Print: 979-8-9914769-3-5

All rights reserved.

By payment of required fees, you have been granted the *non*-exclusive, *non*-transferable right to access and read the text of this book. No part of this text may be reproduced, transmitted, downloaded, decompiled, reverse engineered, or stored in or introduced into any information storage and retrieval system, in any form or by any means, whether electronic or mechanical, now known or hereinafter invented without the express written permission of copyright owner.

Please Note

The reverse engineering, uploading, and/or distributing of this book via the internet or via any other means without the permission of the copyright owner is illegal and punishable by law. Please purchase only authorized electronic editions, and do not participate in or encourage electronic piracy of copyrighted materials. Your support of the author's rights is appreciated.

No part of this book may be reproduced or transmitted in any form or by any electronic or mechanical means, including photocopying, recording or by any information storage and retrieval system, without the written permission of the publisher, except where permitted by law.

Thank you.

Cover Art by The Killion Group

Mysteries by Lana Williams

The Field & Greystone Series:
The Ravenkeeper's Daughter, Book 1
The Mudlark Murders, Book 2
The Gravesend Murder, Book 3

One

London 1883

Nora ran as fast as her ten-year-old legs would carry her. As fast as the terrible pain in her stomach allowed. Heart pounding and chest heaving, she flew along the dark street, oblivious to the cold November air.

A door slammed in the distance followed by footsteps pounding on the pavement behind her. "Nora! Come back at once!"

The voice sent chills down her spine, and she ran harder. Not until she rounded the next corner and yet another did she ease her pace. A strangled whimper escaped her lips as her steps slowed, and her lungs burned. Cramps like knives stabbed her stomach, threatening to bend her over, worsening with every second. Never had she felt such horrible pain.

She shouldn't have gone to the fancy house. Shouldn't have believed it possible to change her future—to reach for the stars.

Those people had tempted her with their pretty words and fine manners. "Come with us," they'd said. "A girl like you deserves better than scrabbling in the mud of the riverbank in search of rubbish."

The offer to train as a maid had been exciting. To work in a grand house with a bed of her own and regular meals was beyond tempting. She was weary of always being hungry and feeling unwanted. And hadn't she always thought herself better and smarter than the other mudlarks?

Nora didn't intend to remain one forever. She had dreams; big ones. But after cholera claimed her mother two years past, leaving her alone, she had to do something to eat. Flowersellers were a close-knit bunch, hiring only daughters as they rarely trusted outsiders, so that wasn't an option. Nor did she care to steal. Not every day, at any rate. Finding treasures on the mudflats by Blackfriars had been exciting at first, an adventure of sorts. Yet soon her back ached, the stench of the river never left her nose, and the mud had seeped into her skin.

She didn't notice much of that anymore. At least, that was what she told herself until the offer to leave it behind had come.

"I should've told Carl where I was goin' 'stead of sneakin' off like a thief in the night," she whispered to herself. Her boss would be angry with her when she returned, but once he learned what happened, he'd be angry with *them*.

She pressed a hand to her roiling stomach as the urge to vomit took hold. Maybe that would help get rid of what ailed her.

Nora paused in an alleyway and slumped against the brick wall. The stench of rotten vegetables and human waste, along with the wrenching belly pains, were enough to have her vomiting.

Once she'd emptied her stomach, she wiped her mouth with the back of her hand, hoping to feel some relief. None came. She felt worse than ever, her skin clammy yet hot, her body drained of energy.

A rat scurried past, startling her, its form barely visible in the dim glow of a nearby gas streetlight. The building she leaned against tilted alarmingly.

She blinked to clear the dizziness, shoving away from the wall to return to the street, staggering with the effort. She couldn't give in to the exhaustion tugging at her.

Not when she needed to warn the others.

After sucking in a shaky breath of the cold night air and rubbing her bare arms—where was her cloak?—she brushed past the few people out on the street, too scared to ask for help.

Running was out of the question, her feet instead stumbling toward home. She trembled, the dizziness yet to subside.

The moment she had been invited to sit at the table where she'd placed the fine china and crystal goblets should've warned her something was amiss. She'd known she didn't belong there, yet still she remained, unable to resist the lure of the appetizing meal and the fancy setting.

"There's a pretty girl," a man cooed as he staggered toward her in the moonlight. "How 'bout a tussle?"

"Leave off," Nora bit out as she straightened to hurry past him, pulse racing.

"Don't be like that." He reached for her and caught hold of her arm, tearing the faded fabric of her best dress. "I only want to make ye feel good."

"No!" She jerked away and quickened her pace as tears filled her eyes. Sobs soon followed and her body shuddered with them as fear seeped into her bones just like the mud.

Something was terribly wrong. A weakness filled her limbs, and it was becoming all she could do to place one foot in front of the other.

Only the thought of her friends, Agnes and Pudge, kept her going. Charlie, too. She had to warn them not to make her mistake.

The house just off Carey Street had not been as fancy as those in Mayfair, but the food had been just as delicious. They'd served wine, too, encouraging her to eat and drink her fill since she was their only guest. She hadn't liked how they watched her but thought they wanted to see if she had good manners. Her tears fell harder at how proud she'd been to have remembered what her mother taught her, how pleased her mother would have been.

Had they put something in her food or drink? She could not tell, not having eaten such dishes before. They'd been much different than the simple fare to which she was accustomed.

It had not been long after they'd finished dinner and she'd helped to clear the table that the cramps had started. Fear crept over her, and the urge to escape had taken hold.

She should've listened to the skin crawls she'd experienced upon arriving, the creepy feeling coming over her too frequently to ignore throughout the evening.

Hadn't Pudge always told her to listen to that feeling—how it would save her? She had to tell Pudge she was right.

Feet faltering and head spinning, the buildings gave way to the mudflats and Nora breathed a sigh of relief. Home wasn't far now. She could make it. Carl wouldn't be angry when he saw how sick she was. Charlie could fetch Pudge and Agnes, and they'd help her, even if Carl wouldn't.

Yet each step was harder than the last, the dizziness adding to her nausea as malaise set in. Maybe she wouldn't go all the way home. She'd rest first. It wouldn't be so terrible if she slept under the stars. The night was frigid, but the cold air felt good against her flushed skin.

The lure of the River Thames lapped at her, a familiar sight that opened its dark arms in a welcome embrace. Moonlight glimmered on its surface, like a path toward the heavens, beckoning her.

Nora stumbled once, twice, the third time taking her to her knees in the cold mud along the riverbank. Yes, she would rest for now. She was close to home. Her friends would find her come morning.

She fell onto her back, the stars swinging above worsening her unsettled stomach, and she closed her eyes.

So tired. She licked her dry lips, wishing for a bit of water to quench her thirst.

Her breath shuddered as tears returned. A deep knowing gripped her. Death was coming for her, and there was nothing she could do to fight it. Not when each breath required effort.

Nora opened her eyes once more, blinked away her tears, and turned her head to see the river. Would anyone care that a mudlark had died? Would they ever find the ones who had done this to her?

She reached into her pocket and pulled out the pretty crystal perfume bottle she'd taken from the kitchen of the fancy house, clutching it tight in her fist.

She closed her eyes again, fear easing as an image of her mother appeared. "M-Mama?"

The familiar face stretched out a hand in welcome, a smile curving her lips. Nora sighed as she reached for her mother, pleased not to be alone any longer.

Two

Amelia Greystone gripped the barge's rail as the wind caught its rust-red sails, sending the large, flat boat skimming across the water. Exuberance rushed through her, a feeling she hadn't experienced in a long time.

"Hold tight, Mrs. Greystone," Captain Booth called with a grin. "She's moving us quick today." He'd told her the barges could sail up to twelve knots per hour, but she hadn't realized how fast that was until this moment.

The River Thames might be known for its stench, tides, and murky depths which hid all manner of refuse, but today? It was magical.

The wind tugged at her cloak, sending it flapping about her. Luckily, Amelia had pinned her hat on with care and secured it with a ribbon beneath her chin for just such an event.

She stood at the front—the bow, she corrected herself—of *Venture* and soaked in the moment: the sights, the sounds, the feelings, hoping she could do them justice in her article for *London Life*.

Never could she have guessed that her position as a correspondent for the periodical would lead to a morning like this. How lucky she was to have been given this assignment.

Captain Richard Booth was proving to be delightful company and an easy person to interview. He tugged on the wheel, his brown cap low on his brow. A red kerchief knotted at his throat lent him a jaunty appearance. Lines marked his tanned face, making his age difficult to determine though she considered him perhaps in his late thirties.

The annual barge race held each summer was a tradition Londoners had enjoyed since 1863. The race was meant to show the advantages of the burly barges to the public and provided an entertaining competition for the captains, as well.

"As I was saying," Booth continued with an eye on the river ahead, "the barges ferry enormous loads, including coal, bricks, timber, and rubbish among other things, and have done so for decades. Though steamships have taken some of our business, you can see why the barges are still used given the speed with which they move up the river despite their heavy loads."

"Impressive." Amelia committed all he said to memory, not wanting to release her hold on the railing to retrieve her notebook.

"They are built with good English oak, often cut green, and have flat-bottomed hulls, making them effective in the shallow waters of the estuary. Not many boats can say that. They can be docked shoreside, even in the mud, to load or unload. They float in as little as three feet of water and are capable of sailing farther afield."

"It's truly amazing." Amelia grinned as the wind billowed the sails.

Captain Booth laughed, the carefree sound swept away on the stiff breeze. Amelia shared a smile with him, appreciating that he still enjoyed the thrill. How wonderful to experience this every day. What a gift that would be.

"Do you take cargo to other countries?" she asked.

He shook his head. "A barge is unlikely to go that far, though I don't think I would want to even if I could. I prefer to remain in England. Nothing but trouble abroad."

Before she could ask why he believed that, they neared the mudflats close to Blackfriars, and Captain Booth turned away to wave at two rather bedraggled-looking girls searching for bits and bobs in the mud to sell.

"Mudlarks," he said by way of explanation as the girls returned his wave.

Each carried a bag with a leather shoulder strap to hold their finds and a stick with which they were digging, their clothing already adorned with mud.

The sight hurt her heart, thinking of how cold and miserable they must be by day's end.

Some of her concern must've shown on her face as the captain shook his head, seeming resigned to their presence. "The tidal river uncovers the banks each day and brings both refuse and treasures near the surface. The dark mud preserves items remarkably well, and those with the tenacity to search might find items dating back to Roman times."

Though she didn't like to think of how difficult their lives were, their discoveries might be an interesting story for the magazine and aid them in the process. Amelia made a mental note to mention the idea to her editor.

Captain Booth frowned as the girls moved toward a mound on the shore a short distance from them. He gestured for his first mate to ease back on the sails to slow their speed as he watched the pair.

"What is it?" Amelia asked as she carefully made her way toward him, the unsteady movement of the barge foreign beneath her feet.

"Looks as if Agnes and Pudge found a body." He shook his head, lips twisting to the side with displeasure. "Though I'm sure it's not the first time, the girls shouldn't have to see such a sight."

Based on his calm reaction, the captain must've witnessed a similar discovery on more than one occasion.

Alarm filled Amelia as she watched the two squat next to something that appeared to be a small form, though at this distance, it was difficult to tell. Her breath caught as one girl scrambled back, nearly losing her balance in the mud.

Had the child not realized what it was until she'd got close—or was there another reason for her surprise?

The other girl remained near the still form and bowed her head, hands clasped together as if she prayed for whoever it was.

"Apologies, Mrs. Greystone, but I have to cut our time short." Captain Booth's eyes held on the two figures. "Someone has to help those girls."

"Of course," she readily agreed. "There isn't an adult watching over them?" She searched the shore for a parent or a supervisor or the like.

The captain scoffed. "No. They have an aunt and uncle, or so they claim, but the girls are on their own more often than not. I help them when I can, usually with a meal or two each week. I tend to suspect they're orphans, but it's hard to know when they won't say."

Amelia should have guessed as much. London could be a cruel place for a child, even more so if they were on their own. "Perhaps we should alert a constable."

"I suppose." Captain Booth shook his head. "Though...it depends on who it is and how it happened."

Amelia bit back a protest. Surely he knew best; the man was familiar with this part of the river. Bodies must wash up on the shores of the Thames more often than they should.

They sailed back to the dock where he and his two men secured the barge with practiced ease. Though Amelia told herself to take note of his movements for her article, her thoughts were with the girls and the body they'd discovered.

The pair looked to be between ten and twelve years of age, though it was difficult to tell at this distance and with such muddy faces. Definitely too young to bear witness to such a sight.

Amelia knew firsthand that children couldn't always be protected from the harshness of life. A girl she'd guess to be close in age to the two mudlarks had recently stayed with her for a time. Maeve, the daughter of the ravenkeeper at the Tower of London, had witnessed her father's murder before her very eyes, an unthinkable tragedy for a child—particularly one who was deaf and mute so had no easy way to communicate the horror she'd seen.

Amelia said a silent prayer for Maeve, now living with her aunt and uncle in the countryside. The aunt had recently sent a letter to advise that Maeve was adjusting well to her new life and enjoying time with her cousins. Though pleased by the news, Amelia missed the girl's quiet presence, though only two weeks had passed since her departure. Her house felt incredibly empty of late. She had been tempted to ask if Maeve wanted to remain with her in London, but the girl was better off with family, and other young children to play with.

Amelia blew out a breath. In truth, she missed the way Maeve had reminded her of her own daughter, Lily, who'd died three years ago from scarlet fever. Allowing others in after losing Lily and then her husband, Matthew, a year ago had not been easy. But Maeve had touched her deeply, the girl's silent world drawing her sympathy. The child had proven her resilience more than once, and that had given Amelia reason to think the girl would thrive no matter what else life tossed at her.

If only she could believe the same about herself.

Captain Booth stepped off the barge and offered her a hand. "If you would like to wait a few minutes, I will know better how long this will take."

THE MUDLARK MURDERS

"Would you mind if I accompanied you?" Amelia asked. At the captain's doubtful look, she added, "I am not squeamish, and I would like to help if I can."

"If you're sure. I wouldn't want you to be overly upset by the scene." He lifted a brow, his protectiveness touching. The tall captain was broad of chest, his boots planted wide as if still bracing himself against the motion of the barge.

"I am sure."

He gave an approving nod and led the way down the dock and around to the mudflats. The girls still stood near the body, clearly uncertain what to do next. That alone was enough to make Amelia pleased she'd joined the captain. The poor mites.

"Agnes. Pudge. What's happened?" he called to the girls as they drew near.

They turned their tear-streaked faces to watch them approach. The taller one pointed to the body and shook her head, lips pressed tight to keep from crying.

The other girl, slightly shorter, sniffed. "It's N-Nora."

Amelia caught her breath at the sight of the small body.

A young girl of a similar age to the pair lay on her back, eyes staring unseeing at the sky. Her face was pale, and her thin form was impossibly still.

Amelia looked away, images of her own Lily taking hold. She pressed a hand to her racing heart and blinked to clear her thoughts. The girls needed help, not a distraught strange woman caught up in her memories.

"Do you know what happened?" Captain Booth asked as he squatted beside the dead girl.

"N-No," the taller one answered. "We haven't seen her since yesterday."

"She's truly...gone?" the other one asked as she stared at their friend.

"I'm afraid so." The captain's voice was quiet as he reached out to shut the girl's eyes. His gaze raked over the body. "No obvious sign as to the cause. Had she been ill?"

"No." The two girls answered too quickly and shared a look, making Amelia wonder if they knew more than they were saying.

"Why don't we send for the constable to help?" Amelia suggested. She was no expert, but it seemed unlikely Nora had died peacefully. A bit of dried vomit was visible in the corner of her mouth and had splashed on the toe of one shoe. Something was definitely amiss.

Amelia knew it might be unusual for a woman to notice such details in the face of such tragedy, but her study of science, chemistry in particular, had trained her to search for anything out of place. Details mattered. Details told the true story.

Once a policeman arrived, she'd request Scotland Yard Inspector Henry Field be sent for. He'd know what to do.

After all, murder was his business.

Three

Henry Field walked alongside a constable toward Blackfriars where the body of a young girl had apparently been discovered, curious why his presence had been requested.

One could make certain assumptions about the victim if she'd been found in this area near the Thames, though he tried not to. Children on the streets faced all manner of challenges and tragedies, from those of their own making to ill-treatment at the hands of adults. Orphans, and those without siblings, were especially at risk.

Unfortunately bodies of all ages washed up far too often on the riverbank. Some were accidents, a few were murder victims, and others chose to end their lives in the murky waters of the Thames.

But they were rarely children.

"It's just over here, Inspector." Constable Gibbons was relatively new to the force, and this was the first time Henry had worked with him.

It? Henry grimaced at the term. "You mean the child?" he corrected.

"Er, yes, sir. Sorry, Inspector."

Clearly the man had never worked a case with a child as a witness before. Then again, Henry hadn't either until recently.

That one had reminded Henry of their value when the only witness to a murder had been a young girl. A *resourceful* young girl, he reminded himself, smiling at the thought of Maeve.

The slippery mud as they neared the shore made walking a challenge. However, he knew its consistency was ideal for preserving items. He well remembered finding clay pipes from centuries past when he was a boy. In the distance, he could see mudlarks working even now.

Henry looked up only to halt in surprise at the sight of a familiar form standing amongst the group near the victim.

He hadn't expected to see Amelia Greystone quite so soon.

Pleasure washed through him at the sight of her neat and tidy appearance. She wore a black cloak over her usual gray gown, a nod to her status as a widow, but that didn't detract from her pleasant appearance.

Her presence explained why he'd been called to the scene.

Nearly a fortnight had passed since he'd last seen her after they'd finally solved the ravenkeeper's murder and she'd helped to ensure Maeve's safety. While hesitant to call Mrs. Greystone a friend, he liked to think they were moving in that direction. She had proved more than helpful during the recent murder investigation.

However, one insurmountable issue stood between them—the unsolved murder of her husband a year ago, a case that weighed heavily on Henry. He smothered a sigh as he resumed his steady pace.

Now wasn't the time to worry about it. Not when another victim required his attention.

"Good afternoon, Mrs. Greystone." Henry allowed his gaze to hold briefly on Amelia before taking in the three others as he nodded in greeting, already wondering about their relationship to the deceased.

"Inspector Field." Amelia smiled, despite the grim circumstances. "I'm pleased you were able to come."

Her greeting delighted him more than it should. He nodded and shifted his attention to the body, remorse filling him at the sight of the young girl. Amelia didn't need another reminder of the death of her own daughter, yet fate seemed determined to continually toss one to her.

"Who do we have here?" he asked as he squatted beside the girl, careful not to touch her until he'd looked over the area thoroughly.

"Nora." The man who stood next to Amelia looked to be a sailor or the like, based on his clothing and his tanned complexion. He shook his head. "Can't say that I know her last name."

"And you are?" Henry asked, withdrawing a notebook from his pocket.

"Richard Booth." He gestured toward the dock where a barge was tied up. "Captain of the *Venture*."

"Ah, your interview?" He looked at Amelia for confirmation, and she nodded. She'd mentioned the story for the magazine when they'd last spoken. He wrote down the captain's name. "Your relationship to the...girl?" He hesitated to call her a victim when he had yet to see any sign of foul play.

"Well." The man shrugged. "An acquaintance, I suppose." He gestured to the two girls standing silent nearby, their gazes riveted on the body. "I see the mudlarks regularly as I sail by and have come to know some of them."

The pale, distraught faces of the two girls suggested they'd known the dead girl well.

"Their names?" Henry asked, uncertain if they were following the conversation or were too shocked to do so.

"Agnes and Pudge," Captain Booth supplied, pointing first to the taller girl and then the shorter one.

The girls looked up at their names, the taller one staring at Henry.

"Who d-did this to her?" Agnes asked, lower lip trembling.

Henry's chest tightened at her question, sorry for her distress when her life was already clearly so harsh. Yet he had no answer and wasn't sure he would, as no indications of injury were visible thus far. What appeared to be vomit crusted at the corner of her mouth, but there were no other signs of trauma. "She was in good health when you last saw her?"

The tall girl—Agnes, was it?—nodded. "Just yesterday afternoon. She left a bit early. Said she had somethin' to take care of." The girl shook her head as she gestured toward the body. "Must've been important fer her to dress like that."

Only then did Henry realize the dress must've been one of Nora's best. Or her *only* best. The faded red cotton fabric with tiny white flowers stretched taut across her chest as if she'd nearly outgrown it. He glanced at the two girls, noting their plain brown woven tunics. One didn't wear nice clothes to dig in the mud.

Deciding it was best to try to determine what had happened to the girl before he asked more questions, he studied the victim more closely for any obvious wounds but still avoided touching her.

Her pale face held a faint blue tinge, though that could be from the cold night. A drop of dried vomit was visible on the toe of her worn shoe. One sleeve was torn, though thin as the fabric appeared to be, it wouldn't take much to rip it. Her brown hair had come loose from a single braid that lay along one shoulder.

From the appearance of the body, she had been there most of the night. She wore no cloak or shawl. No hat. One shoe was missing but a quick glance around showed it a few steps away as if it had come off in the mud and she hadn't bothered to retrieve it.

Henry rose and walked slowly around the body, but no other footprints were indented in the mud. Of course, they would've been washed away when the tide came in. "Gibbons, follow the footprints to locate where she entered the mudflats."

"Yes, sir." The constable nodded and slowly followed them, pausing once or twice as if losing track in a few places.

Henry returned his attention to the girl—Nora, he must remember her name. Her arms were at her sides, her hands in loose fists. A glint of something in one hand caught the weak sunlight. With care, he opened her stiff fingers and found a small crystal perfume bottle. He took it, holding the container up to the light but finding it empty.

"Was this something she might have found in the mud?" he asked the girls.

They both shook their heads. "Too clean," Pudge offered.

Henry retrieved a handkerchief to wrap it in, then tucked it in his pocket and continued the examination. He gently lifted one of her shoulders to roll her onto her side to look for signs of injury but there were none. Next, he ran his fingers over her scalp in search of a bump or the like. Again, he found nothing. How odd.

"Does she have family?" he asked the girls.

The shorter one remained silent and still, but the taller girl said, "Only us. She's one of Carl's, but he ain't family."

"Carl?"

Booth cleared his throat. "He runs a group of mudlarks and splits the profit with them." His expression suggested he had doubts about the arrangement.

"There's no one else?" Henry asked, heart heavy as his gaze briefly met Amelia's. No wonder she'd stayed to see the situation through. The world needed more like Amelia Greystone.

"Her mum died a couple of years ago," the shorter girl, Pudge, supplied in a quiet voice.

"How long have you known her?" Henry asked.

The two looked at one another. "Four years or more," Agnes said. "We knew her mum, too."

Henry glanced around, wondering what might have brought her to the mudflats in the dark—though the moon had been well over half full last night, enough light to see the way, especially if one was familiar with the area.

He looked back to Nora's still form. She was reed thin, much like the girls who stood nearby. What had the tide already washed away that might've helped determine what happened to her?

Constable Gibbons paused at where the mud gave way to the street and waved his hand to signal that was where her path entered the mudflats.

Henry nodded, deciding he'd have a look on his way out. The area near the dock was rough with numerous businesses along the street and a tavern or two. No obvious clues would be there. Plenty of eyes but all would swear they saw nothing, something he knew from experience.

While it seemed unlikely the girl had succumbed to a sudden illness in less than a day, such things happened. The vomit suggested as much. With no obvious trauma, there was no indication of foul play. Just a tragedy that happened all too often.

He pushed to his feet, aware the group around him wouldn't like what he had to say. But such decisions weren't his to make.

"We'll have her taken to the morgue," he began, hesitating to offer anything more.

"And then what?" Amelia asked, brow furrowed as if she sensed what he was going to say.

He hated having to disappoint her when he'd already done so. How could she see anything other than the man who'd failed to solve her husband's murder when she looked at him?

He shifted on his feet in the mud, pushing away the thought. "Difficult to say. The coroner will take a look." Hopefully. He knew Mr. Taylor's caseload was heavier than his own and didn't want to mislead Amelia or the others. "As terrible as it sounds the death of someone, even a child, living on the streets is not unusual. I can't promise an investigation will follow." Henry studied the girl again. "It's a pity." His gaze swung to meet those of the two girls. "I'm sorry you lost a friend."

Agnes nodded, but Pudge's attention remained fixed on the victim.

"We appreciate anything you can do, Henry." Amelia's steadfast gaze suggested she expected more than what he'd offered.

Unfortunately, he didn't think he could provide it.

Four

I can't promise an investigation will follow.

Henry's words circled through Amelia's mind after he departed to pursue another case. She stewed over the comment upon returning home, all evening and into the night. She could not shake it, no matter what she tried.

While she appreciated his honesty, no one should die so unexpectedly without someone discovering the cause and providing closure for those who knew the deceased. She understood that all too well.

The shock and despair on Agnes and Pudge's faces had pinched her heart, yet clearly they hadn't been surprised by Henry's comment. It was almost as if they'd expected it. The resigned look the girls shared had been laced with fear and made Amelia wonder if they were frightened for their own lives.

What if they had reason to be? How would anyone know for certain unless the young girl's death was investigated?

"I trust you slept well, Mrs. Greystone?" Fernsby, her longtime butler, asked as Amelia ventured downstairs the next morning. His upright bearing and tall frame belied his gray hair, but it was the kindness and good humor in his brown eyes that never failed to warm her.

"I did not." She had already told him of Nora's fate and Henry's involvement upon her return home the previous day.

"I am sorry to hear that." He shook his head. "I confess that what you shared with us disturbed Mrs. Fernsby and myself as well."

His wife served as housekeeper, and Amelia didn't know what she would do without the older couple. They were far more than servants to her. They'd become a family of sorts, along with Yvette, the maid. Their steadfastness and support, especially over the past few years, as well as that of her parents, had allowed Amelia to regain a semblance of her footing after first Lily and then Matthew's deaths. They had encouraged her to pursue her interests when otherwise she might have sunk into melancholia.

"Perhaps you will be able to spend time in your laboratory later," he suggested. "That tends to lift your spirits."

"Yes, it does." Her attic laboratory was one of her greatest joys and where she found peace. But at her parents' insistence, she also sought activities that took her out of the house to interact with others, including her position as a special correspondent for the magazine.

However, after days like yesterday, she questioned whether the position was worth the upheaval it caused. A previous interview with the ravenkeeper had resulted in her involvement in the man's murder investigation. Would it happen again with the mudlark?

"I think what upsets me is that I fear little will be done about it." She shouldn't be disappointed if Henry couldn't pursue the case. The death of an orphan was not unusual, yet it bothered her all the same.

Amelia would've liked to speak with the coroner herself to ask him to look for poison. Between the small bottle in the girl's hand and the vomit, not to mention the faint tinge of blue around her lips, she couldn't get the idea of poison out of her mind. If only she'd thought of it before Henry had departed. She was hardly an expert in such things, and she hadn't seen many dead people. Yet still, questions—and suspicions—circled in her mind, refusing to let go.

"Perhaps Inspector Field will discover the cause of the child's death," Fernsby suggested.

The inspector had earned the butler's respect for his considerate treatment of Amelia after Matthew's death, and that had doubled when the ravenkeeper had been murdered and Maeve had come to stay with Amelia for a time. Henry had done more than they expected to protect them, including watching over the household himself.

"I'm sure he has more pressing cases to see to than that of an orphan with nothing to her name, but something should be done." Amelia was to meet with Captain Booth later that morning to continue their interview from the previous day. "Perhaps I can speak with the other two girls again when I meet with the barge captain."

"Do take care," Fernsby said with a worried look. "It sounds as if something foul might be afoot given the unusual circumstances."

"I will." She smiled. "Though few look twice at a widow." Her attire was often a disguise of sorts, a barrier between herself and others. In truth, she welcomed that distance, which allowed her to choose when she wanted to interact with others and when she didn't.

Too often, she didn't.

Grief had taken more out of her than friends and acquaintances realized. Widowed and childless yet still so young, she had lost her purpose and had allowed the label of widow to take over her identity.

"If I may say so, you are more than that, madam." Fernsby offered a stately bow when Amelia thanked him for his kind words.

While she liked to think she was rediscovering herself, progress was slow. Fernsby's reminder bolstered her confidence.

She continued down to the kitchen for breakfast, taking comfort in the familiar routine.

Her house on Bloomsbury Street matched the others on the neat and tidy street with a redbrick exterior, three stories, and a small but lovely garden. It was too big for a woman by herself, as was the staff, but Amelia wasn't yet ready to consider moving.

She'd started the habit of eating the first meal of the day in the kitchen not long after Matthew died. Doing so provided the opportunity to speak with the staff about meals and other issues. In truth, she didn't enjoy dining alone. She missed having Maeve and Henry's company, especially in the evenings, though she didn't miss the tension and fear that had gripped the entire household for a terrifying week.

The aroma of freshly baked bread filled the air, and her stomach grumbled in response.

"Good morning, Mrs. Greystone," the cook said, nodding as she briskly stirred batter in a bowl.

"How is your morning, Mrs. Appleton?" Amelia asked.

"Quite well. I've some fresh bread if you'd like."

"Yes, please." The mouth-watering scent demanded it.

"Would you like some sausage and eggs as well?" the cook asked.

"No, thank you." She ignored the woman's frown. Mrs. Appleton tended to think she didn't eat enough but her appetite could sometimes be fickle.

"Good morning, Mrs. Greystone," Yvette said as she bustled into the room with a rag in hand and a warm smile on her narrow face. Her slender form radiated energy.

"And to you, Yvette."

The maid collected a few supplies and departed, always moving on to the next task.

Amelia rather envied the maid's routine. Tuesdays she dusted the drawing room. Wednesdays the bedrooms. Thursdays the study. That was only a small portion of her duties, but Amelia thought the routine would be comforting. One knew what was expected each day, whereas Amelia struggled with how to spend her time.

No Lily to care for. No Matthew to assist. Only her.

The hole in her heart couldn't be filled, but that didn't mean she had nothing to live for, she reminded herself. She refused to succumb to the dark thoughts that threatened. Doing so didn't bring relief and rising from the depths was too painful, not to mention difficult.

Amelia lifted her chin. *Not today.* She'd learned it was best to take each day as it came. One battle at a time. Better to stay busy and keep her thoughts occupied on something—or someone—other than herself.

"Thank you." The plate with a slice of toasted bread placed before her brought a smile to Amelia's face, along with the cup of tea. Black for the morning. Sugar in the afternoon.

She buttered the thick slice of toast and savored a bite. "Delicious, Mrs. Appleton. As always."

The cook nodded, a hint of a smile on her face. "I'm pleased to hear it."

Simple pleasures, like freshly baked bread and a perfectly steeped cup of tea, had taken on new importance in Amelia's life. If she had to force away the faint echo of a child's giggle or a masculine tone coming from the corridor, no one else need know.

"I will be going out shortly," Amelia said, as much to herself as to Mrs. Appleton. No matter that the cook likely didn't care how she spent her day.

"Looks like a fine day for it." Mrs. Appleton tipped her head toward the window as she paused to add more ingredients to the bowl with efficient movements.

"Yes." All the more reason to step out and try to discover the reason Nora had died on the mudflats with a perfume bottle clutched in her hand.

An hour later, Amelia walked alongside Captain Booth on the dock. "Thank you for seeing me again so soon."

"My pleasure. I'm sorry our time yesterday was ended by such unfortunate circumstances."

"As am I." Amelia shook her head. "Poor Nora. I can't put her from my mind."

"She always had a smile on her face and something pleasant to say." The captain's expression took on a paternal look.

"You knew her well?"

"As well as I know any of the mudlarks." He gestured toward the mudflats. "There are several I see nearly every day. Some I have spoken to only on occasion. Others choose to keep to themselves."

"You must see many things as you traverse the river."

"Yes." He perused the length of the water up and down. "But it's the people who matter."

She nodded, appreciating the captain's sentiment.

"I can't help but wonder why Nora was dressed as she was," Amelia said, with a nervous glance at him from beneath the brim of her hat. Would he think her odd for bringing up such an inconsequential detail? "She must've gone somewhere out of the ordinary."

"I only see them when they're working, and their clothes tend to take on the same hue as the mud."

Which made it all the more unusual for Nora to be wearing her best gown.

She forced her thoughts from Nora to follow the captain to the barge, where she asked him the remaining questions she hadn't had the chance to the previous day. She jotted down notes but took care to listen carefully as well, wanting to remember not only what he shared but also his expression and gestures.

The pride he took in the barge and his work, regardless of whether the cargo he hauled was timber or rubbish, was admirable. As they finished, Amelia's attention caught on the two girls in the near distance whom she'd met yesterday.

Captain Booth followed her gaze. "Good to see them out after discovering poor Nora." He turned to look at her. "Any word from the inspector?"

"No, though I wouldn't expect it as of yet." She hoped Henry would send word if he learned anything. If he was able to pursue the situation, that was. Then again, perhaps he wouldn't since she wasn't directly involved in the case like she had been with Maeve. Surely their previous collaboration meant something to him. It certainly did to her. "Do you think I could have a word with the girls?"

"I don't see why not." He frowned. "Best not to let Carl see you speaking with them if possible. He's not particularly nice."

"I didn't think they worked for him, do they?"

"No, but he's a bit territorial about the mudflats and what happens on the banks."

Amelia nodded but already knew she also wanted the chance to speak with Carl, despite the kind man's warning. The sooner, the better. She refused to allow the mystery of Nora's death to remain unanswered and intended to do all she could to discover what happened to the girl.

Five

"Morning, Mr. Taylor." Henry paused in the doorway of the surgeon's examination room at St. Thomas' near Scotland Yard.

He had found it wise over the years to take a moment to brace himself against the stench of death—not just from the bodies the surgeon examined, but the chemicals used in the process.

He couldn't imagine why Arthur Taylor had chosen to use his skills to investigate death. Then again, some might wonder why Henry had chosen to become a detective unless they recognized his last name.

Henry's father and grandfather had also been constables and then detectives, both retiring as well-respected chief inspectors. Henry had always known what he had wanted to do, though living up to his family's reputation had proven more difficult than he'd anticipated. Unfortunately, he didn't have the same natural instincts they did.

"Field." Mr. Taylor frowned and glanced at the body on the exam table before him, a lock of dark blond hair falling onto his forehead. "Is this one of yours?"

Henry glanced at the victim but quickly averted his gaze from the pale white skin with its chest cavity pried open. "No."

His version of investigating death was preferable to the doctor's and easier on the stomach most days.

"Ah." Taylor nodded and returned his attention to the corpse. "I didn't think so. What brings you by?"

"I need a favor of sorts."

Taylor lifted a brow. "What might that be?"

"A young girl was brought to the morgue yesterday."

"I saw her on the list." He shook his head. "Too young. How unfortunate."

"Indeed. I'd like to know the cause of death."

Mr. Taylor's hands paused as he met Henry's gaze, brow furrowed. "For an orphan?"

"Yes. The circumstances were...unusual." He hesitated to call them suspicious, at least not aloud. Yet questions lingered in his mind. Why had she been on the mudflats at night dressed as she was? What had caused her to vomit? And the perfume bottle she'd held raised questions as well.

He refused to believe the girl's death remained in his thoughts only because of Amelia's involvement. However, he would readily admit he hadn't liked the disappointment that had tightened her expression when he'd expressed doubt about pursuing the girl's death.

People were murdered daily in London and not everyone received justice. There was little he could do to change that. He already had more cases than he could hope to look at, let alone solve.

Yet here he stood, asking Mr. Taylor for a favor.

"Unusual? In what way?" the surgeon asked as he continued his work.

"She was a mudlark found on the mudflats," he began.

"And?"

"She went there at night in her best dress." Henry pulled the perfume bottle from his pocket, unwrapped it, and held it up. "This was found in her hand."

"Hmm." Taylor paused, his gaze darting about the room as if searching for possible answers. "Well, I'm intrigued. What do you suspect?"

"Poison, possibly. She was seen the previous day in fine health, but vomit is visible on her lips, as well as her shoe."

Mr. Taylor frowned. "I can't imagine why anyone would bother to poison a mudlark."

"Nor can I." Though he might be wasting both his own and Mr. Taylor's time, he wanted to know what had caused the girl's death.

"I will have a look. If it's poison, it shouldn't take long to determine. Has her body been claimed?"

Henry sighed as sadness gripped his heart. If loved ones didn't claim the deceased, they were relegated to a pauper's funeral. But if the victim was claimed, the family didn't always appreciate having the body examined for a cause of death since it meant conducting an intrusive search for clues.

"I don't believe so. I would be curious about her last meal." Had she been invited somewhere—was that the reason for her choice of attire? If so, the contents of her stomach might provide a clue.

"Very well. You've piqued my interest. I'll have a quick look."

"Any idea when?" Henry didn't mean to press the busy surgeon but the sooner he knew the results the better for a multitude of reasons.

The surgeon sighed. "After I finish with poor Mr. Wilson." He gestured toward the body before him. "A student is coming to assist me soon, so that should speed the process."

How Mr. Taylor managed to make notes about his findings while conducting the exam, often without help, was impressive. Henry knew he committed as much to memory as possible.

"Thank you. I will stop by again." Henry hesitated. "No need to send word to the Yard." Reynolds, the Director of Criminal Investigations, wouldn't approve of Henry pursuing an investigation of his own accord, especially one involving an orphan. Henry had doubts that a case would be opened.

Mr. Taylor offered a knowing smile and nodded. "Understood."

Henry tipped his head and departed, eager for a breath of fresh air—at least, as fresh as London could offer. He'd take soot-filled air over the odors in St. Thomas' any day.

He cleared his thoughts, redirecting his focus to the other cases that vied for his attention. *If only there weren't so many...*

His next stop was at Hopkins Bank to interview the supervisor of a man who'd been reported missing two days ago. The case was perplexing. It seemed as though Mr. Adam Spencer had disappeared into thin air.

Henry had spoken to Spencer's landlady, who said he'd eaten breakfast and departed for work as usual. She'd advised that he walked to work each day, no matter the weather. However, the man had never arrived. The woman had been quite distraught over his disappearance but equally concerned about how long she would need to hold his room as she had only been paid through the end of the week. After searching the man's room without finding much of interest, Henry had been compelled to ask the landlady not to clean it. From the concerned look on her face, he wondered if she already had.

At the bank, he was shown directly up the stairs to the supervisor's office.

"He was a good employee, always punctual and efficient."

Henry chose not to question why the man referred to him in the past tense. Everyone reacted differently in these situations, some holding out hope even when it was clear there was no cause for it, while others gave up before any answers were found.

"Did he seem worried about anything? Any unusual conversations or a change in his work habits?" Henry asked, notebook in hand.

The man considered the question but shook his head. "No. He managed several accounts, and I have checked to make certain he completed his work on them. All is well."

"Was he friends with any other employees?"

"One, in particular. They took luncheon together on occasion."

"I'd like to speak with the man and look over Mr. Spencer's desk."

"Of course."

Another hour of inquiry provided few answers. The man's desk was tidy, with few personal effects other than a stub of a lottery ticket. His fellow employee shared what little he knew of the man's habits, including his normal route to work, but had nothing new to offer.

Henry took his leave, no closer to discovering what had happened to the missing man. He couldn't linger; he had an appointment with Sergeant Adam Fletcher at a pub for luncheon to learn what he'd discovered from the missing man's aunt. Fletcher assisted Henry with the majority of his cases. His calm, logical approach came from years of experience and a decade in the military.

Fletcher settled into a chair with a pint after they'd both ordered through the hatch. He smoothed his impressive brown moustache before taking a sip. "The aunt is quite distraught. Seems her nephew was expected for dinner the evening he went missing."

"Hmm. It seems unlikely he chose to walk away from his life."

"Agreed. No change in his routine. Nothing unusual reported by the few who knew him."

"Why prepare for work and leave his room if he didn't intend to go to the bank?" Henry liked to talk through cases with Fletcher as doing so often provided clarity—connections neither of them alone could discover.

"Exactly. It seems as if he intended to go but was kept from doing so."

"This was in his desk drawer." Henry slid the lottery stub toward Fletcher.

Lotteries were held on everything from horse racing to boxing to other matches. They were a way for those unable to attend such events because of work or other reasons to still place a wager of sorts on the outcome. Henry had an uncle with a penchant for gambling, including lottery tickets. Henry's father had expressed his frustration about it more than once, stating he didn't understand the lure of tossing away money to feel a flicker of hope.

Henry had never bought a ticket but hesitated to condemn those who so longed for their life to change or for excitement that they bought a chance for it to happen. However, he had a strong aversion to swindling of any kind.

The sergeant scowled. "Those schemes are a waste of money."

"Odd for a man in banking to play."

"No sporting papers in his room?" Fletcher asked.

"Not that I found, though I wonder if the landlady would've tossed any she found. She seems to run a tight ship."

"Could be that he got in over his head with the wrong sort." Fletcher bit into the steaming meat pie, seeming to savor the taste. "It happens."

Henry did the same, enjoying the pie and time off his feet along with the company. Neither spoke while they finished their meal.

Only after Fletcher had wiped his mouth and finished his pint did he look at Henry. "What's next?"

"I'm going to speak with Mr. Taylor on another matter." Henry didn't share any details. Not until he knew if there was a reason to pursue Nora's death. He didn't want to explain why he felt compelled to look into the matter when it was due in part to Amelia.

Fletcher nodded, waiting for orders but not questioning Henry.

"Might be worth visiting the pub where our missing man often had luncheon. Press the lottery angle to see if anyone else there tends to buy tickets. Find out who the winners were of the last two or three drawings and see if that leads to anything."

"Good idea." Fletcher pushed to his feet and put on his hat. "Here's hoping Mr. Spencer makes a sudden reappearance."

Henry nodded, though he had the feeling that was as likely as finding an easy answer for the young mudlark's death.

Six

Amelia gingerly lifted her skirts as she walked toward Agnes and Pudge, hiding a grimace at the mud on her boots. Neither of the Fernsbys would be pleased when she returned home with them in such a terrible state.

The two girls paused in their search for treasure to watch her progress, sharing a worried look with one another. They clearly weren't excited to see her again.

She halted as the slippery mud only seemed to be growing deeper. The tide must've recently gone out, revealing new objects to find if one took the time to look.

"May I have a moment of your time?" she called to them.

After a moment's hesitation, they retrieved their bags and, with sticks in hand, made their way toward her, still searching the ground as they walked. No doubt it was a habit since that was how they spent most of their days when the tide permitted.

She smiled when they drew closer. "Any good discoveries today?"

Agnes, the taller girl, lifted one shoulder in half of a shrug. "A few."

"What sort of items do you often find?" Amelia's curiosity was genuine, but she also hoped a few minutes of conversation would make them more inclined to share what they knew. There had to be a reason for the hint of fear she'd witnessed on their faces the previous day.

"Lots of pins, of course. Pipes and bits of pottery." She retrieved a small clay pipe from her bag and held it up for Amelia's inspection.

"How interesting." Smoking pipes were sold pre-filled with tobacco and were considered disposable, especially by the dockworkers, something Amelia had noted the previous day when she'd been there. However, the one Agnes held looked older. Perhaps that meant it had some value.

"What's the best thing you have ever found?" Amelia asked.

"A gold coin." Pudge shared a smile with her friend. "That was an excitin' day."

"We don't find 'em often," Agnes quickly added. "Those are rare. Sometimes we find jewelry."

Amelia nodded as she looked over the shoreline, where nearly a half dozen small forms bent low to search. "You're not the only ones hunting today, are you?"

Agnes followed her gaze. "No. There's almost always others."

"I keep thinking of your friend Nora," Amelia said gently. "Have you learned anything more about what might have happened to her?" Was it too much to hope that one of their associates had told them something helpful?

Agnes shook her head. "No one seems to know much."

"Much?" Amelia latched onto the word. "Anything could be helpful. The smallest piece of information could prove important even if it seems like nothing."

Agnes pressed her lips together for a long moment as if undecided whether to share. "Charlie...Charlie said Carl was mad at Nora for somethin', but he didn't know what."

"Who's Charlie?"

"Another of Carl's mudlarks." She gestured toward the others, leaving Amelia to assume he was among them.

"Is this Carl nearby?" Amelia asked as she glanced around the area for someone supervising the mudlarks.

"More than likely." Pudge lifted onto her toes to gain a better view as she searched the area. "He's usually 'ere somewhere."

Agnes did the same. "Carl is never far. He keeps a close eye on his workers."

"Why don't the two of you work for him?" Amelia had wondered that yesterday and it seemed a natural time to ask.

"He keeps askin'," Agnes shared a meaningful glance with her companion.

"But we don't like him much," Pudge added, flipping a thin braid of brown hair over her shoulder. "He ain't always nice."

"We tend to think he doesn't share the money proper-like. It ain't fair." Agnes' scowl was fierce for such a young girl.

Amelia imagined he took a significant portion of any profits, and her sympathies were squarely with the girls.

"We mean to make as much as we can, so we don't have to do this long." Pudge's throat moved as she swallowed hard. "Just like Nora wanted."

The idea of a child having to work in order to survive was heartbreaking, but sadly expected in this neighborhood. "She talked about doing something different?"

"We all do." Agnes shifted to scuff a toe of her oversized, worn boot on a rock. "Can't do this forever. The taller ye are, the more it hurts."

Amelia nodded, imagining how sore their backs and fingers must be by day's end. It would be a challenging way to make a living. One might spend days searching with little to show for it.

"There's Carl," Pudge declared as she pointed behind Amelia.

Amelia turned to see a hunch-shouldered man with a low cap dressed in a brown jacket and trousers with a pipe clenched between his teeth.

He hollered at one of the workers, the words lost in the breeze, but the little boy quickly nodded in response. As if feeling the weight of their stares, the man glanced at them and started in their direction.

Agnes and Pudge didn't look pleased but remained where they were.

He might've been close to Amelia's age but time in the sun and wind had taken a toll. Creases marked his face, giving him a permanent scowl.

"Girls." He nodded to them before shifting his attention to Amelia. "Ma'am." He tugged the brim of his hat, brown eyes glinting with curiosity.

"Good afternoon." Amelia wasn't certain how to begin the conversation but offered a friendly smile. It didn't require her knowledge of chemistry to know honey would prove more effective than vinegar in this case. "I happened to be nearby when Nora was discovered yesterday. I am sorry about her unfortunate death."

The pipe still clenched in his mouth, he nodded. "Ain't we all. The girl should've listened."

"Oh?" Amelia's breath caught. "How so?"

"Thinkin' she was better than the rest o'us."

Between the pipe and his accent, Amelia had to listen closely to understand him.

"That's not true," Pudge countered, chin quivering with emotion and blue eyes flashing. "Wantin' more isn't wrong."

Carl fixed the child a steady glare. "Best to know yer place in this world and stay put. Reachin' for more only ends in trouble."

Ire had Amelia lifting her chin, despite her internal commitment to honey. "I would have to disagree. Wanting something better for yourself and those you love is a noble quest."

Carl scoffed. "Noble, eh?" He gestured toward the mud with the pipe. "Nothing noble about life around 'ere."

"All the more reason to reach for more." Anger would gain her nothing from this man, so she pushed it back. "Is that what Nora was doing? Searching for something better?"

He waved a dirty hand in dismissal. "She was always puttin' on airs, thinkin' she wouldn't be 'ere long." He gestured toward Agnes and Pudge. "Yer know that as much as I do."

The two didn't deny it. Did that mean it was true, or did they simply prefer not to argue with Carl?

"Was there a specific dream she mentioned?" Amelia included the girls in her question.

"Too many to name. She was always comin' up with crazed ideas and runnin' her mouth about 'em." Carl shook his head. "Hope the others learn from 'er mistake."

Amelia gasped as outrage took hold. "That's a terrible thing to say." She wanted to cover the girls' ears and box Carl's in equal measure. Every child should have the opportunity to dream. She swallowed against the lump in her throat at the knowledge that Lily had never had the chance to do so. That made it all the more important that these girls did.

"Yer won't find me lyin' to my kids." He took a step closer to Agnes and Pudge. "If yer knew what was good fer yer, yer'd join us. We are safer together."

"No, thank you," Agnes muttered, her gaze fixed on the ground.

"We appreciate yer thinkin' of us, Carl." Pudge's blue eyes met his. "We'll be all right."

"Nora isn't the first one to die, and she won't be the last." Carl gestured toward the mudlarks with his pipe once again. "God only knows who will be next."

"How do you mean?" Amelia asked, horrified at the thought of another child dead, lying lifeless in the mud. "Who else died?"

"Bitty." The pipe returned to Carl's mouth, but it didn't change the way he spoke. "Been a month or more."

"What happened to her?"

"No one knows fer certain."

Agnes bit her lower lip as if the matter bothered her considerably.

"Was her death looked into?" Amelia wished this would've been brought to Henry's attention yesterday. Why hadn't the girls mentioned anything?

"Never found 'er." Carl scanned the river's shoreline, seeming to search the surface from afar. "Besides, the bobbies don't care about the likes of us."

"Maybe she left on 'er own," Pudge suggested, though doubt roughened her tone.

Amelia could hardly fathom the thought of two children gone. Didn't they have any family? A mother who mourned them like she still mourned Lily? Her heart ached at the thought.

If Nora didn't have anyone other than her friends to grieve her or determine what had happened to her, then Amelia would do what she could.

Perhaps the news of a second child missing might allow Henry to investigate the situation, because she knew she couldn't do it on her own.

Seven

The terrible odor hadn't improved when Henry returned to St. Thomas' that afternoon, not that he had expected it to. He was careful to breathe through his mouth, relieved not to see Nora on the surgeon's exam table. Instead, an older male lay upon the cold slab. Even though he didn't know the man, Henry averted his gaze.

Normally he could set aside his feelings while working on cases, but the sight of the young girl had touched him. He didn't like the thought of her body sliced open and organs removed, even if it was necessary to learn what had happened. For the first time, he understood why a family sometimes protested the coroner's examination.

Setting aside his personal thoughts, he nodded at the student who stood beside the doctor with paper, pencil, and board clip in hand.

"Field, you have excellent timing." Taylor nodded at Henry but returned his focus to his work.

"Oh?"

"I have just finished my notes on the girl." Taylor continued to work as he spoke, a testament to how many victims awaited his attention.

"Anything of interest?" He almost hoped there wasn't.

"Poison."

Surprise gripped him, both at the news and its abrupt delivery. Taylor usually preferred to draw out results, lingering on tangents and other details before sharing the conclusion Henry wanted to know the most. While he had wondered if poison had been the cause, he was still shocked. "Arsenic?"

That was the most common, though the number of murders caused by it had been reduced since improved scientific methods made it easier to discover. Criminals were not completely stupid.

"No." Taylor frowned. "Something more unusual."

"Such as?" Henry couldn't imagine how that could've come to pass—or why.

"I'm not sure. The first tests were inconclusive. Running more will take time." His gaze lifted to meet Henry's. "If it's important?"

"It might be." Had the girl taken whatever it had been on her own, tired of the struggle of her existence...or was something more sinister at work?

"Her last meal was impressive, given her occupation, though little remained in her stomach of it." Taylor returned to his work, lifting the victim's heart out of his chest and after a cursory look, setting it in a waiting dish. "Roasted beef with potatoes and carrots. Bread pudding with cream. And wine."

Where would she have had such a fine meal wearing that faded dress? The possibilities were few. A restaurant seemed unlikely, considering the expense and potential witnesses. Had she gone to someone's home and been given the poison in the meal? Perhaps in the wine?

Henry couldn't begin to guess why. Better that he focus on the details he knew with the hope the motive eventually became clear.

"Any ideas as to why she would've taken poison?" Taylor asked, a question he rarely posed. Apparently he was as disturbed by the case as Henry was.

"Not as of yet. Hard to believe anyone would deliberately poison a child."

"Especially an orphan who searched for items along the river's shore," the doctor added. "What harm could she have ever caused?"

"Excellent question." Had the girl found something of value? If so, why hadn't it simply been taken from her?

"I have no doubt you will uncover the truth, given that you're a Field." Taylor's steady gaze met his, the confidence in his expression causing Henry to shift his feet. "You always do."

"Not always." Matthew Greystone's murder weighed heavily on him. Over a year had passed, and he hadn't uncovered any new clues in months. The trail had gone cold though not for lack of trying.

It was surprising Amelia still spoke to him, considering he hadn't been able to bring her either justice or closure. Perhaps she wouldn't if not for the ravenkeeper's case.

"I have complete faith in you, Henry." The surgeon's attention returned to his grisly task. "The report is on the corner of my desk."

"Thank you." Would Taylor have that same faith in him if he knew the truth? That Henry was not a true Field, only an adopted one? The day he'd discovered that had shaken him to the core.

Pushing aside thoughts of the past and circumstances beyond his control, Henry found the report and departed for Scotland Yard to speak to Reynolds about the girl's death. He'd been reluctant to do so the previous day—the death of an orphan hardly warranted an investigation.

Perhaps the poisoning of one did.

He entered the Yard, nodding to Sergeant Johnson at the front desk and continuing down the short hallway that led to the main office where each inspector was assigned one of the desks lined up in rows. Henry had already spent time at his desk earlier, completing notes and reviewing new cases, and gave it no more than a cursory glance as he walked to Reynolds' office.

John Reynolds polished his gold-rimmed spectacles on a handkerchief and put them back on as Henry knocked on his open door. "Field. Any luck with the missing man? Spencer, wasn't it?"

"Not yet, sir. Fletcher and I are still pursuing a few clues." He didn't mention how few there were. After all, one was all it took to break open a case. "There's another matter I wanted to discuss."

Reynolds scratched his bare chin, the only part of his lower face that wasn't covered in dark whiskers. His brown hair was parted in the middle and smoothed down, giving his face a pleasing symmetrical appearance. "What is it?"

"A young girl was found dead on the mudflats near Blackfriars yesterday. The coroner has confirmed poison—and not arsenic."

"How young?"

"Ten."

"Any reason to believe foul play was involved?"

"It seems unlikely she took the poison on her own."

"Family?"

"Orphan," Henry reluctantly answered. That shouldn't matter, but it would.

"A mudlark then?"

Henry nodded. There was no other reason for an orphan to be in the area.

Reynolds shook his head. "We can't justify spending resources on the case of an orphan. For all we know, she drank something she shouldn't have."

"I think there's more to it than that."

"And until you're handed proof, we'll leave it be."

Henry wasn't surprised by the Director of Criminal Investigation's answer, but that didn't keep disappointment from filling him. "Yes, sir."

Arguing would be pointless while he had little to go on.

Henry sighed, pleased he'd at least advised the constable in the area to keep him apprised of any trouble. That would have to be enough for now.

He took his leave, trying to put Nora from his thoughts and focus on the missing man. He was the one who apparently mattered. Unfortunately, that was easier said than done, especially when he needed to tell Amelia he wouldn't be pursuing the case.

Eight

Darkness had fallen though the hour was still relatively early when Henry knocked on Amelia's—Mrs. Greystone's—door. The difference in daylight seemed to be noticeable each day this time of year.

"Inspector Field." Fernsby's welcoming smile had Henry smiling in return. "How good of you to call."

"I hope you are well." He entered Amelia's home, appreciating the inviting scents of lemon, beeswax, and a hint of something delicious for dinner. The latter caused his stomach to grumble in response.

"I am, and you, sir?" Fernsby asked as he reached for Henry's damp coat and took it along with his hat and gloves.

"Quite well." He hadn't intended to stay and felt awkward leaving his things with the butler, as if he were inviting himself to remain for a visit when he had no reason to other than delivering unfortunate news.

He'd made it a point to call on Amelia frequently in the past year, despite not having any updates on her husband's murder. He had wanted her to know that the case was uppermost in his mind. He'd also held the faint hope that she might have news of her own to report.

When the ravenkeeper's daughter Maeve had come to stay with her, he'd spent several nights here to protect both the girl and Amelia. The situation had been dire, but he'd still enjoyed those few evenings spent in her well-appointed and comfortable home, conversing with her. Amelia was excellent company, intelligent and well-read with a quick mind. Her skills in chemistry intrigued him, too, and...well. He was not blind. She was a beautiful woman.

"Mrs. Greystone is in?" Henry asked, though Fernsby would have already told him otherwise.

"Yes, in the drawing room." The older man gestured toward the stairs. "She'll be delighted you came by."

Henry sighed as he followed Fernsby, certain that delight wouldn't last long once he told her his news.

"Inspector Field, madam," the butler announced in the doorway then stepped aside to allow Henry entrance.

It came as no surprise to see Amelia working at her desk in the corner; she always seemed to be busy doing something. Perhaps she was working on her article about the barge captain. He'd managed to read most of the ones she'd written and enjoyed them. She offered a unique perspective about the people she interviewed, and it was clear she found their stories fascinating.

She rose with a smile. "How good to see you, Henry. I assume you received my message?"

"Actually, no. I was out much of the afternoon," he said as he stepped forward, drawn in by her presence along with the welcoming fire and cozy room. There was no comparison to his rather spartan rooms at the lodging house.

"I wanted to speak to you about Nora." She rubbed her hands and glanced out the window. "A chilly night, even for November."

"It is. A fine mist is falling and makes it even colder." No doubt she was eager for any news he had about the mudlark's death—and what was this about a note?

"Have you finished work, or do you have additional duties this evening?"

"I am finished for the night."

"How nice. Would you care to stay for dinner? As you know, Mrs. Appleton tends to prepare far too much food."

"I...I wouldn't want to impose." Henry wanted to stay more than he should. The fare would be much more appetizing than the simple meals his landlady served, not to mention allow him the pleasure of Amelia's company.

"It's no imposition. Allow me to alert Fernsby." Rather than pull the bell, she walked to the doorway to look down the stairs and requested an additional place setting.

Henry heard the butler's muffled reply and tried not to stare as Amelia returned, skirts shifting as she paused before sitting.

"Fernsby says dinner will be served within the hour," she advised as she studied him, eyes narrowing slightly. "Would you care for a drink?"

Did she see his weariness from the day or the reluctance to share his news? "Thank you."

That weariness eased as the prospect of a pleasant evening spent in her company took hold.

"It has been rather quiet without you and Maeve here." She poured a short whiskey for him and a sherry for herself. After handing him the drink, she gestured toward the wingback chairs flanking the fire and sat.

Henry followed suit. "I confess to thinking of her often. I hope she's doing well."

"Her aunt wrote to say she's been enjoying time with her cousins, two of whom are of a similar age."

"That is good news." He wondered if Amelia had pursued the idea of assisting the girl with a special education for those with similar challenges. She'd mentioned the idea after they'd said goodbye to Maeve. "I suppose they will be thinking of school next."

"Indeed. Her aunt and uncle are excited by my offer of schooling for Maeve, but they suggested waiting until after the Christmas season, since she's already had so much turmoil in her life."

He should've known she would follow through with her offer. "That sounds wise. Is there a place near them?"

"Unfortunately, it's far enough that it will mean monthly visits rather than weekly." Amelia frowned, suggesting that concerned her. "While I think it would be beneficial for Maeve to learn skills to help her make her way in the world, not to mention be able to better communicate, I worry whether January will be enough time for her to adjust to the numerous changes in her life."

"I'm certain her aunt and uncle wonder the same. Surely they will suggest waiting longer if they don't think Maeve is ready."

"You're probably right." She took a sip, her brow still furrowed. The question must be truly bothering her.

"Then again, children seem to be amazingly resilient," he added, hoping to reassure her. He took a drink as well, appreciating the taste of a good whiskey. "Waiting overlong could prove equally problematic if she becomes too attached to her cousins and new home."

The furrow eased and she nodded. "True. I suppose I worry that my offer will cause problems rather than opportunities."

"I think that doubtful. We shall have to hope for the best." He lifted his glass in a salute of sorts, still reluctant to raise the reason he'd called.

She returned the gesture with a smile. "Indeed, we shall." She tilted her head to the side as she studied him. "You had your hair trimmed."

Sudden awareness had him repositioning in his seat. "I did. A little shorter than normal."

"I like it."

"Such things go by the wayside during pressing cases," he confessed.

"I can imagine."

He cleared his throat as he forced himself to share his news. "The reason I called is because I spoke with the coroner earlier today about the mudlark's cause of death."

"Oh?" Her eyes lit with curiosity. "And?"

Her obvious interest only made him worry more about her reaction to what he had to tell her. "Poison."

Amelia's quiet gasp filled the room as she took in the news. "I wondered. How terrible to hear."

"It is." He sat forward in his chair and forced himself to hold her gaze. "Unfortunately, Scotland Yard won't be pursuing the matter."

Her mouth tightened with displeasure as she shook her head. "But if it was murder—"

"We don't know that it was," Henry added before she finished the assumption.

"You can't believe she would take poison of her own accord."

"It is possible." Though part of him wanted to agree with her, he also felt compelled to point out other options.

"But unlikely," she persisted.

He nodded, silently appreciating and respecting her opinion.

"The poor thing." She tapped a finger on the edge of her glass as she considered the news. "Agnes and Pudge won't be pleased." She sent Henry a pointed look. "Or surprised."

"I suppose they have little faith in the police, much like half of London."

"Only half?" Amelia asked with a teasing glint in her eyes.

"I stand corrected. I should've said *most*." He smiled.

While the reputation of the Metropolitan Police had improved in recent years, they were still regarded by some as a necessary evil, and the conviction of several inspectors for accepting bribes a few years ago hadn't helped. But since then, the entire department had been reorganized. Reynolds ran a tight ship. It was a shame that few outside their offices knew that.

Amelia laughed as he'd intended, something she rarely did, at least not in his presence. "I am sure that isn't true, but I couldn't resist teasing you."

"I suppose it depends on who is asked." He'd never allowed the public's view of the police to affect his work. After all, his grandfather and father, who had both served as chief inspectors of Scotland Yard, had faced far worse opinions and still managed to find success.

"Who is asked, and which side of the law they are on," Amelia added.

Henry nodded. "I do wish more could be done for the girl." Did Amelia understand his sincerity?

"As do I." Amelia set her glass on the side table. "In turn, I have additional news to report. I spoke with Agnes and Pudge again today."

"Oh?" Henry frowned, not liking the idea of Amelia in the area by herself, especially not after the girl's body had been discovered.

"I needed to finish my interview with Captain Booth, and the girls were on the mudflats."

"Did they say anything more?"

"Yes, that was why I sent you a message. To speak with you about it. I spoke with Carl, who was Nora's...supervisor, if that is what he could be called."

Curiosity and concern warred within Henry. He could imagine what 'Carl' might be like. He'd met many men of the same ilk—but what was done was done. "What were your impressions?"

Amelia gave a mock shudder. "He is a harsh man. He blamed Nora for making the wrong choices because of her determination to better herself. He certainly seems capable of nefarious behavior."

"I'm not sure what motive he would have to harm one of his own workers. An experienced one can be replaced but not without effort."

"True. But I do think he is quick to anger. Perhaps she said or did something that caused him to lose his temper."

"If that were the case, he would be unlikely to choose poison in anger," Henry pointed out.

Amelia sighed. "I suppose you're right, but I still don't like or trust the man."

"Nor should you." He emphasized the words, wanting her to take care. Wandering about on the mudflats and talking to strange men, honestly! What was she thinking?

"Of course," she said with a nod. "Carl did mention another mudlark, Bitty, who went missing a month ago."

"Hmm." Henry didn't like the sound of that, yet a missing orphan was unfortunately a common occurrence. "I will have the morgue records checked."

Again, Amelia nodded. "I can't keep Nora's death from my thoughts. Doesn't everyone deserve justice? Even an orphan?"

"Yes." The thought bothered him as well. "But for all we know, she chose to take the poison. Perhaps she was tired of her life and sought to end it."

"Then why not simply walk into the cold numbing Thames rather than choose an uncomfortable, if not painful, death? Not that either would be pleasant. And where would she have got the poison? I can't imagine someone of so limited means spending money on it."

"True." Henry hesitated, but as there was no formal investigation it surely could not hurt to share this detail with his friend. "The coroner mentioned that her last meal was out of the ordinary for a mudlark. Quite a fine one from what little was left in her stomach."

"Doesn't that suggest something suspicious caused her death?"

"Perhaps." Though his curiosity was roused, he had enough cases assigned to him, some of which he had yet to investigate. "I wish there was more I could do. Perhaps…no, it is no matter."

"What is it?" Amelia asked as if sensing his hesitation.

"You remember the bottle in the girl's hand?"

"Of course."

"Would it be possible for you to discover what it contained?" Her laboratory in the attic was impressive, but he knew nothing of what was required to examine any residue in it.

"If it hasn't been washed, I might be able to tell what it held." Her eagerness spoke of her desire to help.

A tight knot in Henry's chest loosened. He would much rather she pursued that potential clue instead of speaking to men like Carl. "I shall bring it to you tomorrow if that's acceptable." He'd placed it in his desk for safekeeping, unable to put it in the evidence room since the case wouldn't be pursued.

"I look forward to it."

He should let the matter go, as Reynolds had ordered, and encourage Amelia to do the same…but he couldn't. As Amelia had said, the girl deserved justice just as anyone who died by someone else's hand.

Nine

"Good morning, madam," Fernsby greeted Amelia as she descended the stairs the following day. "A constable delivered this earlier." He handed her a cloth-wrapped bundle.

"Thank you." She started to open it, moving with care as anticipation filled her. "Was there any message?"

"No. He only said to be sure you received it."

Disappointment twisted her lips. She'd rather hoped Henry would bring the bottle himself—a ridiculous notion, when she knew how busy he was.

Their time together the previous evening had been enjoyable, though it also confirmed how lonely she'd been of late. How empty her home had become. Hopefully she would soon re-adjust to her quiet life—it was just that she missed having Maeve in the house as well as Henry.

Her mother and father had asked her to come for Christmas, something she hoped to do even if travel during midwinter was often challenging. She could always take the train to see them sooner if she wished. The reminder that she was only as alone as she wanted to be comforted her.

For now, the mystery she held in her palm would provide the perfect distraction and, hopefully, help bring justice for Nora in the process.

She unfolded the last bit of fabric to reveal the familiar crystal bottle with its narrow neck and round stopper.

"It looks fine enough to sit on a lady's dressing table in Mayfair," Fernsby remarked.

"Indeed, which makes it all the more puzzling how it came to be in the girl's possession."

"Take care, madam. The idea of it holding poison is most concerning." The butler eyed the bottle with plain distrust.

"Have no worries. I intend to do just that." Using the cloth in which it had been wrapped Amelia held the crystal up to the light, but the faceted design prevented a clear view of any remaining contents.

That didn't mean the vessel was empty. At the very least, some residue might remain. Hopefully the stopper had been on tight enough to prevent river water from entering and contaminating anything still within it.

She relished the chance to help answer the mystery surrounding Nora, and she appreciated Henry's confidence in her skills more than she could say.

"Can you please ask Mrs. Appleton to hold breakfast?" Amelia wrapped the bottle back in the cloth and started up the stairs. "I want to see to this first. The sooner I attempt to discover what the bottle contained, the better." Though she feared it might already be too late.

Fernsby nodded. "Of course, madam. I'm sure the cook won't mind."

Excitement had her hurrying up the two flights of stairs to her laboratory—ridiculous, when for all she knew the girl had simply found the bottle somewhere, and it had nothing to do with her death.

Yet Amelia couldn't set aside the idea that it was a clue, that perhaps it contained a remnant of the poison which had killed Nora. Why else would the girl have held onto it despite the terrible cramps and nausea, not to mention the vomiting, that must have plagued her final minutes? Dying from poison was apparently an unpleasant end, to say the least.

Testing for poison wouldn't be straightforward, especially if there wasn't enough for a significant sample. So where should she start?

Arsenic, one of the most common toxins, was readily available as it was used to eradicate rats and other pests. However, the coroner had already confirmed arsenic had not killed Nora, according to Henry. What else could it be, then? She and Henry would have to attempt to discover it on their own.

If only her father lived closer. This was one of his areas of interest, and he would undoubtedly have suggestions. As an apothecary in a small village north of London, he'd stirred her interest in chemistry when a young child, though she'd quickly realized she had no desire to dole out remedies for upset stomachs or headaches. She preferred to delve into the adverse effects that occurred in organisms in response to chemicals.

Breathless by the time she reached the uppermost level of the house, Amelia set the bottle on the counter and reached for her apron that hung on a peg inside the door. After donning it, she lit several lamps. The tall bank of windows allowed in natural light, but the hour was early and the day cloudy.

Working in the laboratory always lifted her spirits—*almost* always, anyway. It had served as a sanctuary during difficult times, providing purpose and fueling her thirst for knowledge, and Amelia took pride in her work. Matthew had never understood her 'hobby' and thought it ill-suited for a woman. Whether her insistence on spending time in the lab had driven a deeper wedge between them was something she often wondered...but his late nights and secretive behavior hadn't helped.

Amelia pushed aside the dark thoughts and retrieved a notebook and pencil to document her steps, along with any results. That was vital in all her experiments, but especially one of this nature. She could not afford to miss a single clue. She gathered a few supplies before carefully removing the stopper of the bottle to peer inside.

To her disappointment no liquid was visible, only a gray residue. With meticulous care, Amelia used a small scalpel-like knife and scraped some of the substance onto a glass slide, then repeated the process with another miniscule sample.

Though concerned whether there was enough of the stuff to reveal anything, she wouldn't know until she tried. Nora deserved justice, and her friends were owed an explanation for her death—and whether they had reason to fear for their own lives.

Deep inside, Amelia knew she was trying to help the mudlarks because she hadn't been able to save Lily, but she couldn't help it. She might not be able to answer the question of what had happened to Nora, but she had to try. As she'd learned during the ravenkeeper's investigation, one unexpected clue often led to another.

Holding onto that thought, she jotted down her initial observations. It didn't take long to confirm that the substance wasn't an opiate, and a negative answer was nearly as important as a positive one.

Cyanide, perhaps? That also seemed unlikely. Though usually a gas, it could also be made by crushing the kernels of apricots…but a substantial number of the pits would be needed in order to produce enough of the poison.

What else?

She walked to her bookshelves along one wall and retrieved one of her reference books, turning the pages to the brief section on poisonous substances.

Mercury. Unlikely but possible. Strychnine seemed unlikely, as well. Various fungi were a distant possibility. With so little to test, she needed to consider each option carefully.

But which one should she look for?

Amelia stared at the bit of residue, wishing it would reveal its secret. If someone had wanted an orphan dead, why not use a method which didn't require such forethought and a certain amount of cooperation from the victim? There had been no sign of force used. No marks on her wrists that suggested she'd been restrained.

Had she been given poison for some specific reason? Perhaps in some manner which had disguised it from the girl? With food or drink would be the most obvious way to get anyone to take it.

Logic suggested a more common poison, such as cyanide, yet Amelia hesitated, a distinctly unscientific voice in her head suggesting she try something else. It was a risk though, to trust her gut with such little evidence remaining.

She consulted her book one more time to review the options and then went with her instinct, hoping it would yield results.

A half-hour later, she had a puzzling result—fungi. Precisely what kind remained to be seen. She didn't know enough about mushrooms to conduct further testing to determine exactly which one. Yet there was no logical explanation as to why ground mushrooms would be stored in a perfume bottle under normal circumstances—at least, not in her mind.

Satisfaction filled Amelia: her instinct had proved correct and her skills, though limited, had confirmed it. But how this might help solve the case wasn't yet clear.

She jotted a message to Henry, telling him of her discovery and suggesting they meet to discuss it further at his convenience. She looked forward to hearing his thoughts and intended to do additional research on the topic.

Her stomach growled as she reviewed her notes a final time to make certain she hadn't forgotten anything. Then she took the message to Fernsby to have it delivered and continued to the kitchen, pleased with her day thus far.

Unfortunately she doubted the news would allow Henry to pursue the girl's death in an official capacity—but Amelia intended to do all she could to find justice for Nora, with or without his assistance.

Ten

Henry spent a frustrating morning speaking with a few other employees at the bank regarding the still missing Mr. Spencer. Their lack of knowledge about a co-worker who spent nine hours a day at a desk within arm's reach was astounding, although the supervisor made it clear conversing during business hours was frowned upon by the management.

Working through potential clues was still productive even if he didn't gain any direct answers, but on mornings like this, it was difficult to believe. Hopefully Fletcher was finding more success.

A quick look at his pocket watch revealed Henry still had well over an hour before he and Fletcher were to meet at a pub for luncheon to share what they'd found. His portion of the conversation would be ridiculously short.

While he considered his next steps to locate Mr. Spencer, Henry decided to seek out and speak with Carl. Guilt nudged him as he caught a hansom cab and directed the driver to Puddle Dock near Blackfriars. Working on a case he hadn't been assigned—that was not even considered a case by his superiors—didn't sit well. If Director Reynolds found out there would be hell to pay, especially since he'd already been told directly not to pursue the girl's death.

But between Amelia's fixation on Nora and the questions running through his own mind, taking an hour out of his day to further look into the matter seemed reasonable. He just couldn't dismiss the feeling that something foul was afoot.

Half a dozen small figures were visible along the river's foreshore when the hansom dropped him off, their small forms bent double to scour the dark mud for anything of interest.

Though he'd thought it great fun to search the sand and mud for trinkets when he was a boy, he couldn't imagine doing so for hours the way these children did; not when their next meal depended on their success, not to mention the roof over their heads. He arched his back at the thought of the soreness they must feel.

It wasn't the children who interested him this time, though he could see the two girls who'd discovered the body searching near the shore. He scanned the area for anyone who appeared to be watching over things and quickly found a candidate who fit what little description Amelia had given him.

The man wore his cap low, hiding much of his face, and was dressed in brown from head to toe. He shook a finger at a small lad who stood at his side, clearly unhappy about something. The man turned, his gaze catching suspiciously on Henry's approach.

"Might I have a word?" Henry called, doing his best to ignore the cold. He'd best grow used to it as the winter had hardly begun.

The boy scuttled away with a furtive look, clearly anxious to make use of the distraction Henry provided.

"Depends." The words were hard to distinguish with the pipe in the man's teeth. "What is it y'want?"

"Information." Henry didn't bother trying to be friendly. This was not a man who would appreciate it.

"What sort?"

"About the young mudlark who recently died." Henry shrugged, already feeling the damp cold seeping through his layers and wondered how the children withstood it.

"Nora?" The man scowled, emphasizing the wrinkles around his eyes and mouth in his leathered face. "What was she to yer?"

"Only a child who died under suspicious circumstances." Henry didn't come right out and say murder. It was too soon to say that for certain and doing so might put the man on the defensive. "I assume you're Carl?"

He nodded, looking over Henry. "Yer a copper then?"

The man's study of him didn't particularly bother Henry. He'd dealt with his share of ruffians and wasn't intimidated.

It was tempting to lie, or at least obscure the truth of his identity, but it wouldn't help in the long run. "An inspector with Scotland Yard."

The man chortled. "Yer can't expect me to believe the Yard is takin' an interest in what happens 'round here. Yer might as well tell me the second comin' is upon us."

"Your full name?" Henry asked, preferring to direct the questions to him. Never mind the man was close to the truth.

"Carl Jeffries."

"And how did you know Nora?"

"She worked fer me along with the others." He made a vague gesture toward the young mudlarks who'd paused their efforts to watch. "Get back to work! All of yer!"

The children returned to their search but kept a watchful eye on the men.

"What was her full name?"

"Nora Murray. She said."

"Where did she live?"

"The laundress down the way let her sleep there most nights." Carl gestured toward a nearby street. "Nora helped with the wash when she weren't mudlarkin'."

"How long did Nora work for you?" Henry didn't bother to take out his notebook, doubtful he'd receive enough information to warrant it. Besides, he was more interested in gaining an impression of the man.

"Two years. Three." Carl shrugged. "Since her mother took ill. Some of these kids would be lost without the likes of me." He gestured to himself with a dirty thumb.

From the pride in his voice and demeanor, Carl clearly believed it. Yet Henry felt certain the man took advantage of the situation.

"How exactly do you help them?" Henry couldn't help but ask, allowing doubt to color his tone.

"Give 'em a job and the chance to earn their keep, just like I did at that age. They're lucky. Anyone could've found 'em."

Henry glanced toward the children searching the ground. "They bring their finds to you and..." He paused for the man to finish the sentence.

"I sell 'em and pay a share."

"Is there a pre-determined split?"

"Don't get me wrong, I take a portion. Finding the right buyers for the odds and ends they find ain't easy."

Henry was sure Carl already had buyers for every possible valuable they found. "And did you and Nora have a disagreement prior to her death?"

Carl's eyes went wide. "Ye're not thinkin' I'm to blame, are yer? I didn't kill the girl."

"I'm only trying to discover the facts surrounding her death. Any information you provide would be much appreciated, no matter how small."

"Hmm." Carl considered him for a moment, evidently weighing whether it was a good idea to irritate a policeman. "Well, Nora had a few grand ideas, thinkin' she could better herself. I told her to be grateful for the work she had. Can't allow the kids to believe they're more than they are, ye know. Bad for business."

"And if one does, what happens?" Henry watched him carefully. It didn't make sense for the man to kill a worker because she wanted to do something else, but Carl might have become angry if she were upsetting the other mudlarks. Yet it seemed unlikely he would take time to poison the girl. Something like that took forethought and planning. Carl didn't strike him as the sort to bother with such things.

"I give 'em a talkin' to. Can't have 'em sourin' the rest of the workers now, can I? Spreads a poor attitude."

"When did you last see Nora?"

The man's gaze shifted to the kids as if thinking over the question. Whether that was to try to remember or to provide himself with an alibi remained to be seen. "Tuesday, late afternoon. We were about to finish work for the day as the tide was rollin' in. She left early without a word to anyone about where she was goin'."

"Was that unusual?"

"For her, it was. She always minded her manners and listened. Only the last couple of weeks, she'd started to act a bit…rebellious."

Henry's hackles rose. "Did you see her speaking with anyone? Any strangers?"

"Hmm. Now that you mention it, a man spoke to a few of the kids a week or so ago. Better dressed than most around 'ere or I might not have noticed."

"Can you describe him?" Gaining details from the man was like pulling teeth, but Henry did his best to hide his irritation.

Carl shrugged. "Only saw him from a distance as I was arrivin'. He took his leave when he saw me. Tall, dark hair with long sideburns. Black suit. 'Bout my age."

"Which is?" Given the man's time out of doors in the elements, it was difficult to say. His hunched shoulders and uneven gait were more common in old men.

"Forty-three." Carl looked at him as if shocked Henry couldn't tell.

Henry took care not to show any surprise, though it was even younger than he'd expected. "You didn't speak with him?"

"Nah. As I said, he hurried off when he saw me. Told the kids he was lookin' fer someone, but I have my doubts. Can't imagine what a man like him would want with the mudlarks."

Nor could Henry. "Have you seen him since?"

"Nope." The man shifted away, clearly tired of the conversation. "If ye're done, I've got things to do."

"I'd like to ask your workers a few questions."

"Now ye're costin' me money." Carl adjusted the pipe between his worn-down teeth with a scowl.

"It won't take long." Henry refused to take no for an answer and glanced at the children. "Is there one who was close to Nora? Or perhaps someone who spoke with the stranger?"

Carl heaved a sigh, clearly put out. "I suppose ye can have a word with Charlie. He spent more time with Nora than the rest, an' he talked to the man." He turned to look over the kids. "Charlie!"

The same boy Carl had been berating earlier stilled then slowly straightened, his stiff movements making his reluctance clear.

"Come 'ere." Carl gestured him forward.

The boy couldn't have been more than eight or nine, a mop of curly brown hair peeking from beneath his dirty cap, face smeared with mud in several places. His wide brown eyes were wary in his thin face as he looked between Henry and Carl. "Sir?"

Henry would rather speak to him without Carl listening, but this would have to do for now. He smiled in an attempt to put the boy at ease. "Hello, Charlie. My name is Henry. I want to ask you a few questions about Nora."

Grief pinched the boy's features even as his eyes watered suspiciously. "What about her?"

"Do you have any idea what happened?"

Charlie lifted one shoulder and gestured toward the two girls who had found the girl. "Agnes and Pudge told me that it looked like she'd been sick."

"Did she mention being ill?"

He shook his head. "She was fine earlier."

"Did she say where she was going that night?"

"No." He frowned, clearly distressed. "I wish she would've." The lad glanced at Carl as if wondering what more to say.

"Agnes and Pudge mentioned that she was wearing her best dress," Henry pressed. "Do you know why?"

He shook his head. "I can only think she was goin' to meet someone. Maybe that man who was talkin' to her." The boy sent a questioning look at Carl, clearly worried he'd said too much.

"I'm sure Carl wants to know what happened to Nora as much as you do." Henry sent a pointed look at the man. "Don't you, sir?"

"Yeah. Fine." Carl sighed. "Tell him what yer know."

Charlie's lips twisted, suggesting he didn't completely believe his boss. "He spoke to a couple of us. Told us he had a better position if we was interested. I didn't listen to him much. Why would some bloke come to the mudflats lookin' for workers? Seemed odd to me. Gave me skin crawls, the way he looked us over." He gave a mock shudder.

"Did Nora seem interested?" Henry asked.

"Hard to say. I told her to pay him no mind."

"Did he provide an address or any way to contact him?"

"Not that I heard." Charlie's mouth tightened, hands now twisting together before him. "I should've paid more attention."

"If he comes around again and you happen to get a name or address, I'd be pleased to pay you for the information." It wasn't done, not really, but Henry consoled himself with the fact that as this wasn't an official investigation, it surely would not matter if he spent a little of his own coin on the problem.

"Oh yeah?" Again, Charlie glanced at Carl as if for permission.

"We all want to know what happened, as I said." Henry glared at Carl until the man nodded. His easy agreement made Henry think he would take a portion of any payment the child received.

"Charlie?" Henry put a hand on the boy's shoulder, wanting to make certain the child heard him. "Take care. Don't put yourself in danger to find out more." The surprise in the lad's face struck Henry square in the chest. Did the boy not realize his life was of value? Henry bent to look him in the eye. "My grandfather's name was Charlie, so I wouldn't want anything to happen to you."

Though he didn't want to frighten the children, they should know to take care until more could be discovered about Nora's death.

A corner of the boy's lip curled upward, hinting at a smile underneath all the mud. "Was it truly?"

"Indeed it was."

Charles Field had been larger than life and well-known on London's streets. He'd been a constable for years, finishing his career as a Chief Inspector with Scotland Yard. His long friendship with another

Charles, Charles Dickens, had made him even more popular. Henry had adored him and wanted to be just like him.

No matter how hard he tried, he would never be as good as his grandfather with his blithe assurance, or his father who had meticulous attention to detail. The two were legends in Scotland Yard, their shadows forever falling over Henry as he was often compared to the two.

Unfortunately he was only a Field by chance and so had not inherited their many fine qualities. That didn't mean he didn't seek to imbue them.

If not for his adoption, he might've spent his childhood much like these orphans, doing whatever he could to earn his next meal and a warm corner in which to sleep. The thought was a sobering one.

"If you discover anything tell Constable Gibbons, and he'll pass the message to me," Henry advised. "He'll be around."

"Yes, sir." Charlie dipped his head.

"Get back to work," Carl ordered, clearly done with the conversation.

"Thank you for your time," Henry called after the boy as he watched him trot back to the others.

"I don't make a habit of helpin' the bobbies." Whether Carl meant his words as a warning wasn't clear.

"Perhaps, but we wouldn't want any more of your workers to disappear. That would cost you money too, wouldn't it? Let me know if you see the man again." Henry nodded and departed to visit with the laundress. He remained convinced that Nora had died under suspicious circumstances, and he was determined to discover why.

Eleven

Deciding it was unlikely Henry would call until the evening, Amelia took time to read the news sheet, something she liked to do to keep abreast of current events, though the continued news of unrest abroad was concerning. The remainder of the morning she worked on the barge article, pleased with what she had thus far.

Her position as a correspondent for the periodical provided an excellent opportunity to indulge her curious nature. She loved learning new things, and interviewing the unique and unusual allowed her to do just that. She found it fascinating to discover people and places in London she hadn't realized were there.

Directly after luncheon, Amelia changed into an afternoon gown—gray, of course—and prepared for an outing she'd been looking forward to for some time. Elizabeth Drake, a female chemist, was lecturing at South Kensington Museum. Amelia had followed her work for some time since she was not only a chemist but a woman. It was thrilling to know she wasn't alone in her interest in the field.

"I shall return in a few hours, Fernsby," Amelia advised as she affixed her hat in the hall.

"Are you certain you don't want Yvette to accompany you?" the butler asked, never liking her to venture out on her own, particularly not after the trouble the household had so recently been through.

"No need. The poor dear would be bored to tears." Yvette preferred to stay busy and waiting for Amelia tested the limits of her patience. With a smile, Amelia strode to the waiting hansom cab Fernsby had ordered and settled inside.

The drive to the museum on Cromwell Road was pleasant, if chilly, traffic snarling their progress in only a few places. Within a half hour Amelia was alighting at the museum and making her way toward the lecture theater, a place she'd been to on several other occasions to listen to speakers on architecture, art collections, and paleontology. Those had been interesting, but she had especially high hopes for this one.

She followed other attendees, mainly men but more women than usual, to the lecture hall, a separate round brick building, and paid for a ticket.

Though accustomed to being alone, it was times like this when Amelia felt the weight of that status. Her few female friends were more interested in fashion and gossip, their children, and the goings on of high society, than lectures of any sort. Matthew had rarely accompanied her as he'd been busy with his import-export business. While she wondered if Henry might enjoy a lecture like this, his job took up much of his time—and besides, she would not wish to appear forward by inviting him.

Amelia lifted her chin, determined to enjoy the afternoon despite being alone. After finding a seat, she didn't have to wait long before the museum director introduced the speaker.

Elizabeth Drake was well-known in the field of chemistry, specifically the study of organic compounds and materials. Amelia had followed her analyses in publications the last few years on chemical structures, a concept which had only been discovered in 1858. Certain carbon atoms were found to link to one another in a pattern of sorts. Amelia had only a limited understanding of the idea but looked forward to learning more, especially from a fellow woman.

The fact that so many men were in attendance was surprising. In her experience, many men continued to believe females weren't capable of such things, a ridiculous notion as far as Amelia was concerned.

Mrs. Drake took the stage, her stride to the podium confident as was her demeanor. Her long, narrow face was pale, her brown hair drawn into a tight knot at the nape of her neck, giving her a no-nonsense look. She appeared to be in her early to mid-forties. A gray gown with white lace trim and a high neck neither enhanced nor detracted from her appearance.

Amelia understood her choice of attire. Wearing anything overly feminine would only draw criticism, but the reverse would also be true. She had been caught before in the same trap.

"Good afternoon." Mrs. Drake surveyed the audience as if to gauge those who had chosen to attend. "During the next hour, I will be sharing my latest research on organic compounds. As we all know, carbon is the principal element of these substances. My particular field of interest pertains to compounds from biological sources. To date, we still know very little, but these compounds have the potential of aiding humanity in numerous areas."

As the lecture continued, Amelia reached into her reticule to retrieve the small notebook she'd brought, relieved to see she wasn't the only one taking notes.

"...metabolites provide a defense mechanism in living things. These can be found in everything from plants to insects. Studying metabolites will allow us to not only understand their organic structure but to possibly use them to improve our defense against disease and illness..."

Amelia's interest deepened as the lecture continued. Mrs. Drake didn't try to convince the audience of any specific agenda but rather presented the facts followed by her conclusions, which were few to date. Clearly, she had only dipped her toe in the field and there was much more to learn, but the potential the woman described was staggering. A rush of excitement poured through Amelia's heart. So much to discover, so much to explore! Was this not wonderful?

The rest of the audience seemed as intrigued as Amelia saw numerous rapt faces around her. She soon gave up on taking notes and instead listened closely with the hope of drinking in as much as possible. The hour passed quickly and in the blink of an eye, Mrs. Drake was concluding her lecture.

"In summary, while plants have been used to aid in healing since the beginning of life, determining what particular part of the plant provides that benefit and how it does so still remains a mystery. If we can understand these minute compounds, we could expand the benefits and harness their power to save lives."

Applause filled the room, and Amelia found herself pushing to her feet to clap enthusiastically. How invigorating to hear of someone using their knowledge for the good of all rather than personal gain or to feed an ego. The fact that it was a woman only pleased her more.

Mrs. Drake offered a polite smile to the crowd and stepped away from the podium.

Amelia lingered as the audience slowly filed out of the theater. Though tempted to speak with Mrs. Drake, she wasn't sure what she would say. She hesitated to mention that she herself dabbled in chemistry. On the one hand, Amelia knew she did more than dabble, as her study in the field was fairly extensive. On the other hand, she hardly wished to compare herself to someone like Mrs. Drake, who had impressively devoted her life to the field.

With a sigh, Amelia moved toward the stage, unable to resist the urge to speak with her. How often did one have the chance to visit with a hero—or heroine? She wasn't the only one wanting a word with the speaker, and she waited patiently in a queue with half a dozen others. The time allowed her to observe Mrs. Drake while deciding what to say.

A man with a beard stood to one side just behind her in a black suit, clearly waiting for her to finish. Whether he was her husband or an assistant was difficult to tell. Amelia offered him a polite smile when he glanced at her. He nodded but didn't return the smile, his cold blue eyes less than friendly.

Amelia returned her attention to Mrs. Drake. The woman's confident demeanor never faltered, even when a man questioned her about whether studying such minuscule compounds and understanding them was truly possible.

The chemist was firm in her response, suggesting she had fielded similar comments before. Rather than becoming defensive, she pointed out several discoveries that had been believed impossible only a year ago. "It is only by pressing the boundaries of what we believe that we can learn more."

"Humph." The man remained obviously unconvinced. "We shall see. Sounds like a waste of time when we already know certain plants provide benefits."

The lady leaned forward and held the man's gaze. "But what if we can do more?" Then she turned her attention to the next person in line, elegantly dismissing both the man and his doubts.

Amelia nodded in approval, wishing she had even a portion of Mrs. Drake's certainty. She waited a few more minutes before it was her turn, her fingers inexplicably shaking. "I wanted to express my appreciation for you sharing your knowledge and…and applaud you for your endeavors," she began, nearly breathless as nerves took hold.

"You are leading the way not only in chemistry but also as a woman, and I admire you so much for it."

A brief smile appeared which swiftly departed. "Thank you."

Amelia waited, hoping for a moment of connection or even further conversation, but Mrs. Drake turned to look at the next person in line.

Though asking about the woman's expertise on fungi was on the tip of her tongue, Amelia eased back, the feeling of dismissal hard to shake.

With a resigned sigh, she turned away, realizing it was her own fault. She should've made it clear she had more to say, then Mrs. Drake might have further engaged in conversation. Her own confidence must be more fragile than she'd thought.

The man behind her asked a specific question regarding one of the plants Mrs. Drake had mentioned during the lecture. Amelia paused a short distance away to listen as the woman answered.

"Consider digitalis purpurea or foxglove, which is poisonous—yet Sir William Withering discovered how to use it to treat heart failure. The contrasts in nature are fascinating, are they not?"

Amelia pondered that idea during the trip home. The power in some plants was indeed miraculous. If that power could be better understood and isolated, the potential to aid humanity would be endless. Yet the danger of those same compounds, including fungi, couldn't be overlooked.

Perhaps that might be something she could study herself. Testing the reaction of organisms to various fungi would be a challenge, but perhaps it could lead to a breakthrough to what had happened to Nora.

"How was the lecture?" Fernsby asked upon her return, taking her things.

"Very informative. In fact, I shall be in the laboratory for a time." What better way to improve her confidence than applying what she'd learned?

"Splendid."

"I am in need of a variety of mushrooms, including poisonous ones."

"Oh?" Fernsby's brows raised, his concern obvious. "Right. Well. Allow me to see what I can procure."

"Thank you." Amelia climbed the stairs, pleased the lecture had inspired her even as she hoped Henry would call soon to discuss the result of her testing. If he had the time, she would enjoy sharing some of what she'd learned at the lecture.

Twelve

"Any luck?" Henry asked as he joined Fletcher at the Three Pigeons on Stafford Street after placing an order at the bar. The familiar scent of fried food and spilled ale lingered in the air, the warmth of the pub welcome after spending time in the frigid November air.

The sergeant had already claimed their usual table near a window in the crowded place and heaved a sigh. "Somewhat. No sign of Mr. Spencer, though a few said they knew him, and that he regularly purchased lottery tickets. Those I spoke with said he kept to himself but given that he was better dressed than most others in the place, he drew attention."

"And no one has seen him since he was reported missing?"

"No." Fletcher withdrew a notebook from his pocket. "A Mr. Jones said he was at the drawing on Saturday night. They briefly spoke to commiserate after they both lost."

"Any idea how much?" Money issues, mainly the lack thereof, were a common reason people suddenly changed their routine.

"Not specifically. The few I spoke with had the impression he didn't spend beyond his means."

"Isn't a record kept of the tickets sold?" At Fletcher's nod, Henry added, "Can we request specifics on how much he wagered over the past six months?"

"I did ask the barkeep, but he said the man with that information won't be there until Saturday evening."

"We can't wait that long." Henry shifted on the stool, frustrated by their lack of progress. "For all we know, Mr. Spencer could be in danger. Kidnapped. Injured. Worse."

"I pressed for his name and address, but the barkeep insisted he didn't have it. I'll check with the lottery company's office after lunch. Surely they can provide it."

"Good idea."

Fletcher took a long sip of his pint then raised his brows as he studied Henry. "You think he might've stepped off a bridge into the Thames? Perhaps we should be combing the shores for a body?"

"Perhaps, but we'll leave that to the dredgers. Until we know for certain, we must keep searching. A look into his finances could prove helpful. I found a letter in his desk that listed the bank he used."

"He didn't keep his money in the one where he worked?"

"Apparently not."

Fletcher frowned. "Doesn't that seem odd?"

Henry shrugged, his stomach grumbling. "I suppose it's wise to keep one's work and personal life separate. It would be awkward if you lost your position."

"True." Fletcher shook his head. "Still seems strange."

"There could be a simple explanation. Maybe he had the account in place before he got the job, or that was where his parents banked." Henry already had the impression that Spencer was a man who liked his privacy. "I'll stop by the bank in the morning."

"His parents didn't have any suggestions about where to look for him," Fletcher advised. "In truth, sir, I thought their reply to our telegram seemed surprisingly unconcerned."

"It was puzzling. Most parents would have made the trip to London to help with the search by now."

They dug into their lunch of eel pie and fried potatoes, each alone in their thoughts. Henry's strayed from the missing man to Nora and what he'd learned earlier. There was so much to consider, so much to—

"Care to share what has you so preoccupied?" Fletcher asked as he finished his pie and wiped his moustache with a napkin.

Henry debated whether to tell him about Nora. The case wasn't his to pursue, and it was wrong to involve himself with it, let alone Fletcher. It wasn't even technically a case.

Yet before he could further consider the matter, the details spilled from his lips. "A young mudlark was found dead on the mudflats near Blackfriars. Poisoned."

Fletcher's eyes narrowed. "Why would anyone poison a mudlark?"

"Good question. Reynolds doesn't intend to spend resources to look into the case."

"Logical, since the victim was more than likely an orphan. No parents, no one to advocate for justice. I assume she was an orphan?"

"She was," Henry reluctantly conceded. Not that it should make a difference. "Mrs. Greystone is the one who sent for me when the girl was found."

"Greystone? How is she connected?" Fletcher asked, clearly surprised.

"You may remember she works for a magazine. She was interviewing a barge captain who knows some of the mudlarks when the body was found."

"Ah. Small world."

"Indeed." Henry stared across the pub but didn't take in any of the other patrons. His visit with the laundress hadn't taken long. She'd been saddened to hear of Nora's passing but had no idea where the girl could have been or who would wish to harm her. She'd handed over the few possessions the girl had stowed in a corner of the back room, which hadn't revealed anything other than abject poverty. He'd left them with the woman to give to another as she saw fit.

"The girl wore her best dress, and Mr. Taylor found the remains of an impressive meal for a mudlark in her stomach. Or at least what little was left of it, as she was sick before she died."

"Odd." Fletcher nodded. "No wonder the death has caught your interest. The details don't add up."

"No, they don't. The girl had a small crystal bottle in her hand, an expensive one. She worked for an overseer of sorts, and I spoke with him, but it doesn't make sense that he would bother to poison her."

"True. Hit her, yes, more's the pity. But poison? No."

"Exactly. But who then, and why?"

Fletcher smiled. "Those are always the questions, aren't they?"

"I confess her death is difficult to let go of despite what Reynolds said. Seems like a child, even with no kin, deserves justice as much as the next person."

"Yes, but there are only so many inspectors and so many hours in a day," Fletcher pointed out.

"You're right. But I might delve into the situation further on my own time."

"That wouldn't have anything to do with the fact that Mrs. Greystone is involved, would it?"

Henry bit back a denial since there was some truth to Fletcher's question.

"I know you're frustrated that we haven't solved her husband's murder."

"I am, and I suppose that is part of it." His friend's comment was a reminder to go back through Matthew Greystone's file to see if any of the notes jarred something loose in his mind. It had been months since any clues had emerged, but as in all cases, someone had to know something. Someone out there knew who had murdered Amelia's husband.

Fletcher reached for his hat. "I confess that the violent death of a child is always troubling. To think someone would deliberately poison an innocent is...disturbing." His friend leaned closer, his gaze holding on Henry's. "And it makes you wonder if another victim will soon be found."

Henry nodded. "That is my concern as well." Especially after seeing the children searching along the shore and meeting some of them. No doubt Amelia felt the same.

Once again, a flicker of worry that Amelia would decide something more should be done and take matters into her own hands sparked down his spine. That wouldn't do, especially given how dangerous the area was.

"Let me know if there's anything I can do," Fletcher offered. "I don't mind looking in on a lead while I'm on my way to another."

That was one of the many reasons Henry liked the man. "Thank you, Fletcher. I'll do that."

The dinner hour had come and gone by the time Henry called on Amelia. Darkness had fallen, bringing a damp cold along with it. Despite her message requesting him to stop by, he didn't want to impose by sharing a meal with her again so soon. Better that he didn't grow accustomed to such pleasant evenings.

"Good evening, Inspector." Fernsby greeted him with his customary smile. "May I take your things?"

"Fernsby." He shook his head. "No need. I won't be long. That is, if Mrs. Greystone is available?"

"I believe she is." The butler led the way up the stairs. "Inspector Field, madam," he announced at the doorway of the drawing room.

Amelia sat in a wingback chair before the fire with a book on her lap. She smiled as she marked her page and set aside the book to stand, her gray gown flattering her slender frame. "Good evening, Henry."

"Amelia. I received your message and hope I'm not intruding," he said as Fernsby departed.

"Not at all. Please join me."

He waited for her to return to her chair before taking the one opposite, careful not to dwell on the warm fire or the cozy room which looked far too inviting. "I only have a few minutes but wanted to hear more about what you discovered."

The light of enthusiasm in her eyes made him smile. Her obvious pleasure in the task of testing for poison surprised him, though by now he supposed it shouldn't.

"Given how small the sample was, I hesitated as to which poison to look for. After a little research, I decided on fungi." She paused for a moment. "And I was right."

Her message had mentioned that, but he'd thought there might be more to the result as it was so puzzling. "As in…mushrooms?"

She nodded in response.

"What made you think to test for fungi?" Henry didn't know much about them and had yet to encounter any in his work.

Amelia shifted her attention to stare into the flames of the fire, brow creased. "I'm not quite sure." She met his gaze. "A feeling, I suppose. It's hard to explain."

Henry nodded. Intuition was something he used but hesitated to rely on. His father and grandfather had, but he didn't have the same instincts they did. There was a difference between a sense of knowing and logical assumptions. Only on occasion did the two meet, and he'd found it best to back any hunches with facts.

"At any rate, I found a significant amount of poisonous fungi in the sample, small though it was."

"Well done." Henry was truly impressed with her skills in chemistry, just as he'd been the last time she'd used them at his behest in the ravenkeeper's case.

"Thank you." Her pleased smile warmed him. "The question is, where do we go from here? This proves that something suspicious happened to Nora." She shifted to the edge of her chair as if expecting him to assign her a task in the investigation.

Henry frowned. "All it does is prove she ate poisoned mushrooms—a mistake people sometimes make, however infrequently. Besides, identifying the poison won't change my superior's decision on the matter. The best I can do is continue to look into her death in my spare time."

"I understand, but there must be something I can do—even if it's just having another conversation with Agnes and Pudge to see if they have learned anything more."

"Amelia, that is a dangerous area. The less you go there, the better."

Color touched her cheeks even as a hint of a smile reached her lips. "I will keep my visits to daylight hours, of course. You need not worry on my behalf."

But he did. The idea of her in the vicinity of the place at any time of day, given that she'd be alone, was more than concerning. She wasn't his to protect, Henry reluctantly reminded himself, but that didn't keep him from worrying. He hoped their friendship allowed him to offer advice. "Given the rough characters there, including Carl, I don't think that's wise."

She lifted her chin, signaling he'd already lost the argument. "I appreciate your concern, but I have been there twice in the last few days with no issue." She ran a hand along the fabric of her gown, hinting that she wasn't as confident as she acted. "Please know that I will take care."

"If someone is murdering children, there is no telling what else they are capable of." He hated to resort to scaring her, but she left him little choice. Did she not comprehend the risk she ran?

"I understand, but in turn you cannot deny that we need to discover all we can to keep the other children safe."

While Nora's poisoning could be a one-time occurrence, there was also the chance it wasn't. Which brought him back to his instincts—those told him another death would occur. Until he had a way to prove that, he would keep it to himself. Sharing the concern with Amelia would only encourage her to question those in the area.

"Fine, but within reason." He pressed his lips tight, keeping his other thoughts to himself. "Please consider having Fernsby accompany you."

"I will."

Whether that was an agreement to take the butler with her or simply think about it was unclear.

Amelia was quite independent, something she'd already proven while watching over Maeve. She was stronger than she knew—than he had expected—given what she'd endured before he'd met her. Other people would have crumbled beneath the hand she'd been dealt, between the death of her daughter followed soon by her husband's unsolved murder. Then she'd been tossed into the middle of the investigation of the ravenkeeper's death, lending assistance not only to the victim's daughter but to the case. It was a great deal for anyone.

Henry eased back, realizing he'd been leaning forward to make his point. He had no doubt she'd heard him. She'd never been reckless, and he had no reason to think she would be so now. Yet he couldn't help but add one last plea. "Do take care, Mrs. Greystone. Amelia. This is a serious matter."

"I will." She nodded. "Yet I can't help but think there is more to be discovered there. We shall see if I can uncover anything useful."

"You'll share whatever you happen to find with me?"

Surprise flashed across her face. "Of course. I will keep you informed."

Somehow her promise did little to reassure him that she would take reasonable precautions to stay safe.

Thirteen

"To the mudflats again, madam?" Fernsby stared at the boots Amelia wore, his displeasure evident.

"Well, yes." Amelia followed his gaze, all too aware of the muddy mess she'd brought home after her last two visits. "I did remember to wear an older pair of shoes." She glanced at the butler to see if that relieved his concern.

"So I see." Obviously it did not.

The morning was clear for the moment, but clouds loomed on the horizon. With luck, she would return before the weather took a turn for the worse.

"I am sorry, Fernsby, but it can't be helped. Something must be done to discover what happened to the girl."

"Is that not Inspector Field's job?"

"Not unless his superiors come to their senses and assign him the case. Or give it to someone else in the department."

That brought to mind Inspector Perdy, one of Henry's coworkers. She'd had the *displeasure* of meeting the arrogant man while Maeve had stayed with her. She nearly shuddered at the thought of him being involved in Nora's investigation; she'd never met a more irritating and inept man in her life.

"But the girl was poisoned," Fernsby protested, deep concern in his eyes. "Does that not warrant an investigation?"

"One would think." Amelia shook her head and adjusted her gloves before reaching for her reticule and the basket she'd asked the cook to fill with ham sandwiches and biscuits for the mudlarks. "Until then, Henry—Inspector Field is looking into the matter on his own time, and I am lending assistance."

Henry's concern for her wellbeing had touched her last night, but it had also been clear he'd been anxious to leave. She had decided against mentioning the lecture she had attended. *Silly to think he would find it interesting just because she did.* She'd been reading too much into their association. They might have become friends of a sort, but his interest in her was due mainly because of Matthew's unsolved murder, something she had allowed herself to ignore the past few weeks.

She appreciated his suggestion that Fernsby accompany her, but she couldn't imagine having him waiting nearby while she spoke with the mudlarks. That would only draw more attention, something she preferred to avoid.

"I do hope you will take care, Mrs. Greystone," Mrs. Fernsby requested as she paused on her way to the stairs with a neatly folded stack of linens in hand. "That area of London can be dangerous, even if you come bearing gifts." The housekeeper glanced at the basket Amelia held.

"Yes, it can. I will most definitely be careful." It was on the tip of her tongue to mention that if she didn't return by luncheon, they should send word to Henry, but she decided against doing so. No need to worry them when she had no doubt they would do exactly that if she didn't reappear in a suitable period of time.

Amelia nodded at the couple, grateful as always that she had them to look after her. Their overprotectiveness might drive her crazed at times, but they helped ease her loneliness. They'd been through so much with her, sharing her grief and offering unwavering support that provided a column on which she could lean when needed.

With a fortifying breath, she shook off her thoughts to focus on Nora. She didn't know if she could discover anything by returning to the area, but she certainly wouldn't find any clues if she remained home.

"I shall return soon." She stepped through the door and strode toward the hansom cab, saying a silent prayer for the blessings in her life, including Mr. and Mrs. Fernsby.

The day marked a year since Matthew's death. All the more reason for her to step out. She preferred to remember more pleasurable anniversaries, but this one had to be acknowledged. She'd woken with tears and said a prayer for herself, and then another that justice would eventually be found for him, though she didn't know how after so long.

Then she'd brushed away her tears and risen to face the day. What better way to spend it than to be productive rather than mourning her previous existence as a wife and mother, when she'd felt whole?

The cab ride was uneventful and soon deposited her on Puddle Dock, a narrow street that linked several wharves. She paused to look about, shivering against the chill in the air. An immense flour mill, which Amelia had read was one of the largest in the world at over eight stories high, had once stood nearby but had burned down over a decade ago. It was difficult to imagine what it must've looked like. The area didn't appear to have recovered, based on the worn look of the buildings.

The mudflats were narrow this morning, the tide higher than the past two times she'd visited. Making a mental note to pay more attention to such things before her next visit, she searched the dock for Captain Booth's tall form.

Her motives were not entirely mercenary; she truly did have a couple of questions for the man before she turned in her article. But Amelia also thought it wise to advise him that she was in the area again with the hope he'd keep an eye out for trouble—not that she was expecting any.

Unfortunately, Captain Booth and his barge were gone, although others were docked nearby. No matter.

Amelia walked to where the mudflats spread toward the river's shore. Half a dozen children bent low, including Agnes and Pudge, some squatting, all focused on sifting through the mud and pebbles.

She continued toward the two girls, who were working off to one side, taking care not to step in the worst of the mud as Fernsby's disapproval remained vivid in her mind.

"Good morning," she called to them as she drew closer.

Both girls slowly straightened and shared an inexplicable look with one another.

Amelia didn't want to know what they were thinking. It was probably something along the lines of: 'Here comes the crazed lady again. Doesn't she have anything better to do?'

No, she didn't. The reminder weighed on her, leaving her heart heavy. She was no longer a mother. No longer a wife. She conducted interviews, wrote articles, and puttered in her laboratory. She was a busybody poking her nose in situations which shouldn't necessarily concern her.

She shoved aside the depressing thought and forced a smile. "I hope the day finds you well, girls."

"Well enough," Pudge said with a small shiver as she rubbed her hands together as if to warm them.

"And yerself, ma'am?" Agnes added, as if sensing Amelia's hesitation.

"Quite well. Thank you." Amelia glanced around again. "I hoped to speak with Captain Booth, but he must be away." Saying that made her feel a little better, as if she truly did have a purpose.

"He left earlier. Not sure when he'll be back." Pudge bent to pick up something, then held a piece of blue and white pottery with a smile. "Pretty, eh?"

Agnes bent closer to look. "Oh, that is nice."

The floral pattern was clearly visible, though Amelia doubted the broken chunk had value. "Are you likely to find the rest of it?"

"Nah. The tide churns up the mud. Hard to say what we'll find next."

"I brought some sandwiches for you and the others," Amelia said, lifting the basket.

Voices in the distance kept them from replying. The three turned to see a man hailing one of the other mudlarks as he approached, his laughter floating on the light breeze.

"Oh, no." Pudge's lips tightened as she and Agnes shared another look. The silent communication between the girls was truly impressive.

"Who is that?" Amelia asked as she studied the jovial newcomer.

The man's gray muttonchops and moustache hid much of his face and his low cap hid the rest. He was tall and slender, his navy jacket and trousers roughly woven, and he appeared to be in his late fifties as far as she could tell from this distance.

"Captain Salem. He runs a barge, too." The lack of enthusiasm in Pudge's tone not to mention her scowl made Amelia wonder.

"You don't care for him?"

"No." The girls didn't hesitate, answering in unison.

"But we like the pennies he gives us." Agnes didn't sound excited in the least.

"Pennies for what?" Yet as Amelia watched the man speaking with a young girl, he reached into his pocket and pulled forth a coin, holding it up for the mudlark to view.

The girl lifted onto her toes, looking up at the man who bent to kiss her on the lips. Then the man laughed and handed her the coin.

"Dear heaven." Horror poured through Amelia's tight chest.

"It's not so bad, 'cept his breath smells of tobacco," Pudge said quietly.

Agnes shook her head. "Smells worse than that. His teeth are nearly as black as the mud."

Captain Salem held the girl's shoulder as he glanced around in search of his next target. His focus shifted to the three of them, and Amelia braced herself as he approached.

"Mornin'," he called when he neared, a smile on his face, his teeth in poor condition just as Agnes had described. Pale blue eyes gave him an unsettling appearance, nearly making Amelia take a step back when they fixed on her.

"Good morning." She straightened her shoulders, unused to being addressed by strange men to whom she hadn't been introduced, but the rules of polite behavior evidently did not apply here.

"Ain't ye a pretty thing." His gaze swept over her from head to toe and back again. "What brings a woman like yerself to a place like this?"

"I was looking for my friend, Captain Booth." Surely mentioning the man's name would serve as a warning to the newcomer.

It appeared not. "What do ye need him fer when ye can have me?" He pulled off his cap with a flourish to bow. "Captain Michael Salem at yer service."

"Thank you, but only Captain Booth will do." Amelia didn't mention her interview for fear of encouraging the man. She already didn't care for him. Young as they were, Agnes and Pudge were good judges of character.

He shook his head and replaced his cap over stringy gray hair that was combed over the top of a pale bald pate. "Suit yerself."

His smile returned as he looked between the girls. "I've come fer a kiss," he declared as he held up a shiny penny.

"You pay the children for kisses?" Amelia asked, making her disapproval clear.

"Wouldn't be right to request a kiss without givin' somethin' in return," he advised as if his impaired logic made it all right. He frowned when Amelia's expression didn't change. "I give 'em a choice, don't I? They could refuse if they don't want a kiss from Captain Salem." He tapped his chest, his nails overly long.

"It doesn't seem proper for a...grown man to solicit kisses from little girls." How could he not see how wrong this was?

His scowl nearly had Amelia taking a step back after all, unease tightening her stomach. "Who are yer to be sayin' such things? I have nothin' but good intentions fer these girls." He gestured toward Agnes and Pudge.

Yet based on how uncomfortable they seemed, Amelia had to wonder. She wouldn't want a creepy man giving her a coin in exchange for a kiss as a grown woman, let alone when she was but a child. How could he not realize he wasn't truly giving the children a choice when all their age were taught to respect their elders and do as they said? Besides, the mudlarks were desperate for money of any amount. It wasn't a fair trade.

Unfortunately, Amelia didn't think her protesting would do any good. It would take a man to confront Captain Salem and even then, she doubted whether he would see the error of his ways. Men like him were in all walks of life, dressed in fine suits with diamond signet rings on their fingers, living on the street, and everywhere in between.

"Good intentions? I should hope so," Amelia said quietly, holding the man's gaze with a steely one of her own.

He shrugged off her concern and smiled again, though with less enthusiasm. "Now then, who wants a penny?"

Agnes's gaze held on the coin as she rose onto her toes and offered her mouth. The captain kissed her with a smacking sound that caused Amelia to grimace. He laughed and handed her the coin then looked to Pudge who repeated the process.

Though she knew the girls would take any coin they could get, given their circumstances, Amelia wished deeply they didn't have to endure this.

Pudge discreetly wiped her mouth with the back of her hand after the kiss—a wise precaution, as far as Amelia was concerned.

"What about yer?" Captain Salem asked Amelia as he held up a coin.

Amelia gasped in outrage, but the man only chortled with glee.

"No coin fer yer then." He tucked away the coin once he regained control of his mirth.

"No, indeed." Amelia continued to glare at him for good measure.

"Why are ye pesterin' these girls when they're tryin' to work?" he asked.

Something about the way he watched her, suddenly possessive and with absolutely no morals, had Amelia wondering if she could be facing Nora's killer. She tightened her hold on her reticule, wishing she had carried an umbrella or some other item that might serve as a weapon.

Next time, she would.

Though unease crawled along her spine, this was her chance to ask a few questions; to aid Henry with the investigation and help Nora find the justice she deserved.

"If you are a frequent visitor with the mudlarks, you must have known Nora."

Captain Salem's eyes narrowed as he nodded. "I did. A shame what 'appened to her."

"It is. How well did you know her?"

"As well as I know any of the girls." He placed a hand on Pudge's thin shoulder, rubbing his thumb back and forth, seemingly unaware that the girl stiffened in response. "I see 'em out 'ere nearly every day, workin' their fingers to the bone while Carl watches over them to make sure they don't steal from 'im."

Based on his sneer when he said the overseer's name, he didn't care for Carl.

"If yer ask me, I would be lookin' at him," Captain Salem continued. "He don't like it when his workers talk of movin' on."

"You see nothing wrong with them wanting to improve their circumstances?" Amelia asked, hoping he'd keep talking and perhaps incriminate himself.

"Why would I?" He tapped his chest. "I came from nothin' and am now a barge captain. Ain't many who can say that." The pride in his voice couldn't be denied.

He had every right to be proud of himself, as far as his raised social standing was concerned. It still disgusted her that he demanded a kiss from a child for a penny.

"Now then, I have others to greet. I wish yer a good mornin'." He tugged the brim of his hat and turned away, walking toward where a young boy with a mop of wavy brown hair visible beneath his cap searched.

"Poor Charlie hates it worse than we do," Agnes murmured as she watched the captain.

"But he needs the coin just like us," Pudge added.

Amelia's stomach turned as she watched Captain Salem kiss Charlie on the mouth just as he'd done with the girls. *Dear God, all the children?*

There were problems in the world that she couldn't fix, and this was one of them. Despite Captain Salem's denial of any wrongdoing, he would go on her list of suspects. Perhaps it would be wise to keep Carl on it as well.

Fourteen

It took several conversations with one manager after another at Mr. Spencer's personal bank before Henry was finally permitted to see his records.

After reviewing a year's worth of them, a pattern began to emerge—or rather, a new pattern. Regular deposits of approximately the same amount coincided with pay dates from his position at the other bank. Withdrawals for rent and meals, so far fine. However, other withdrawals varied by amount and dates. They appeared to have increased over the past three months.

Did that mean he was gambling more heavily? Henry knew some people had difficulty with the pastime, much like drinking and other such vices. Perhaps Mr. Spencer enjoyed more than merely purchasing lottery tickets? He might have a taste for horse racing or fights or the other sporting events on which people wagered.

Though more money had been coming out of the missing man's bank account in the past couple of months, he still had more than sufficient funds remaining. It seemed unlikely he would've felt the urge to end his life because of gambling debts. That was, unless his bank account didn't provide the whole story…

Henry spoke with several bank employees but was told much of what he already knew—Mr. Spencer was polite, quiet, and not inclined to converse. He hadn't acted any differently in the past two or three weeks when he'd come by to do his banking business than in the months prior. He'd been alone each time he'd stopped in.

After thanking the last manager for his time, Henry took his leave, choosing to walk so he might sort through his thoughts on the case.

So. What could have occurred?

Had Mr. Spencer run into trouble, possibly caused by his gambling? He might've owed some unsavory character more than he could repay, more than was in his bank. Then again, he could've ended his life for a reason yet to be determined—or met with an unfortunate accident that had claimed his life.

It seemed unlikely a man with a decent position and what appeared to be at least a satisfactory life would choose to end it or simply walk away without a trace.

Given that he'd left for work the morning of his disappearance as usual and hadn't acted out of the ordinary in the days leading up to that, Henry tended to think he'd owed money he couldn't repay. He could've been the victim of an accident but more than likely, someone would have witnessed it and reported it. Since that hadn't happened, logic had Henry returning to his previous idea—the man had encountered trouble as a result of his gambling.

Perhaps the landlady could shed more light on the situation now that Henry better understood Mr. Spencer. He had a few more questions for her and needed to search the man's room again. There might be a clue he'd overlooked the first time—something that would point him in a direction to pursue.

"I'm sorry, but I had to clean out his room," the landlady advised a half hour later, wringing her hands. "Another person inquired about renting, and as I'm sure you can understand, I couldn't pass that up."

The older lady, a widow with a narrow face and wide brown eyes, watched Henry as if worried he might arrest her for the offense.

With a frustrated sigh, Henry politely nodded. "But you still have his personal effects?"

"Oh, of course." She gestured for Henry to come in and led the way to a small sitting room off the front door. "I gave the room a thorough cleaning, of course. I found a few papers I almost threw away before I remembered you asked me not to."

"I appreciate that." If only she'd remembered he'd asked her not to clean it as well. He waited while she retrieved the items, wishing the room was still intact so he could search it again himself.

It didn't take long for her to return with a wooden crate. "I have a trunk with his clothes, though I already made sure nothing remained in his pockets, so I'm not certain you need those."

"Not at the moment." Not if she'd already checked the pockets, probably for any loose coins. Henry attempted a smile and gestured to the crate. "I'm sure you have other duties to see to while I look through this."

"I'm happy to wait," she advised as she took a seat, peering into the crate as if she weren't familiar with each and every item inside.

"If you're sure." Henry started with the papers, a combination of receipts and a few letters, all of which he'd seen before. None of them were revealing. It was clear Mr. Spencer hadn't been sentimental based on how few items he saved.

"Do you have many clues?" she asked as she watched him work with obvious interest.

"Not as many as we'd like." He supposed it was only natural that she was curious, given that Mr. Spencer had been her tenant for nearly two years. Besides this might be as much excitement as she'd experienced in some time.

"I thought his mother might come for his things, but she hasn't."

Henry paused in his search. "Are you acquainted with her?"

"We've met. She lives in Shropshire, you know. Comes to see him when she's in town, though that's not often."

"When was the last time she was here?"

"Must've been...two months ago or better. She and her new husband took Mr. Spencer to supper. He said it was a fine meal, although he didn't seem especially happy about it."

"Did he mention why?"

"I had the impression he didn't care for his stepfather." She stared across the room as if trying to remember the details. "I suppose it would be difficult at his age to see his mother remarry." The lady pointed to the crate. "There's a letter in there from her."

Henry frowned. A letter from Mr. Spencer's mother? He hadn't come across it during his last search.

"It might have arrived after you were here the first time." By the woman's guilty look, he wondered if she'd already read it.

"I see." He sorted through the other papers and found an envelope in neat feminine script with several other papers stacked together. "Are all these new?"

"Oh. I believe I found those under his mattress when I cleaned out the room. I turn them over when I have new tenants, you see."

A good place to keep confidential items when one had a snoopy landlady who could come and go from one's room whenever she pleased.

"Seems like most of it could be thrown into the rubbish bin, but since you asked me not to, I kept it all." Again, she clutched her hands in her apron nervously, making Henry wonder if she'd already thrown out some things—or taken a few items of value.

He didn't comment but reviewed the papers one by one. Several lottery ticket stubs. Another letter, this one written by a man. Henry glanced at the signature. "Do you know who sent this?"

"Can't say that I do. Mr. Spencer never mentioned him, and I don't think he'd written before."

At a glance, the letter requested a meeting to discuss a problem but offered few details. Henry set it aside to take with him. The other papers included a laundry receipt and a shopping list as well as another letter from his mother.

Henry took the items he wanted to review further and asked the landlady to hold the remaining belongings until the end of the month, along with Mr. Spencer's clothes. He couldn't take the whole trunk. There simply wasn't room at the Yard at the moment. It wouldn't do for them to locate the man only to tell him that his possessions had been discarded and his room let to another.

"I suppose I can." She glanced around the sitting room as if looking for a place to put them. "I don't really have the extra space, as I'm sure you understand."

"Just until the end of the month."

"You don't think you'll know anything until then?" she asked with a frown.

"Difficult to say." Though Henry was tempted to tell her just how many people went missing daily in London and how few were found, he held back. Better if the public didn't know, else they might not sleep at night.

"You'll send word? I confess that the more I think about it, the more concerned I am about what might have happened to Mr. Spencer."

"Oh? What makes you say that?"

"I suppose those lottery tickets for one." She shook her head. "Why someone would spend their hard-earned pay on such things is beyond me. Might as well hand it out to any stranger on the street for all the good it would do you."

Her remark made him wonder if perhaps her late husband had gambled. "You disapprove of gambling?"

"As any good Christian does. No wonder Mr. Spencer hid those things under the mattress. I don't know that I want someone involved in such unsavory activities living under my roof."

"Perhaps it was nothing more than a little innocent fun." Henry couldn't help but play the devil's advocate to see her reaction.

"Innocent? Gambling?" Her outraged tone suggested that was impossible to believe. "Wagering of any sort should be illegal."

Henry didn't bother to mention that some lottery tickets were. That didn't stop them from being popular, especially among the working class. Who could blame them for wanting a better life than the one they had?

The thought brought little Nora to mind, dressed in her best outfit hoping to change her fortune.

"I will take the papers and leave the rest with you for the time being." Henry pushed to his feet, wondering if he had time before meeting Fletcher to visit the mudflats again.

He only hoped Amelia hadn't already decided to do so.

Fifteen

Amelia's breath caught at the sight of Henry's tall form approaching, an unsettling sensation fluttering in her chest. She'd been about to leave Blackfriars—although she had distributed the food she'd brought, she had yet to speak with Captain Booth, and lingering in the area any longer than necessary seemed unwise.

She squelched the feeling of joy at Henry's arrival, not wanting to appear overeager. She wasn't so naïve—or desperate—to think the inspector's interest in her extended beyond the unusual circumstances that had forced them together, starting with her husband's murder.

Yet she couldn't hold back a smile as Henry joined her. She enjoyed his company and though it sounded terrible, she also enjoyed the mental challenge of helping to determine what had happened to the ravenkeeper, and now Nora. In truth, anything that kept her thoughts from straying to the past was welcome.

"Amelia." He nodded. "I must say I'm not particularly pleased to see you here." The warmth in his brown eyes took the sting from his words.

His strong jaw and cleanshaven face were a pleasant change from the numerous bearded men around the docks. She supposed he was handsome with straight brows that framed brown eyes with their long lashes. Prominent cheekbones lent his face character as did the thoughtful intelligence in his eyes. He was broad of shoulder and taller than Matthew had been, for the top of her head barely reached his chin.

"You didn't really expect me to stay away," she countered.

After a long moment that left her wondering at his thoughts, his gaze caught on the basket she held.

"I brought some sandwiches and biscuits for the mudlarks." Heat filled her cheeks as she was certain he would disapprove of her presence there alone.

"That was kind of you." He turned to peruse the area. "Anything of interest today?"

She followed his gaze to where the children worked. They wouldn't be able to continue much longer as the tide was coming in and would soon hide the ribbon of shoreline. "Yes, as a matter of fact. Another potential suspect."

"Oh?" Henry's brows lifted as he met her gaze.

"In addition to Carl, we should add Michael Salem, another barge captain, to the list." She didn't bother to hide her poor opinion of the man in her tone.

"You spoke with him?" The displeasure in Henry's expression was touching. She appreciated having someone other than the servants fret over her.

"I did." She shook her head. "He pays the mudlarks a penny for a kiss."

In his thoughtful way, Henry silently processed this information before responding. "While unpleasant and concerning, it doesn't necessarily mean he gave one of them poison."

"No, but you must admit his behavior is suspicious."

"True." Henry glanced around. "Is he still nearby?"

"Unfortunately, no. He left on his barge. I'm not the only one who doesn't care for him. Agnes and Pudge don't like him either."

"But they like the pennies he offers," Henry countered.

"Of course. None of them are in a position to refuse a coin, even if the price is too high."

"Do they think he had reason to kill Nora?"

Amelia paused as regret filled her. What a poor detective she was. "I-I didn't think to ask."

"I'm glad you didn't. I would rather you left me something to speak with them about." A teasing light glinted in Henry's brown eyes.

"Oh, please." She waved a hand in dismissal, though her stomach lurched in a strangely pleasant way. "I have hardly touched the surface of the investigation." And she wasn't quite sure what to do next, other than linger in the area to see if someone else appeared to question. In truth, the noon hour was approaching, and she was ready for a hot cup of tea and a warm meal.

"We don't have much of an investigation as of yet, given the limited time I have to dedicate to it."

"All the more reason I am doing what I can to help." She didn't want another lecture on how dangerous it was for her to do so. Her gaze held on Agnes and Pudge. "I worry another child will be lost if we don't act."

"We must hope they are on guard after what happened to Nora." His less-than-confident tone suggested he didn't think that was enough to keep them safe.

Nor did she. "Indeed, though it's difficult for them to watch for trouble when we don't know from what direction it will come."

"They're clever. For now, I was hoping to speak with Charlie again." Henry searched the mudlarks.

"Charlie? Oh, yes. The girls pointed him out, but I have yet to meet him." She followed his gaze to a young boy, his head bent low as he worked.

"I spoke with him yesterday, since Carl advised he and Nora were friends. However, Carl listened to every word of our conversation. I thought the lad might share something more if his boss was absent."

"Excellent idea. May I join you?"

Henry hesitated, and Amelia feared he intended to send her on her way. But after a moment, he nodded. "That might be wise. If those in the vicinity are reminded of our acquaintance, it might offer you some limited protection."

Again, his thoughtfulness touched her, warming her despite the cold breeze. They walked across the way to where the children worked the shore.

"Nearly time to call it a day?" Henry asked the young lad.

He looked up and then straightened, arching his back with a grimace like a man five times his age. "Almost, sir. Tide's comin' in quick." He glanced at the water gently lapping at the shore.

"Have you had luck today?"

The child shrugged. "Nothin' much."

"I hope that changes. Anyone in the area today who doesn't belong?"

"No, sir." He glanced at Amelia as if suggesting 'no one other than her'.

"This is my friend, Mrs. Greystone," said Henry politely, as though the lad were twice the age he was.

Amelia smiled warmly. "A pleasure to make your acquaintance, Charlie."

The young lad looked nervous as he glanced at her, which tugged at her heart, but then turned his attention to the tall inspector who he was clearly more concerned about.

Henry appeared to see that, for he smiled. "Did you remember anything more about the man you told me about, Charlie? The one who spoke to Nora?"

Amelia's breath caught as she waited for the boy's answer.

After a long moment that suggested he was reviewing his memory, Charlie shook his head. "Can't say that I do. Have yer found out anything more about what 'appened to her?"

"Not yet." Henry gestured toward Amelia. "Mrs. Greystone and I are doing what we can to look into the matter. Any details could be helpful."

"I keep tryin' to 'member what that man looked like and what he said, but I didn't pay much attention." He bit his lower lip, a scowl on his thin face. "I wish now I would've."

"Do you think he was about my age? My height?"

Amelia admired the way Henry used comparisons to bring out a few details. He'd done something similar with Maeve.

The boy's brown eyes narrowed. "A bit older and shorter. Bigger." He patted his stomach as he eyed Henry's form. "Spoke fancy-like."

"That's very helpful. If you see him again, tell Constable Gibbons and he'll send word to me. I'd be most grateful."

Charlie looked back at the ground and gasped. As quick as a fox, he squatted to pull what appeared to be a circle from the rocks near the water's edge. "Oh! This is a good 'un."

"What is it?" Amelia stepped closer to see the small gold object he held.

"A fastenin' loop, like they used to keep clothes together." With his free hand he gestured down the front of his own shirt, moving it back and forth in a zigzag pattern.

The loop was covered in mud, and Amelia's untrained eyes found it difficult to recognize. Charlie bent down to rinse it off in the rising tide, scrubbing it with his nail to remove the last bit of stubborn debris that clung to the circle.

With a grin, he held it out for them to see, his excitement contagious. It was about the size of a ring, gold, but the small twist where the two ends came together confirmed its purpose.

"How interesting," Amelia marveled, peering closer for a look. "That must be from around the fifteen hundreds. They were often used in pairs to fasten garments as Charlie said."

"You and Charlie have an impressive knowledge of historical clothing," Henry said as he looked between them with a smile.

"I've found 'em before," Charlie advised as he continued to study his find.

"And I spend too much time reading. I do enjoy history." Feeling heat stain her cheeks as she practically admitted how dull her life had become, Amelia was suddenly anxious to return his attention to Charlie. "Do you find them often?"

"Once in a while. Carl will be pleased." He glanced at the ground as if hoping to find another.

"It's amazing how bright the gold is," Henry said as he studied the fastener.

"It's the mud," Charlie declared. "Keeps things lookin' near the same as when they was dropped."

"Fascinating." Amelia could see how searching for such things would be addictive. Having found a few, one would continue to hope another might be just under the surface of the silt.

"Good work. You have excellent eyes," Henry praised the boy, then glanced at Amelia. "Mrs. Greystone mentioned that Captain Salem was here earlier."

Charlie's face scrunched with disapproval. "He's an odd duck, but I'll take his pennies."

"Do you think he could have anything to do with Nora's death?"

The boy frowned as he considered the possibility. "I can't see why he would but who knows?" He sniffed, clearly still upset by his friend's death. "But everyone liked Nora. I don't know who would 'urt her."

Henry nodded, asking him a few more questions before bidding him goodbye. He waved at Agnes and Pudge who were working a little farther up the river. The girls waved back.

"I think Charlie would help discover what happened to Nora if he could," Amelia said quietly as they returned to the pier.

"He seems quite distraught over her death."

"I think all the mudlarks are. No doubt they realize it could've easily been one of them." How she wished she could do more to protect them. "Are you in the area because of another case?" she asked.

"Not exactly. I am meeting Fletcher shortly to review details on an investigation and thought I'd come by here before I did so."

"Is it a murder?" A thrill of something Amelia did not care to inspect rushed through her. Honestly, was she excited by the thought of such a crime?

"A missing person, though the circumstances are suspicious, and he has yet to return. I'm starting to think it might be murder."

Murder. Amelia shivered. "That must be difficult to determine if no body has been found."

"Very. It's hard enough even when there is a body, much like Nora." His gaze held hers. "And...and your late husband. Hard to believe it has been a year."

Of course he remembered the date. She nodded, not wanting to think about Matthew at the moment. "I keep thinking about her last meal. Nora's, I mean. Where would she eat like that? A restaurant seems unlikely when she had so little money. She had to have been with an adult. Perhaps a guest at someone's house, since she wore her best dress?"

"Perhaps. I doubt Carl eats so well."

"Captain Salem might." His clothes hadn't been particularly fine, but he'd been about to take a load on his barge, the cargo of which varied. Barge captains earned decent wages from what Captain Booth had shared.

Henry held her gaze. "You truly didn't like him, did you?"

"No. Anyone who takes advantage of children is capable of worse things." She couldn't help but shiver at the thought.

"I will see what I can discover about him."

"Good." Amelia frowned, wondering once again how she could help. "I still need to speak with Captain Booth about our interview, though it looks like it will have to wait until tomorrow since he has yet to return. I will ask him about Captain Salem, too."

"Amelia, I would warn you again of the danger. It wouldn't be wise to let anyone know who you suspect. It could easily get back to whoever did it and place you in danger."

She nodded, aware Henry was right, though she appreciated his concern. "I will take care." As much as she wanted to discover who had killed Nora, she didn't intend to be the next victim.

There were more aspects to the investigation than she'd realized, and she needed to tread carefully—but she still was determined to do all she could to protect the mudlarks.

Sixteen

Scotland Yard bustled with activity as Henry entered the building a short time later. The place was always busy, which was no surprise as crime in London never subsided. He nodded at Sergeant Johnson near the front door and continued along the corridor to his desk. A glance around showed Fletcher had yet to appear, which gave Henry time to look over the new cases he'd been assigned.

While he didn't like to start others before he'd finished the most pressing ones he was working on, such was the life of a detective. There were always more cases than he could possibly see to. Looking into Nora's death took up some of his limited time, yet he couldn't set it aside. The best he could do was use some evenings to make up for the time he'd taken from work.

One of the new cases he'd been assigned, the theft of an expensive painting, caught his notice, but since the crime was unlikely to place anyone in danger he set it aside for now. Murder cases took priority, and the disappearance of Mr. Spencer was beginning to smell like foul play—even if he didn't yet have any proof.

Time passed quickly as he prioritized, made notes, and planned a course of action on several. He looked up to see Fletcher striding toward him.

"I'm starving. Did you already eat?"

"Not as of yet." Henry set aside the files and stood. "Shall we eat and talk?"

"Efficiency is our motto," Fletcher said with a smile.

"Well, if it isn't Scotland Yard's finest." Joseph Perdy, a fellow inspector, strolled toward them with a smirk.

Henry smothered a sigh. He had never cared for the man and, after briefly working with him on the ravenkeeper's murder investigation, his opinion on the man's skills had only worsened. Perdy was too full of himself to listen to anyone else's ideas. How he'd risen from constable to an inspector was something Henry did not understand. Perhaps the man had been lucky enough to stumble into a solution for a case or two—that seemed the only way he could've managed it.

"What are you up to this afternoon?" Perdy braced his feet wide apart and folded his arms over his chest before Henry's desk as if prepared to stay.

"Working." Fletcher just barely managed to keep his tone respectful. "You?"

"Always knee-deep in a case." Perdy nodded, his gaze catching on the folders on Henry's desk. "Looks like you're falling behind again, Field. I suppose that means the Director will request a meeting with you soon."

"Do you only have the one case?" Henry asked as he retrieved his hat from the corner of his desk. "I would've thought a detective of your experience would have more."

"I have my share, don't you worry." Perdy leaned close. "I hope I don't have to help you again, Field. Then again, maybe the Director will soon realize this Field was promoted before you were prepared for the position."

Henry did his best to hide the fact that the remark struck true. The idea concerned him, though he'd solved his fair share of cases in the two years since he'd been promoted to inspector. He'd hoped identifying the ravenkeeper's killers and helping to save the Queen of England had eased the mind of anyone else in the department who agreed with the odious man before him.

"Why don't you worry about your own reputation, Perdy? And keep comments like that to yourself." Henry held the man's gaze long enough to make sure it was understood he wouldn't tolerate them.

"Now, Field." Perdy raised his voice, drawing the attention of the other inspectors in the office. "No need to take offense. I was only jesting."

"That's odd." Fletcher looked at Henry and lifted a brow. "Neither of us seem to be laughing."

"Let's go," Henry said firmly, before Fletcher said something to which Perdy might take offense and then be forced to apologize. "We have cases to solve." He sent a pointed look at the other inspector.

"Good luck," Perdy called as they strode out. "You clearly need it."

"Has he forgotten you recently saved the Queen?" Fletcher muttered as they neared the door. "I'd like to remind him that he nearly bungled the entire investigation."

"*We* saved Her Majesty," Henry corrected him with a smile, appreciating his friend's support. "I couldn't have done it without you." He held the door for Fletcher. "It is enough that we remember."

"I'm sure the other men do as well. At least, I hope so." Fletcher shook his head as if to clear it. "Any success this morning?"

Henry shared his review of Mr. Spencer's bank records as well as the conversation with his landlady as they walked down the street to a cart selling sausage rolls on the corner. The appetizing aroma of the piping hot sausages in a flaky crust drew customers far better than any sign could.

Fletcher frowned. "Why didn't the landlady share those details about his family the first time she spoke to you?"

"Who's to say? That is why we speak with people more than once. You never know what they'll tell you the next time. At any rate, let's send a telegram to a constable in Shropshire and have him speak with Mr. Spencer's mother. I'd like to see if she has any idea as to his whereabouts."

"Do you think the stepfather has anything to do with the situation?" Fletcher asked, after swallowing a bite of the sausage roll.

"It crossed my mind and is worth looking into." Family was always near the top of the list of suspects, more's the pity. "The mother's last letter to him had news of home but little else. But maybe she wouldn't put concerns about her son's gambling habits in writing. If she expressed displeasure over it, the stepfather might have taken it upon himself to have a word with Mr. Spencer and the discussion got out of hand."

"Shall I request a constable to verify the stepfather's whereabouts over the past week?"

Henry would prefer to speak with the stepfather himself. Once someone else asked questions which suggested the man was under suspicion, he'd be more likely to guard his reaction—but Henry couldn't be everywhere at once.

"Yes. Have him inquire about both the mother and stepfather's whereabouts along with the last time they saw Mr. Spencer. We'll see what comes from that."

"Very well." Fletcher brushed the crumbs from his hands as they both finished their hasty lunch.

Henry mulled over what other steps they might take to find Mr. Spencer but leads were few. Who else could he ask? Where else could he go?

"I meant to ask if Mrs. Greystone has heard anything about Maeve and how she's faring," Fletcher said.

Henry smiled, appreciating the sergeant's soft heart. He had taken a liking to the girl as they all had. "Her aunt says she is doing well and enjoying time with her cousins. It sounds as if she will start at a special school after the Christmas period." Henry didn't mention that Amelia was paying for it. That was her business.

Fletcher nodded, a pleased gleam in his eyes. "That's good to hear. The girl is as smart as they come. More schooling might be just what she needs."

"Especially since she will have a challenging road ahead. It can't be easy living in a silent world."

"No, sir, it's hard enough living in this one. So, what's next?" Fletcher asked, wiping his moustache.

"It would be an unofficial assignment," Henry warned.

"And?" Fletcher waited, making it clear he didn't mind.

"Will you check the morgue records to see if there has been a rise in orphan deaths of late? There's always a chance the bodies weren't found, but it would be helpful to know."

"Consider it done."

"Thank you. I found another lottery ticket stub in Spencer's possessions from the Sail and Anchor Public House. A drawing is being held tonight, so I'm going to see what I can find. Someone might remember him. If not, at the very least, I'll know who's involved in the scheme."

"Our missing man might be in deeper than we thought. Want some company?"

"Only if your wife won't mind." Henry grinned. "I prefer to keep on her good side in case I ever have the pleasure of meeting her."

Fletcher chuckled. "It has been some time since I had to step out in the evening. She'll probably welcome a quiet night to herself."

Did Fletcher realize how lucky he was to have someone waiting for him to return home every night? Henry couldn't help but wonder as he smiled at his laughing friend. How sad to be like Spencer, who no one seemed to know well based on the few personal details they had learned.

The thought gave Henry pause. Was he himself so different? He, too, kept his distance from his colleagues. He had few friends. Of course, he had his parents, which reminded him that he was to join them for dinner the following evening. He wouldn't mind asking his father's opinion on Spencer's case to see if there was anything he'd overlooked.

Yes, better that he focused on his work rather than his personal life, or lack thereof.

"At the very least, perhaps we'll meet a few other men like Spencer at this pub. They might shed some light on his habits which could provide a clue."

They arranged to meet outside the tavern later that evening. Fletcher departed to check on the mortuary while Henry called on the man who'd sent the letter to Spencer to see what he knew. The day was going to be a long one.

The Sail and Anchor Public House in East London was located near enough to the docks to draw business from sailors as well as locals, and what might be considered a colorful place during the day took on a more sinister hue at night.

The other shops along the street were locked up tight, their windows dark, but light spilled out from the pub. Based on the noise coming from the door being held open as several people entered, the evening's festivities had drawn a crowd. It seemed the patrons took the lottery drawing as serious business.

Henry wore an older suit with darned sleeves with the hope of better blending in and wondered if Fletcher had thought to do the same. He had no intention of announcing that they were with Scotland Yard unless necessary.

The chill of the November night settled over him, making him wish he was home—or even better, spending the evening with Amelia—rather than preparing to step into the pub. Thank goodness Fletcher had offered to join him. Though he didn't expect any trouble, that was often when it appeared.

"Evening." Henry barely made out Fletcher's beefy form before the sergeant stepped away from a building to join him. A glance at his worn brown jacket with its frayed cuffs revealed Henry shouldn't have worried.

"Quite the crowd, eh?" Fletcher studied the grimy window of the pub.

"Do you suppose they are all here for the drawing or is it always this busy?" Henry asked, amazed to think so many chose to purchase tickets.

"Couldn't say." Fletcher frowned. "If you wanted to bet on an event, why not do so directly rather than through a lottery ticket?"

"Excellent question. I would like to take a look at the mathematics behind the prizes. They claim that only expenses are deducted but several of the lotteries have been uncovered as little more than schemes to part people from their money. Funny how when one lottery is shut down, another opens to take its place."

"And makes those selling tickets rich right at the edges of the law," Fletcher added, his voice low. "Don't forget that part."

"Good point." Henry sighed. "One problem at a time. We're not here to contest the legality of the drawing, only to discover what we can about Spencer and his whereabouts."

"Learning more about those selling the tickets could aid us. There's always the chance Spencer realized it was a scheme, given his background in accounting and banking."

"That crossed my mind as well." Henry nodded. "If he uncovered evidence to prove that and confronted those behind the scheme, he might well have been silenced."

"So we will have a look around, ask a few questions, and get a sense of who is in charge?" Fletcher lifted a brow.

"Precisely." Henry glanced through the dirty window again before looking back at Fletcher. "It wouldn't do to ask too many questions. Don't mention Spencer more than once or twice."

"We are just here for a pint," Fletcher suggested with a smile.

"That's right."

"Are we taking opposite ends of the bar?"

"Might be for the best. We can compare observations afterward."

Fletcher tipped his hat to Henry, his demeanor shifting from the upright bearing of a former military man to a less imposing one with slumped shoulders and a shorter gait. It was truly impressive. "See you in an hour or so."

Then he eased inside and disappeared into the crowd.

Henry waited a few minutes and then followed his example, careful not to look around too much, wanting it to appear as though he'd been in the pub before in case anyone was observing him.

From what Fletcher had learned about the other lottery, a news sheet was printed each week which outlined the details of the weekly drawings. This one was held on Wednesdays and the other on Saturdays. People purchased tickets for who or what they thought would win and various cash prizes were awarded for first, second, and third places in the contests. Though horse racing was one of the more popular lotteries, other sporting events were included as well. Results were printed and sold two days after the drawings. Henry thought it a poor sport to sell the results. Just one more way to take people's money.

He eased through the crowd toward the long, polished bar and ordered a pint. When the barman slid a drink toward him, Henry thanked him, then added, "Busy place this evening."

"Always is, night of the lottery drawing." The barman quickly stepped away to fill someone else's order.

With the drink in hand, Henry turned to peruse the patrons, wondering how many would purchase a ticket. Did some intend to merely watch the spectacle, or did everyone participate?

Excitement filled the air: from an old, whiskered man who sat at the corner table to a young man who looked to be a clerk of some sort, everyone was animated, their spirits high.

If only they could all win a portion of the prize.

Henry allowed his gaze to drift around the room until he found Fletcher, who was already deep in conversation with another man. His friend met Henry's gaze briefly and gave the smallest of nods before returning to his conversation.

A further study of the room revealed a few other men who seemed more intent on observing rather than joining in the excitement. Henry guessed they were the muscle who made certain no one became overly excited. He watched each one for a few minutes before moving on.

"If ye hope to buy a ticket, ye'd better go upstairs," the barkeep advised as he drew another pint.

"Thanks, I will." Henry hesitated. "Do you by chance know a man named Adam Spencer? He often comes for the drawing."

The barkeep shook his head. "Can't say as I do."

With his drink in hand, Henry eased through the boisterous crowd and fell into a queue with a dozen or more who were making their way up the stairs.

"Excuse me," he said to the man before him. "Do you know a man by the name of Adam Spencer?"

The other patron frowned and shook his head. "No, I don't."

Though not surprised, Henry couldn't deny disappointment. Ridiculous to think he'd learn more about the missing man here than at his place of employment.

Well, he was here, so he might as well take in all he could. The upstairs of the pub was a wide, open area and overly warm, partly because of the numerous people and also from the heat rising from the stove on the lower level. The stench of sweat and desperation made for an unpleasant odor.

A man stood on a crate with tickets in hand, his encouraging calls to those waiting to make a purchase filling the air. "Get yer tickets! Time is running out."

Several patrons jostled for position to make certain they were able to buy them, though most looked as if they should keep their money in their pockets based on their simple, worn clothing.

Henry eased to one side and leaned against a railing so as not to be in the way.

The man on the crate continued to hawk tickets and was rewarded by a brisk pace of sales. Another stood beside him carefully counting money and offering change, though more than once, Henry saw him slip an extra coin into his pocket. A small table sat behind the two with a lockbox and a stack of tickets on it, a third man watching over them.

The trio worked smoothly together, suggesting they'd done this many times before.

"Hurry now," the hawker called. "Don't miss the drawin'."

Henry shook his head at the pointless urging. The man's remarks were making those in line anxious. Tempers flared as patience grew short. If the man wasn't careful, he would have a riot on his hands. That would be ugly with so many in an enclosed space.

Though he'd told Fletcher not to mention their missing man overmuch, Henry wanted answers. There was no way to gain them other than ask questions. He made his way to the man at the table. "I'm looking for Adam Spencer. Do you know him?"

The man's gaze raked over his face then he shook his head. "Never heard of him."

After watching a few more minutes, long enough to be certain he had a good description of the three involved in selling tickets, Henry returned downstairs, immediately appreciating the cooler air.

He caught Fletcher's gaze and tipped his head toward the door to indicate they should leave soon. Fletcher nodded. After draining his glass, Henry returned it to the bar and stepped out the door.

He'd only taken a couple of steps when he felt a prick in the middle of his back, causing him to stiffen. The pain sharpened when Henry attempted to look over his shoulder, but it was too dark to get a good look at him.

"Do ye think we don't know a copper when we see one?" The man growled in his ear. "Best that ye go and don't come back."

An even sharper pain pierced his back before he was shoved into the street. The rough cobblestones scrapped his palms as he caught himself. His knee protested at the hard landing, but he was on his feet in an instant to face his attacker.

"Why the concern?" Henry asked as he straightened his jacket, ignoring the aches and pains. He didn't bother to deny he was with the police. "Unless you're doing something illegal."

The large man growled, having already put away the knife. His face was in the shadows, but his large fists were visible and would do plenty of damage. "Don't come back, understand?" He turned and went back inside.

Though tempted to follow the man, Henry decided against it. He and Fletcher would be sorely outnumbered if a physical altercation were to ensue. The question was whether he had struck a nerve by asking about Spencer, or they merely didn't want the police looking into their business.

He pressed a hand to his back, easily locating the cut but didn't think it amounted to much. With a sigh, he found a dark corner to wait for Fletcher and make certain he didn't receive the same treatment.

Seventeen

"Aunt Margaret!" Amelia stared at her mother's younger sister, standing in the doorway of the drawing room, with a mixture of shock and dismay. "What an unexpected surprise."

She'd finished dinner and had settled to read more of her book. When she'd heard a knock at the front door, she listened closely as she hoped it was Henry. Never had she expected her *aunt*.

"Amelia, it's been too long." Aunt Margaret drew off her gloves and tossed them onto a nearby table, then strode across the room to reach for Amelia, who'd finally managed to overcome her surprise and rise. "I decided I was overdue for a visit."

"How...how exciting." Amelia hugged the woman, catching a hint of her familiar violet perfume. "I didn't realize you were coming to London." Why on earth hadn't her mother and father mentioned it?

"I wanted to surprise you." Aunt Margaret leaned back, blue eyes sparkling in her round face as she held Amelia's arms.

"You certainly did."

Amelia adored her spinster aunt, but she tended to take over when she visited. At least, that had proven true the previous times she had come to stay, including when she'd come after Matthew's death.

While Amelia had appreciated her support, her presence now would put a slight damper on Amelia's routine. One thing she knew for certain was that Aunt Margaret would not be excited about Amelia's involvement in the investigation of Nora's death.

Perhaps that was why she had come—because she'd heard of Amelia's connection with Maeve. No doubt her parents had mentioned the situation.

"I hope you don't mind if I stay with you for a few days. I already told Fernsby to place my bags in the guest room." Her aunt's independence and adventurous spirit had always been something Amelia admired, as exasperating as it often was.

"Of course, I'm happy to have you. I just wish you would've told me so I could clear my schedule."

"Oh?" Aunt Margaret's eyes widened with interest as she looked Amelia over from head to toe as if to assess what that meant by her very clothing. "Do you have plans?"

"A-A few, yes." She had intended to return to Blackfriars in the morning to speak with Captain Booth and see what more she could discover. Her conversation with Captain Salem continued to bother her, and she wanted the other captain's opinion on the man. However, Amelia did not share any of those details with her aunt. "Have you had dinner?"

"Yes, thank you. I didn't want to impose so stopped for a meal after I left the train."

"I see." A glance at the doorway showed Fernsby with her aunt's bags, a question on his face. Amelia nodded, knowing the butler shared her mixed feelings about their visitor. "How long will you be staying?" she asked as Fernsby disappeared from view.

"Perhaps a week. Who's to say? I considered taking a holiday abroad but given the turmoil of late, especially in Egypt, I decided against it. Have you read the news sheet? Positively dreadful."

Amelia lifted a brow, wondering if she intended to visit the pyramids, but before she could ask, her aunt moved to stand before the fire.

"My, it is positively frigid out there." Before she could've possible warmed her outstretched hands, Aunt Margaret sank into the wingback chair, smoothing the skirts of her striped gown, her movements restless. "I don't want to interfere with your schedule, of course."

Clearly, she didn't care if she did. Amelia briefly closed her eyes with the hope of shifting her attitude. While she adored her family, including Aunt Margaret, she also appreciated her privacy. Surprises like this weren't necessarily welcome, especially in the middle of an investigation.

But unwilling to tell her aunt she could not stay, Amelia forced a smile, adjusting to her unexpected guest as disappointment filled her at the realization that there wouldn't be any evenings with Henry in the coming days to discuss the case. That was enough to cause her smile to falter.

"Mother and Father are well?" she asked aloud as she returned to her own chair. She already knew the answer as she'd received a letter from them only yesterday, saying as much.

"Quite well. They miss you, of course."

"I look forward to spending time with them over the festive season." It was difficult to believe Christmas was next month, she'd been so busy of late with Maeve and now the mudlark's death. Time was passing quicker than she could've imagined a few months ago.

Though murder investigations were a grim way to pass the time, she couldn't deny how intriguing they had been thus far. A puzzle of sorts with life-and-death consequences. If only she could solve Matthew's.

"You mentioned plans?" Her aunt lifted a brow, pulling her from her thoughts. "Perhaps I can join you."

"Unfortunately, not." Amelia smiled with the hope of keeping her aunt from feeling offended. "I'm in the middle of an interview for the magazine."

"How fascinating. What is this one about?"

"A barge captain and the race they hold each year."

Her aunt frowned. "That doesn't sound very exciting. I thought that was the point of your articles, to share the unique and unusual."

"The barge races are both, as are the captains involved." She knew that firsthand from speaking with Captain Booth. "The idea of barges moving fast enough to race is surprising, and those who guide them are equally interesting."

"If you say so." Her aunt's frown did not diminish. "Surely you won't venture to the docks for the interview. That's no place for a lady."

Amelia kept her smile, not wanting to argue. "It's quite safe in the daylight hours." Heaven knew what her aunt would think if she learned of the mudlark's death.

"But your reputation, dear." Her aunt shook her head. "How do you intend to find another husband if you insist on going to such places?"

"I'm not searching for a husband." That was the last thing on her mind. While she didn't know if she wanted to spend the rest of her life alone, Amelia had no intention of marrying merely to avoid such a fate. "I need only think of you and your many adventures to know I can be happy by myself."

"It is not for everyone, Amelia. In fact, it's not for most." Her aunt's gaze slid to the side, making Amelia wonder if something was amiss. "You should think twice before deciding to remain a widow."

Amelia reached out to touch her aunt's knee, her sympathy and curiosity caught. "I thought you were happy."

Her aunt fluttered a hand in the air then allowed it to fall to her lap. "Of course. Most days." She forced a smile, but it didn't reach her eyes and soon her attention shifted to the fire. "But not all. Loneliness is not a companion I would recommend."

Aunt Margaret's words circled through Amelia's mind as she took a hansom cab to Puddle Dock again the following morning. It saddened her to think her aunt wasn't happy. Clearly her enthusiasm and exuberance hid feelings Amelia hadn't noted before.

That was something she understood. How often in the months since first Lily's death, and then Matthew's, had she pretended all was well? More than she could count. While part of her thought pretending would help her regain balance and find a path to normalcy, that wasn't always true.

Forcing herself to smile and act as if she had the motivation to carry on with the day had helped Amelia avoid the darkest pits of despair. But it was exhausting, and one couldn't pretend forever. Emotions had to be experienced to be released. Constant avoidance didn't solve anything.

It had taken Matthew's death for her to realize that.

Though she knew she would never completely heal after the losses she'd endured, she liked to think she had gained ground.

Truly? a voice inside her head whispered.

Yes, well, she would be the first to admit the situation with Maeve followed by seeing poor Nora's body had brought back painful memories. Grief—never far away—had threatened to return.

However, she preferred to think that was normal. Anyone who had seen Maeve mourn her father, or Nora's lifeless body, would be upset. Of course, Amelia's reaction had been stronger than most given her experiences—but using that upset as motivation to assist with the investigations was a healthy way to manage it. At least, that was her hope.

She would give Aunt Margaret a few days to settle in, and then perhaps a serious conversation was in order. Though tempted to write to her mother about her concerns, Amelia would see if Aunt Margaret would share what was bothering her first.

Her aunt had never mentioned being lonely before, but she was much like a small bird, fluttering here and there, always on the go, making serious conversations difficult. Maybe her aunt hadn't allowed herself to grieve for the life she thought she'd have. In truth, Amelia didn't know what her aunt's hopes and dreams had been when she was younger.

It was never too late to reach for what one wanted. If Amelia could encourage her aunt to pursue her desires, she would do so.

Pleased to have a plan of sorts to aid her aunt, Amelia turned her attention to the scenery, relieved to see Captain Booth's barge tied to the dock. Hopefully, that meant he was there.

She paid the cab driver, not bothering to ask him to wait as she didn't know how long she'd be. She held a hand to the short brim of her hat to shade her eyes from the weak sunshine, realizing she hadn't timed her visit well since the tide was in and none of the mudlarks were in sight.

Still, she started slowly toward the barge, hoping Captain Booth would be nearby.

"Mrs. Greystone."

She turned to see the lanky captain approaching from the street, a smile on his familiar face. "Good morning."

"What brings you back to the dock?" Captain Booth asked as he joined her, his pace slowing to match hers as they continued toward his barge.

"I have a few more questions for you to complete the article if you have a few minutes."

"Of course. I'm happy to help." He glanced around the river's edge. "Fine day for November, isn't it?"

"Very much." No doubt he was used to the damp cold while she was not. "Do you have a busy day ahead?"

"I'm taking a load of bricks upriver. Care to join me?"

She wouldn't deny the idea was tempting, after enjoying the ride the other day very much. "I wish I could, but my aunt has come for an unexpected visit. If I don't return by luncheon, she'll wonder what's become of me."

The captain nodded. "Another time then. The invitation is always open."

Amelia smiled. The chance to experience a journey on his barge again was enough to make a promise to herself that she would take Captain Booth's offer when possible. Perhaps Aunt Margaret would enjoy it as well.

She studied him, wondering if he might like to meet her aunt, despite the probable difference in their ages, only to decide the question was for another time.

"Thank you," she said. "You mentioned the man who started the barge race, and I wanted to include a little more about him in the article."

"That would be Henry Dodd." Captain Booth drew to a halt to share what he knew, and Amelia took notes to make certain she kept the details straight.

"Do you think any of the other barge captains might have known him?" Though curious, the question also provided a way to delicately raise the topic of Captain Salem.

"Most certainly." He glanced around the dock. "I don't see Captain Walsh at the moment, but he did. I'm sure he'd be happy to speak with you."

"Excellent." That would provide her with a reason to return. "I will come back another day to see if he's available." She cleared her throat. "I met Captain Salem yesterday."

A wry look came over the man's face. "I am sorry to hear that. How unfortunate for you."

"You don't care for him?" Amelia was relieved to hear him speak so coldly about the man.

"Can't say that I do, but he's an experienced captain and good at his job."

"I saw him offering coins to the mudlarks in exchange for a kiss."

"I warned him to stop, but he claims it's their choice. As if any of those poor children could refuse a coin."

Amelia hesitated, wondering how honest to be—yet now she knew Captain Booth didn't agree with the man's practice, she would speak plainly. "In all honesty, I thought it disturbing. It made me wonder if he could've had anything to do with Nora's death."

Captain Booth's brows shot up in surprise, but he didn't immediately deny it. "As odd as he is, I can't think he means the mudlarks true harm."

Amelia waited to see if he would add anything more, and liked to think Henry would be pleased with her questioning technique.

His lips twisted as he searched the shoreline, but the tide was only beginning to recede, and none of the mudlarks were in view. "I sure hope he wouldn't."

"Is there anyone else who has come to mind over the last few days? Someone who doesn't look upon the children with as friendly an eye as you?"

"Carl, of course." Amelia nodded and held her silence again. "There's also a dredger who's often yelling at them. Accuses the children of taking things that don't belong to them."

"Isn't that their job?" she asked, confused.

"He seems to think he owns the river and its banks. At least, that's how he acts sometimes."

"His name?"

"Mr. Tobias Watson."

"Can you point him out?" Amelia looked around the pier but realized she wouldn't know a dredge from a barge.

"He's not here at the moment—but don't try to talk to him." The sincerity of his tone had Amelia meeting his gaze. "He's a grumpy old man, set in his ways. While I can't imagine him killing anyone, there are times when he makes even me nervous. He acts a bit...unhinged at times. Too much time on the river pulling up bodies, if you ask me."

"Oh?" Amelia was horrified by the thought. "Bodies?"

"Who wouldn't be unhinged after looking at all those dead people, let alone picking through their pockets in search of valuables?" Captain Booth gave a mock shudder.

"I'm not familiar with dredgers. Is that how he makes his living?"

"He isn't so different than the mudlarks, though he searches the river rather than the shore. He pulls up crates, barrels, baskets, and anything else that fell off a boat. He either claims the reward or sells them."

"Including *bodies*." Amelia couldn't get past that part. It was morbid to the extreme.

"He says somebody has to clean up the river."

"I suppose that's true."

"If someone goes missing, their family might offer a reward. I guess knowing what happened to them brings closure of a sort."

Amelia nodded, understanding that all too well as tension tightened around her lungs, only to gently release. She needed to realize she might never know what happened to Matthew or why.

"But as I said, Watson is not the friendly sort, and I'd advise you to steer clear of him."

"I will do that." But that didn't mean she wouldn't share the man's name with Henry in the hope he would question him. "Is there anyone else? Any strangers in the area you've noticed lately?"

Captain Booth shook his head as he pulled out his pocket watch. Clearly he was anxious to get on with his day. "Hard to say. People are through here all the time and though I am familiar with many, I don't claim to know them all."

"Of course." Amelia placed her notebook back in her reticule, guilt weighing on her for keeping the honest, hard-working man from his job. "I won't take any more of your time. I certainly appreciate your assistance."

"My pleasure." He tugged on the brim of his hat. "It's not often that I have the chance to speak with an intelligent and attractive lady."

The respect in his tone put her at ease, and in all honesty, it was rather flattering.

"Don't be surprised when I return to accept the offer of another ride on your barge," she said with a smile.

"I look forward to it." He dipped his head and strode away with a long gait, clearly comfortable in who he was. Not many could claim the same.

Amelia was in no hurry to return home, though she couldn't stay too long without her aunt wondering where she was. She left the dock and walked along the street in the direction of a hansom cab stand, taking her time to survey the area as she went.

She studied the people passing by and the buildings lining the street, unsure what she was looking for—it wasn't as if she would know whether someone in the area was a stranger or not—yet she felt compelled to search.

The street was by no means crowded, so she discreetly watched each person she passed. Most were rough looking men who must work in the area, hurrying to wherever they needed to be. Others drove carts that hauled loads of bricks, barrels, and timber. Everyone she saw seemed to have a destination in mind and none appeared to be out of place.

Who would choose to poison a young girl, and why? Had Nora gone inside one of these buildings? Amelia paused to consider a red brick structure, the windows too coated with grime to see through them.

What purpose did it serve? Three stories with few windows suggested a warehouse. No one would go into one without a reason. It seemed unlikely that Nora would wear her best dress to venture within.

She continued walking past a few businesses but didn't see any that would appeal to Nora. The Blackfriar Pub across the street, where a medieval Dominican friary had once stood, might have provided the fine meal she'd eaten before her death. But who would've paid for it?

With a frustrated sigh, she pushed on to the cab stand, wishing she had more than another name to share with Henry. She would just have to hope that he was having better luck…

Eighteen

Henry read the message from Amelia, torn between admiration and worry. The fact that she'd returned yet again to Blackfriars was concerning. If her presence was noted by Nora's killer, she could be in jeopardy. The area was dangerous before a child's body had been found. Now it was even more so.

Still, he couldn't deny that each time she ventured to the area, she learned something. Given her curiosity and intelligence, she would've made a fine detective—if women were allowed to do such things.

And now she'd given him the name of another potential suspect—Tobias Watson, a dredger. No other details were written in her neat hand, and he wished she had shared the reason the man should be considered as a suspect to help guide Henry's questioning.

A deep breath made the small cut on his back sting, reminding him to be more careful. Henry was relieved the wound hadn't required stitches as he didn't care for needles or the feel of them. Then again, he hadn't consulted a doctor to know for certain. Luckily, Fletcher hadn't received the same treatment as Henry had upon leaving the pub.

Henry had just returned to Scotland Yard having spent the morning looking into the lottery ticket business. The publisher who printed the drawing results hadn't been of much help. No one there had heard of Adam Spencer, nor had they received any complaints about the drawings. At least, none they would share. Further digging was needed, something that Fletcher was working on.

No other names of those involved had been offered. It seemed clear that the men behind the drawings preferred to remain in the background. That alone raised Henry's suspicions.

The other potential lead regarding Spencer, the letter which had been under the mattress, hadn't resulted in anything of interest. Henry had also checked in again at the bank where the man was employed, but they still hadn't heard from him. The manager wasn't so different from Spencer's landlady, making noises about replacing him.

If the man did eventually make a reappearance, he would find much of his life upended.

Henry read Amelia's message again, debating whether he could take an hour or two to find the dredger that afternoon, though it probably wasn't the best time of day since this Mr. Watson was more than likely done working until dawn.

"Field."

He looked up to see Director Reynolds gesture for him to come into his office. Stuffing the message into his pocket, he stood and followed Reynolds.

"What's the latest on your missing man?" the Director asked as he sat behind his desk.

"Still missing, unfortunately. The only potential leads which have arisen thus far involve lottery ticket stubs and bank records that suggest he was withdrawing increasing amounts, possibly to spend on gambling. It makes me wonder if the man was getting in too deep with the lottery. He also has a new stepfather, who might cause friction." He shared the few additional details of what they had learned to date.

The scowl on Reynolds' face suggested he was less than pleased with the progress. "No signs of problems from his employer?"

"No, sir. The sharing of personal information was something his superior frowned upon, and Spencer took that seriously. His colleagues know surprisingly little about him."

"Hmm. Funny how often it's the quiet ones who end up in trouble of some sort, eh?"

"True."

"Well, keep digging. Someone has to know something." Reynolds removed his spectacles and rubbed them with a handkerchief. "Have you started on that theft of the painting?"

"Not yet."

"Best to look into that one soon before the trail goes cold."

So much for finding Tobias Watson that afternoon.

"Something else on your mind, Field?" the Director asked as he put on his glasses.

"I suppose I have yet to stop wondering what happened to the young girl who was killed."

"The mudlark?" Based on Reynolds' frown, that didn't please him either.

"Yes. Knowing she was poisoned doesn't sit well." Though mentioning it was risky when it might only gain Reynolds' disapproval, he wanted an official investigation into the girl's death.

It appeared he was not going to get one. "Yes, well, it's never good when a child dies but given her occupation and lack of family, you have to let it go."

Resentment surged but Henry was careful to mask it. Pressing his superior wouldn't change his mind when it was already made up.

"Keep me posted on the missing man and work quickly on the theft. The painting is worth a significant sum and the owner wants it found and returned."

Henry nodded and returned to his desk, frustration rising. A painting should never be considered more valuable than a human life. Even if Director Reynolds didn't agree, he knew Amelia would.

The following morning, Henry made a point to wake early. The only chance he had of speaking with Tobias Watson was before dawn. From what he knew, dredgers tended to be out on the river by sunrise, if not earlier, to search for things dropped overboard by ships moving at night or items stirred up by the changing tide.

As he dressed, blinking to remove the grit in his eyes, he told himself that venturing out at this hour would leave him the rest of the day to find the stolen painting...but the reassurance didn't keep him from yawning.

He let himself out of his apartment building then walked briskly to a hansom cab stand, breath visible beneath the occasional lamp light in the cold air. He would much rather be sipping a hot cup of coffee but that would have to come later.

Luckily a cab waited, a bundled-up driver and horse dozing while the night continued to hold firm.

"Blackfriars." Henry hopped in, rubbing his hands together to ward off the chill, wishing he had a warming brick or two at his feet.

"Yes, sir," came the muffled reply as the man adjusted his scarf.

Only a few carts and wagons were on the street at this hour, so they made good time. After alighting, he paid the driver and walked toward the water's edge where several small rowboats were tied, oars waiting. The place was eerily quiet, the lingering darkness causing him to glance around uneasily. His nose twitched with the brackish scent in the air and from the cold.

Pushing aside the unsettling feeling, he asked a few of the men working nearby for direction. It took several tries before one could point him toward a Tobias Watson.

The man was bent low over his boat, visible in the dim light of a nearby lantern. He coiled a rope into the bottom where a boathook rested along with what looked to be a harpoon. Though dawn was slowly lifting the darkness, it didn't yet provide enough light to work by.

"Mr. Watson?" Henry asked.

The man straightened, squinting at Henry, his expression unwelcoming. "Yeah? Who are yer?" he asked as he rubbed his grizzled face.

"Scotland Yard, Inspector Henry Field."

Watson scoffed. "What are ye doin' here at this hour?"

"I would like to ask you a few questions."

"About what?" The dredger returned to his work, seeming unconcerned about Henry and his questions.

"Are you familiar with the mudlarks?"

The man straightened again to stare at Henry as if he were daft. "O'course. Who 'round here ain't?"

"What about Nora, the girl who was found dead on the mudflats the other day?" Henry gestured to the area where her body had been.

"Sure, I knew her. I know 'em all, don't I?" He looked toward the shoreline, though no children were there. "They're in the way, often as not."

"Oh?"

"The river is mine to search, but they're in the water the moment my back is turned." His disgruntled tone made his feelings on the matter clear. "Have to watch 'em like a hawk."

"Did Nora search the water as well?"

"Didn't I just say they all do it?" Again, he fixed Henry with a glare. "That girl, too."

Watson was clearly a cantankerous sort. "Did the two of you argue about the matter?"

"Are ye suggestin' I had something to do with her dyin'?" Watson's eyes widened in disbelief. "Whatever would I kill her fer? She must've fallen ill or the like. Have ye seen those kids? Most would blow over in a stiff breeze."

The man had a point. "Do you live in the area?"

"Not far. Same as the other dredgers."

Henry nodded as he glanced inside the man's boat, noting that the hook or harpoon would make fine murder weapons, though neither of those had been part of Nora's fate. "Have you found anything interesting of late?"

"Depends on what you call interestin'."

"Valuable?" Henry lifted a brow to encourage the man to answer.

Watson shrugged as he adjusted the knot of a handkerchief tied around his throat. "A crate full of fancy vases yesterday."

"How do you know where to look?" Henry had seen dredgers at work and been called to investigate a body they'd found in the river on more than one occasion. He had often wondered how they knew where to throw in their hook since many of the things they found weren't visible from the surface.

"Ye study the water. An eddy or ripple often tells when somethin' is in the depths." The man was silent as he stared at the water. "The river has secrets she doesn't always want to reveal," he continued. "Sometimes, if ye're patient, she lifts them to the surface for a glimpse and other times, she holds 'em down, angry when you try to pull 'em up."

A rather poetic way to describe it. The life of a dredger was not an easy one, and the dangers were real. Becoming hooked on an immovable object under the water when the tide changed could either prove fatal or provide treasure.

"I'm sure there are days when you don't retrieve much of anything," Henry suggested, studying the dark water with a certain dread.

The man chuckled. "Oh, we always find somethin'. It's just not always worth much."

"Bodies?" The fate of the missing Spencer came to mind, though Henry still held a faint hope he'd be found.

"O'course."

Again, Henry waited to see if the man would share more. He was aware of the practice of men like Watson searching the pockets of floaters for anything they could sell. Digging in the clothing of bloated bodies was a grisly way to make a living, but Henry wouldn't deny that at least the bodies were found.

"If ye're done with yer questions, I have work to do," Watson said, his profile barely visible against the dawn's faint glow.

"Send word if you see anything unusual. It could be related to the mudlark's death and help us find who killed her."

"Unusual?" Watson chuckled. "Not a day goes by that I don't see that. It's the valuable I'm interested in."

"Yes, well, while you're out there, look for both," Henry advised shortly.

With a tip of his head to acknowledge the request, Watson pushed the boat into the water and nimbly hopped in, the lantern in the bow lighting a path on the water's black surface. How the man could see well enough at this hour to find anything was a mystery.

Henry turned away, more than ready to find a hot cup of coffee or at least some tea on his way to Scotland Yard. He pondered the conversation with Watson as he walked toward the dock.

"Out early this morning, eh?"

Henry looked up to see Captain Booth approach. "Seemed like the best time to speak with one of the dredgers."

Booth nodded as he looked toward the river. "I suppose I'm to blame for that. Watson, I suppose? Learn anything?"

"Nothing that offers a clue as to who killed Nora." Henry shook his head. "Still a puzzle. Have you seen or heard anything of interest?"

"Can't say that I have, though I've been keeping an eye out. Several of the other barge captains are doing the same."

"Including Salem?"

Booth smiled. "You and Mrs. Greystone must speak often."

"We do." Henry was pleased the man had spotted that, though he didn't care to ponder the reason.

"The tide's going out. The mudlarks will be on the mudflats soon."

The sky lightened with every minute that passed, melting away the darkness. Even as they looked around, several small forms became visible in the distance, all walking toward the river's edge with bags on their shoulders. Henry recognized Pudge and Agnes as well as several of the other mudlarks he'd seen before. He continued watching but didn't see Charlie. Carl would surely lecture the boy for being late.

"Time for me to be on my way as well," Booth said after a moment of silence. He heaved a sigh as if sharing Henry's reluctance to begin what would be a long day. "My load won't haul itself."

"Hope the day goes well for both of us." Henry nodded and started toward the hansom cab stand down the street.

He was nearly halfway there when shouts from the shoreline caught his attention. He turned to see two of the mudlarks running toward the river as a small rowboat drew near. It didn't take long to realize Watson, the dredger, was already returning to shore.

The man shouted, his words muffled to mere noise in the distance. He waved to gain the attention of those on shore and unease crawled along Henry's spine.

He hurried to where the boat neared the bank. Watson was shaking his head as he muttered to himself. His gaze held on the floor of his boat as he rowed, the craft at last bumping onto the shore. The dredger made quick work of stowing the oars then turned to wave away the approaching mudlarks, including Agnes and Pudge, shouting at them to get back.

Henry quickened his pace. Out of the corner of his eye, he saw Captain Booth rushing toward Watson as well. Booth reached him first only to peer into the boat then take two steps back, his body stiff.

Dread knotted in the pit of Henry's stomach. He had the sinking feeling he knew what—or rather, who—was in the bottom of the boat.

Another mudlark joined the other two, the three of them staring into the boat, oblivious to Watson's calls to stay back.

Henry reached them at last, and his chest tightened at the sight of Charlie—Charlie staring up at the sky, mouth agape, his body lifeless.

Nineteen

Henry bit back the oath that nearly escaped his clenched lips. Swearing wouldn't help the boy.

"Where?" he demanded of Watson, finally tearing his gaze away from the child's body.

Watson wiped his coat sleeve across his face though no emotion showed on his features. "Just up the river."

"On the shore or in the water?" Either thought was repellent, but he had to know.

"Just off the shore." The man gestured toward the harpoon in his boat. "I saw him floatin'. Hooked him with the tip."

One of the mudlarks standing nearby, possibly Agnes, gasped.

"I didn't 'urt him none," Watson quickly explained as if guessing what she was thinking. The thought had occurred to Henry too. "Just hooked onto his coat is all."

Henry shared a look with Captain Booth whose distress clearly matched his own. "Will you get the mudlarks back?"

He wanted to examine the body for clues but preferred the children didn't watch when they were already upset.

"Of course." Booth heaved a sigh and placed a hand on one of the girl's shoulders. "Come along, now. Let's give the inspector some room to do his job."

Henry stepped into the boat, which sent it rocking along with Charlie's body. Using the lantern, he took a closer look. Based on the hint of blue around the boy's lips and his pale face, he had been dead for several hours. His body wasn't bloated but that wouldn't happen unless he'd been in the water for days.

"Did you take anything from him?" Henry asked Watson as he bent to gently shut the boy's eyes. He set down the lantern to shift the boy's head, searching for any wounds, before doing the same with his body.

"No. No—what do yer take me fer?" Watson asked even as he looked away.

"Tell me exactly how you found him," Henry demanded as he checked the boy's jacket for evidence.

His pockets were empty except for a penny. The sight of it brought to mind Amelia's mention of Captain Salem, and the coin he offered the mudlarks in exchange for kisses.

"I was just down the river, there." Watson pointed to the location. "And saw somethin' floatin' a foot or two from shore. Thought it was just clothes at first 'til I got closer. He was face up. No injury that I could see." The grizzled man shook his head again as if trying to remove the memory from his mind. "I called his name and shook him when I got 'im on the boat. Didn't do no good."

Charlie's face was ice cold. He'd either been in the water or at least exposed to the elements for some time. Henry had to suspect the timing was similar to that of Nora's death.

"Y'think he drowned?" Watson asked as he narrowed his eyes, staring at the boy again.

No, he didn't, but Henry wasn't going to share that. Proof was needed, not speculation. "Hard to say." He continued his brief examination of the body, noting the details of his attire and appearance. "Nothing near where you found him?"

"Nope. Just him. I confess I was surprised enough that I didn't look much."

Henry glanced up to see the dredger staring across the river as if he'd rather be anywhere else.

Had Watson known where to find him because he'd harmed the boy earlier? While the older man appeared genuinely upset, his emotions could be an act. It wouldn't be the first time a murderer feigned regret.

The cause of death would help reveal the likely suspects. At the moment, Henry didn't see anything that pointed to a reason the boy had died, other than the water—drowning was certainly a possibility. The lad might have been overly distressed after losing his friend and chosen to walk into the water to end his suffering. Chances were he couldn't swim. If he'd ventured too far into the river, he might have been unable to save himself even if he'd changed his mind.

Yet the scenario didn't ring true. Nora's death might have upset him, but why would he have waited several days to join her?

Had Charlie been poisoned as well? The river would've washed away any signs of vomiting, but the surgeon would know once he examined him.

Henry hoped the boy hadn't gone in search of whoever he thought had harmed Nora. His clothing wasn't stained with mud as the mudlarks' attire so often was, but, again, that could be the work of the river. And yet…were the roughly woven jacket and trousers his best clothes? Worn boots that appeared to be too large for his feet were laced tight. His cap was long gone, leaving his wavy brown hair plastered to his head.

Amelia would be very distressed to hear the news.

The thought pained him, mingling with his own distress at the child's death. Too young. Too alone.

Henry glanced over to see Captain Booth still nearby, the children huddled in a group a little farther away. "Can you send for the constable?"

Booth nodded and whistled for one of the men working on the dock.

Less than a quarter of an hour later Constable Gibbons strode toward him, expression grim as he took in the boy's lifeless body. "Another, eh, sir?"

"We won't know if the two are related until a postmortem is done. Watch over him while Watson shows me where the boy was found."

They moved Charlie from the boat to the bank, leaving Gibbons with him while Watson rowed Henry up the river to point to where he'd found the body.

The muddy bank made it nearly impossible to do a thorough search on foot, so Henry had Watson row the boat slowly along the shore while Henry looked for anything out of place. The attempt to search for evidence in such conditions, and without full daylight, proved fruitless. His best hope was to advise the mudlarks to keep watch for anything that could help determine what had happened to Charlie—though what they should be looking for, Henry could not think.

Watson rowed him back to Gibbons and, after thanking the dredger, Henry had the constable fetch a dog cart to take the body to St. Thomas' for Mr. Taylor to examine.

Next Henry spoke with the mudlarks, asking each one when they'd last seen Charlie and if he had mentioned any plans for the previous evening or if he had acted out of sorts. None had anything to offer. Agnes and Pudge were distraught, their silent tears tugging at Henry's heart.

"What is this?" Carl asked as he arrived, hands balled in fists at his sides, no pipe in sight. "They're supposed to be searchin', not talkin' to yer."

"Another body has been found." Henry watched him closely for his reaction. "Charlie."

Carl's shock appeared genuine, eyes widening and mouth dropping open. "No!"

"When did you last see him?" Henry withdrew his notebook from his pocket.

"Late yesterday afternoon. What 'appened to him?"

"We don't know yet. His body was found just off the shore."

Carl muttered a curse and tugged off his hat before briefly bowing his head as if to say a silent prayer. "Was he 'urt?"

"Not that I could see. Did he say anything specific yesterday? Was he still upset over Nora?"

"O'course. We all are. He was mad about it—said someone should pay for what they done."

"Who?" Henry asked, trying not to allow excitement into his tones.

Carl frowned at Henry. "How should I know? Isn't that yer job?"

Henry chose to ignore the remark. It wasn't the first time he'd heard it and wouldn't be the last. "Charlie didn't mention anyone by name?"

"Nah, he thought the man he'd seen around was to blame but no one's spotted him since Nora was...found." Carl replaced his hat as he scowled at Henry. "Now another of my workers is gone. What use is the police?"

None, when they were yet to officially investigate Nora's death. But Henry kept his frustration to himself. "Any and all clues should be reported as they could prove helpful." He glanced at the mudlarks who still stood nearby. "If you find anything of interest, anything at all, advise the constable and he will get word to me."

"Fine." Carl's lack of enthusiasm was palpable. "And if another child is found dead?"

The other mudlarks flinched at his words, making Henry want to shake the man. Could he not see how afraid they were? "We shall hope that doesn't come to pass."

Carl only scowled in response and stalked closer to his mudlarks, putting a hand on the shoulder of one of the younger boys. Perhaps the man had a bigger heart than Henry had realized.

After some polite negotiation, Henry found a few workers to place planks from a shipment of boards on the mud near where Watson had spotted Charlie so he could attempt a more thorough search.

Unfortunately, he didn't find anything other than Charlie's hat along the shore. There was always a chance the boy had gone into the water farther upstream, and the current had brought him in this direction.

The image of him falling ill like Nora had and following her path back to the river kept circling in Henry's mind. If he'd sat down to rest only to die, he could've ended up along the water's edge. The tide might have pulled him into the water.

That would mean that if Watson hadn't come along when he did, the boy's body would've been washed out to sea, never to be found. There was no telling how many bodies had endured such a fate.

Henry straightened, blowing out an angry breath as he studied the mud and pebbles, still looking for clues. The sight of a cigar stub caught his eye, and he bent to retrieve it. The stub wasn't the sort of treasure the mudlarks searched for but could prove helpful. Most of the men around here smoked pipes from what he'd seen.

Henry wrapped it in a handkerchief and continued the search until satisfied he hadn't missed anything, which took a depressingly short time.

The planks were washed off and returned to the dock. Captain Booth had left on his barge to deliver his load while Carl had also disappeared. The mudlarks were working, though they often paused to watch him. He wished he had answers for them.

But he wouldn't find them here.

Henry caught a hansom cab to St. Thomas', not wanting to waste time by walking. Though Mr. Taylor couldn't have examined Charlie this soon, Henry wanted to speak with him about the boy. Until a cause of death was determined, he wouldn't advise Reynolds of the second victim. If Charlie had drowned, the Director wouldn't care, nor would he be pleased that Henry had spent so much of his morning looking into a death that wasn't part of an official investigation.

For once Mr. Taylor wasn't standing over a body, but instead was writing notes at his desk. Relief filled Henry not to find him already examining Charlie. Somehow, he didn't think he could stomach seeing the boy cut open—despite it being necessary to discover what had happened.

Taylor glanced up when Henry paused in the doorway, the surgeon's pencil stub still gripped in his long fingers. "Good morning, Field, though I suppose you don't think it is after your discovery."

"Not a pleasant start to the day," Henry agreed as he leaned against the doorframe. "Thought I'd ask when you anticipate being able to have a look."

The surgeon sighed as he glanced at his desk which bore a rather tall stack of files. "I will move a few things around so I can take a look sooner rather than later." His eyes narrowed. "Do you suspect he met the same fate as the girl?"

Henry nodded. "I do. Though it's possible he drowned, I suppose."

"He was a mudlark, too?"

"Yes, found near where the girl was. He was friends with her and quite upset over her passing."

"The constable didn't give the boy a last name," Taylor said as he pulled a piece of paper closer to review. "Just 'Charlie'."

"That's all I have as well, but I will try to find out more."

"An orphan, I presume?"

"I believe so."

"Never easy to conduct a postmortem on one so young, but I will see what I can find."

Henry had no idea how he managed it. Investigating a child's death was uncommon, at least for himself, and that was difficult enough.

"Shall I send word when I know something?" Taylor asked.

"Why don't I return later in the day to see if you have results?" He didn't want him sending a message to the Yard when there was not yet a case.

Taylor offered a tired smile. "Is this one unofficial, too?"

"So far. That could change depending on what you find."

"I hope so if it's the same cause of death. It is concerning to think someone is poisoning children on a regular basis."

"On that, we agree." Henry straightened. "I'll see you this afternoon."

Taylor nodded and returned to his notes, leaving Henry to wonder how he was going to tell Amelia the terrible news.

Twenty

As Henry walked into Scotland Yard, Perdy rose from his desk and pulled out his pocket watch to stare at it, then looked up at him. "Keeping your own hours these days, Field?"

Henry didn't bother to respond, it would do no good. Why the man was so often at Scotland Yard rather than in the field remained a puzzle. After all, there were no suspects to question or evidence to collect in the office.

Though tempted to advise Reynolds of the discovery of the boy, Henry knew it would serve no purpose. Better that he waited to do so until he knew what happened. Hopefully by this afternoon, Taylor would hand him the evidence that would allow him to do just that.

He checked his desk, relieved not to find any new cases, and left a message for Fletcher to meet him at the Yard at the end of the workday and headed out. It would take effort today to focus on the other cases vying for his attention when all he could see was Charlie staring up at the sky from the bottom of the boat.

Perhaps telling Fletcher the news would settle Henry's thoughts. The sergeant would understand his upset and share his determination to find out who was killing the mudlarks, regardless of whether they needed to solve the case on their own time.

But the thought of telling Amelia filled him with dread. She didn't need to endure any further hardship than she already had. Not only was she still grieving for her daughter and husband, but she'd also been embroiled with the ravenkeeper's murder and his daughter's grief, and now she'd also been pulled into the mudlark murder. Possibly murders.

Something painful twisted in Henry's gut. He felt a certain amount of responsibility for her involvement in his cases, even if he hadn't been the one to initiate it. Protective instincts he hadn't realized he possessed rose to the surface at the idea of causing her more pain.

Would he still feel that way if he'd managed to solve her husband's murder?

The question was for another time. With quick strides—he couldn't afford to keep taking cabs—Henry made his way once again to the home of Viscount Tellington, the owner of the stolen painting.

Though he had yet to find proof, Henry believed Joseph—one of the footmen he'd interviewed—knew more than he'd said. He liked to think himself a good judge of character and the fine bead of sweat on the servant's brow, not to mention the way his eyes had shifted as if in search of an alibi for the time in question, had roused Henry's finely tuned suspicions.

Another conversation with the man was in order, along with some of the other servants. Stopes, the butler, would be familiar with the footman's references, and Henry wanted to learn where else he'd worked and perhaps even speak with his previous employer.

Lord Tellington had gallantly insisted his staff could not be at fault as he only hired the best, but what the nobility believed and what was true were often different.

He knocked on the servant's entrance and requested to speak with the butler. None of the staff looked pleased to see him again but that came as no surprise. Policemen were rarely welcome anywhere.

"More questions, Inspector?" Stopes asked as he appeared in the corridor. "I thought we had covered them all during your previous visits."

The butler was shorter than Henry, which prevented him from looking down his nose, but based on the way he imperiously lifted his chin he dearly wanted to.

"More have arisen, sir." Henry attempted a friendly but respectful tone so as not to put the man on the defensive.

"And? What are they?"

"If we could speak in private, please." Though Henry suspected the footman, it wouldn't do to allow anyone else to know that. He'd have to ask several other servants the same questions as he had no doubt they'd compare experiences once Henry had departed.

"Very well." With ill-concealed impatience, the man led the way to the small room where the silver and sets of china were kept, as well as a small table, chairs, and a few other items.

Henry sat and the butler reluctantly did the same. After retrieving his notebook, Henry went through several of the servants' names and supposed whereabouts at the time of the theft and then asked to speak again with the housemaid who'd been the last to see the painting.

"To what purpose?" Stopes asked with a frown.

"To verify the information she provided." Henry offered an unassuming smile. "You see, people often remember events differently after they've had time to consider the details."

Stopes' lips tightened, but he stepped out of the butler's pantry to request one of the staff to fetch the housemaid.

In short order the young woman—who couldn't have been more than two and twenty—arrived, eyes wide and hands gripped tightly before her. Stopes closed the door when he departed to allow them privacy, shutting it with more force than was necessary.

"You asked to speak with me, sir?"

"Yes, thank you." Henry gestured for her to have a seat and turned the pages of his notes, asking similar questions to the ones he'd previously asked.

As expected, her answers were exactly the same. At four o'clock, she'd begun dusting the small sitting room just off the gallery where the painting had hung. She remembered the time because Lady Tellington had served tea to guests in the drawing room at that hour, which allowed the maid to dust the room where Lady Tellington usually spent her afternoons when she didn't have company. The painting had been hanging in its usual place at a quarter past four when the maid had completed her cleaning and walked by it again.

Henry thanked her for her time and repeated the process with three more servants before asking to speak with the footman again.

The man entered the room and sank into the chair across from Henry, glancing around nervously just like the previous occasion Henry had spoken to him. While speaking with the police often made people anxious, Joseph's reaction was certainly more pronounced than usual.

That didn't make him guilty, but it did suggest he had something to hide.

"I don't believe I asked last time how you came to find employment here," Henry said as he pretended to look over his notes, suggesting it was merely an oversight on his part.

"I, ah, I heard of the opening from a friend."

"Who?"

The man hesitated. "Another staff member."

"I see. Their name?" Henry pressed.

The man's lips twisted, clearly reluctant to answer. "Stopes."

Henry's brow lifted. "You were previously acquainted with the butler?"

"Well, he's...he's my uncle, you see."

That would explain the hesitation. Had Stopes failed to disclose that detail to his employers? The butler certainly hadn't mentioned it to him.

"That explains it." Henry nodded, hoping to put the man at ease. "Where were you previously employed?"

He shifted in his chair. "At another household."

"The name?"

"Does it matter? Why would you need to speak with them?" Once again, sweat beaded on his brow.

"I probably don't. It's just for my notes." Henry gestured to them with a languid shrug.

"Stanwich. Mr. and Mrs. Stanwich."

"Address?"

The man cleared his throat. "I'd rather not say."

"Oh? Is there a problem?"

"They...they wouldn't provide a reference. That is why I came to my uncle."

"Understandable. Some people can be quite difficult, can't they?" Henry felt certain he was on to something and wasn't about to let it go.

Joseph nodded eagerly. "True, sir."

"And how long have you worked here?" He led him through several questions before moving to the issue of the missing artwork. "When did you last see the painting?"

"As I told you last time, before I retired for the night." The footman shifted with impatience.

"What duties do you perform prior to going to bed?"

Joseph appeared to be breathing more quickly, his distress worsening. "I check to be sure the windows are locked in the main rooms."

"Does that take you through the gallery?" Henry felt his own heartbeat quicken as he pushed for answers, hoping instinct hadn't led him astray, especially when he had no proof.

"Yes, sir."

"The painting was there?"

He licked his lips. "I can't say for sure. I didn't pay much attention."

"Hmm. It's a rather large painting. You must've noticed the blank space."

"I-I suppose I was focused on my duties."

Henry nodded. "What did you do after you checked the windows on that floor?"

"I retired for the night."

"When were you first made aware of the missing painting?"

"The following morning. One of the other footmen noticed it was gone and alerted Stopes—my uncle. The entire staff was in a flurry over it."

"I don't suppose Lord Tellington was pleased." Henry sent him a sympathetic look.

"No, sir."

"Do you know anything about art?"

"Can't say that I do."

"Did you like the painting?"

The footman frowned. "Sir?"

"I'm just curious if you found it appealing." Henry leaned forward with a conspiratorial air. "Between you and me, valuable paintings often tend to be ugly."

"Can't say that I cared for it." He shrugged. "I wouldn't have known it was valuable if not for one of the maids mentioning it."

"No great loss that it was stolen as far as you're concerned," Henry suggested.

"They do have many others." A faint light of resentment glinted in his eyes.

"Indeed," Henry agreed. "I saw that for myself. A shame that your uncle will be the one blamed for it."

Joseph frowned. "What makes you say that?"

"The servants are his responsibility. It seems clear one of the staff took it. If none come forward, Stopes will have to be held responsible. He'll lose his position." Henry widened his eyes as if a new thought just occurred to him. "I suppose that means you will, too, being his nephew and all."

"They don't know I am," Joseph protested instantly.

Just as Henry suspected. "Why wouldn't Stopes have told them?"

Again the man hesitated, so Henry pushed him. "I will have to check the references of all the staff if the investigation continues."

"There was a...situation. At my last place of employment." He shifted in his chair, clearly wishing he were somewhere else.

"What sort?" Another missing painting perhaps?

"I'd rather not say."

Henry nodded, heart racing. He had to be getting close now. "Understandable. Of course, I'd rather hear it from you than your former employer."

The man grimaced. "A theft," he said with reluctance. "They blamed me."

"And were you responsible?"

The man only glared, lips pressed tightly, making it clear he didn't intend to answer.

Henry stood. "Why don't we have your uncle join us for the rest of this conversation?" Pulse pounding, he started toward the door, nerves taut. Would the other man confess?

"Wait!" Joseph jerked to his feet. "That won't be necessary. I-I'll tell you. I'll tell you everything."

Henry released a quiet sigh of relief. A familiar feeling of satisfaction ran through him, something that would never grow old. In moments like this, he felt a connection with his grandfather and was certain his father would be proud when he had the chance to tell him the details of the case.

Hopefully wrapping up this investigation would keep him in Reynolds' good graces and allow him to devote more time to investigating Nora and Charlie's deaths. They were far more important than a painting, no matter the artist.

Twenty-One

Amelia stared out the window of her laboratory, debating the wisdom of venturing to Blackfriars again. The gloomy afternoon matched her mood. Restlessness had caused her to seek solitude in her lab that afternoon rather than politely keeping her aunt company in the drawing room.

She'd intended to continue her experiments on mushrooms but couldn't focus. In truth, she wasn't certain what she was looking for. Experiments were more meaningful when a hypothesis was set forth to examine. Merely studying the advantages and disadvantages of various fungi felt pointless when there were so many poisonous types.

There was fly agaric, which looked like something out of a fairytale with its bright red top. The deadly dapperling commonly found in Europe was often mistaken for an edible mushroom. Destroying angels or fool's mushrooms were similar in that they also resembled an edible variety. There were also death caps, autumn skullcaps, and ink caps, the latter of which was only fatal when combined with alcohol...

What she'd learned thus far hadn't proved to be particularly helpful or answered the question of why someone would give any of those to a child. She was beginning to fear the subject was too immense for her skills. If only she'd asked Mrs. Drake for advice after listening to her lecture.

If she were to venture to the mudflats again, what purpose would it serve? Amelia assumed Henry had spoken with the dredger, though if he hadn't the time, she would offer to do so. He already had so many pressing cases to investigate, and...and unsolved ones.

Yet Captain Booth had advised against speaking with Watson. And she couldn't forget Henry's warnings about how dangerous the area could be. She didn't want to worry him, only help. She felt certain if he had learned anything of interest, he would've called on her.

Movement on the street below caught her notice, and she leaned closer to the window to see a familiar figure striding along the pavement toward her house.

Henry.

A mix of relief and excitement filled her. He must have news to share, or he wouldn't call during working hours. Perhaps he'd learned something from the dredger.

Yet the thought of attempting to have a meaningful conversation with her aunt present dampened her anticipation. Aunt Margaret still didn't know about the mudlark death, let alone Amelia's involvement in the investigation.

While she was a grown woman with a life of her own, she wasn't anxious to share the details of the case with her aunt—or field her presumably numerous questions and concerns.

Her aunt hadn't been her usual self during the visit thus far, but Amelia had yet to determine the nature of the problem. Since she had a few secrets of her own at the moment, she hadn't pried. Hopefully, her aunt would soon share what was bothering her.

For now, Amelia was anxious to hear what Henry had to say. It would be best if she asked Fernsby to show Henry up here so they could speak in private.

Impatient, she walked to the door and opened it, moving to the top of the stairs to listen. Male voices drifted up from the front entrance but were too indistinct to reveal any of the conversation.

She waited until Fernsby came into view at the foot of the stairs, not wanting him to make the trip to the third floor if she could prevent it. "Fernsby?"

The butler looked up. "Inspector Field is calling, madam."

"Please send him straight up."

"Of course." Fernsby retreated and Amelia returned to her lab, leaving the door open for Henry.

It wasn't long before she heard his footsteps on the stairs and he stood in the doorway, hat in hand. "Good afternoon, Amelia."

"Henry," she said with a smile. "I hope you don't mind if we converse in here." She gestured for him to close the door. "My aunt is visiting for a few days."

"Ah. I see." He complied, walking slowly forward. "Is that good or bad?"

"Mostly good, though unexpected."

He nodded. "Conducting any new experiments?" He glanced around as if hoping to see what she was working on.

"I have been doing several on fungi to better understand them." She glanced at her notes on the worktable. "I find it fascinating that some can be beneficial and others deadly."

"Yes, most interesting." Henry pondered the idea a long moment.

It took no longer than that to realize something more serious was on his mind. The somberness in his expression spoke of bad news.

"What's happened?" she asked, bracing herself for what he had to say.

He released a long sigh, not responding immediately as if trying to find the proper words. "Another mudlark is dead."

Amelia's mouth dropped open even as her stomach fell. "Who?"

"The boy. Charlie."

"Oh, no. How terrible." She relaxed the fist she hadn't realized she'd clenched. Her relief that it hadn't been Agnes or Pudge made her feel guilty. But how horrible that it had been Charlie. "What happened?" A closer look at his face told her the answer. "Poison?"

Henry nodded. "I just learned the results from the Scotland Yard surgeon."

Amelia turned aside, pressing a hand to her mouth as she tried to digest the news and what it meant. "It...it doesn't make any sense. Why would anyone harm those children, let alone with poison?"

"Do you think they suffered?" Henry asked, almost as though it were against his better judgment.

"Many poisons cause a painful death." She turned back to look at him, certain he already knew that. Perhaps he had hoped he was wrong. "Where was Charlie found?" she asked, hoping Agnes and Pudge hadn't been the ones to discover him.

"I was at the mudflats early this morning with the hope of speaking to the dredger you sent word of. I did so briefly before he rowed out onto the river. He found the boy minutes later just upstream from the dock."

"In the water?"

"Yes, though I tend to think his body washed into the river when the tide came in."

"So he died near the same place as Nora." Her thoughts raced while trying to make sense of that as well. "Did the surgeon share anything else?"

"He enjoyed a fine meal that evening, much like Nora had."

"That is surely no coincidence."

Henry shook his head. "Why feed them such a meal only to poison them?"

"The effects of poison can change if taken with food or alcohol. How that fits into the puzzle, I don't know."

"Improving or worsening them?" he asked.

"Depends on the poison, and the weight of the person taking it." She shared a worried look with him. "Could someone be trying different dosages to get the desired result?"

"Seems unlikely they'd do that on children." Henry's skepticism was clear.

"True," she admitted. "The results would be quite different than for an adult, though they are less likely to protest."

"One could make the argument that orphans even less so." Henry stared out the window, but she was sure he wasn't seeing the view. "And to what end?"

"Excellent question. If both Nora and Charlie ended up in the same area of the mudflats, they must have been near enough to walk." She shook her head. "I have looked over the neighborhood but didn't see any obvious place that would appeal to them."

"Amelia, may I once again remind you of the dangers—"

She held up a hand to hold off the well-intended lecture. "I only looked as I walked from the dock to the cab stand, I took no unnecessary risks."

"Good." Henry still looked less than pleased. "Charlie often stayed in the back of the pub in exchange for doing some cleaning after hours. The owner couldn't shed any light on where the boy might have gone, nor could the other lad who stays there. They said he never spoke a word about anything unusual."

"Such a tragedy. How did Agnes and Pudge seem?" The question was pointless, but she couldn't help but ask.

"Upset. Everyone was, including Carl."

"I can imagine. Will there be an official investigation now?"

Henry's features tightened as anger flashed across his face. "Not as of yet."

"Two children have been callously poisoned, and the police aren't going to look into the matter?" Amelia couldn't hide her astonishment, her fists once again clenching.

"They were orphans with no family to raise concern over their deaths. My superior pointed out that as far as we know, they might've taken the poison of their own accord. They could've found it somewhere—"

"But you don't believe that." She drew a relieved breath when he shook his head. "What is wrong with people to not value children, regardless of what sort of life they've lived or whether they have family?"

"I couldn't say. However, I intend to do all I can to investigate their deaths. I just wish I had more clues to lead the way."

Amelia nodded, holding back the urge to tell him that she would help however she could. He would only advise her it was too dangerous.

Yet how could she stand by and allow another child to die while whoever was poisoning them continued their barbaric acts?

"I do hope you will keep me apprised and tell me if I can be of assistance." She bit her lip to keep from telling him that she would definitely return to the mudflats to speak with the other mudlarks. Surely he knew.

Perhaps they would tell her something different, particularly now that another of their number had died. Something they wouldn't mention to the police.

"Of course." He sighed as if the weight of the world sat on his shoulders, and his somber expression tightened her chest painfully.

"I'm sorry to bring you naught but bad news. Unfortunately, I must go."

"Have you found the missing man you mentioned the other day?" she asked. How did he sleep at night, with so many cases demanding his attention?

"No. He didn't leave much of a trail to follow, but we're continuing to make inquiries." How frequently did he use a similar phrase over the course of a week? "There's a chance he may have got in over his head with gambling."

"Oh, dear. That doesn't sound promising."

His lips twisted. "No. We shall see. I did manage to resolve a stolen painting case, so that will provide me with a little more time."

"Well done." She tended to think the police in general didn't hear that often enough, though the press and the public were quick to criticize them.

A hint of a smile flashed across his face before quickly disappearing as he dipped his head to acknowledge her remark.

"Thank you for coming by to tell me." She pressed a hand to her aching heart. "I shall hold Charlie and Nora in my prayers."

"Perhaps hold the other mudlarks in them instead. I hope those two are now in a better place."

Amelia nodded, knowing he was right. But that didn't keep her from saying prayers for Lily every night. It was only in this moment that she realized those prayers were for herself as much as they were for her daughter.

If they couldn't find this murderer soon…how many other children's names would be added to that list?

Twenty-Two

Amelia's stricken expression at hearing of Charlie's death was etched indelibly in Henry's mind as he returned to Scotland Yard to meet Fletcher. He had no doubt the news brought back memories of her daughter's death and the sorrow that accompanied it. How he wished he knew the right words to comfort her.

While the day had been productive in several ways, that did not erase his own upset over the boy's murder or his frustration at not being allowed to officially pursue the case.

Mr. Taylor's finding poison as the cause of death wasn't a surprise, yet it was still unsettling.

Why were the mudlarks being poisoned?

Obviously orphans of any sort were easy targets, and no one would cause much of a stir if they suddenly disappeared. But why bother to poison them at all?

Could Amelia be right—someone was testing various poisons and assumed the orphans wouldn't be missed? To what end? He couldn't find the logic or think of a motive.

Daylight was already fading, the temperature dropping along with it as the November days grew steadily shorter. That tended to make investigations more difficult as everything from pursuing leads to searching for clues became a challenge under the blanket of cold and darkness.

How did the mudlarks manage to search the mud in colder temperatures? Their fingers had to be numb well before the tide changed and their work ended for the day. It made his own fingers ache to think about it.

When Henry had told Reynolds of Charlie's death, the director had again suggested the children might have taken the poison willingly. The notion was preposterous. Something more was going on; Henry felt it deep in his bones.

Thankfully Reynolds was pleased Henry had solved the stolen painting case. Joseph had been taken into custody as his uncle watched with grim anger. The butler was clearly enraged that his nephew had done such a thing. The footman had reluctantly confessed to the crime, not wanting to put his uncle in more of a precarious position than he already had, going so far as to tell Henry where to find the painting. Luckily he had stashed it, intending to wait to sell it after the uproar over its disappearance had calmed. The artwork had already been returned to Lord Tellington.

Whether the painting's homecoming had saved the butler his position was something that remained to be seen. Since the man hadn't revealed his relationship with his nephew prior to hiring him, it seemed doubtful the lord would want to keep him on—but Lady Tellington had mentioned how difficult it was to find efficient butlers. Perhaps Stopes would be forgiven.

"Fletcher," Henry called to gain the sergeant's attention across the street from the Yard and waved him over. Given his tumultuous thoughts, discussing the case with Fletcher while they walked might bring forth clarity. It would at least make him feel less alone.

"How did Mrs. Greystone take the news?" Fletcher asked after he crossed the street and fell into step alongside Henry.

"As well as could be expected." Henry scowled. "Hopefully she won't take it upon herself to question the mudlarks or those who work in the area about Charlie's death. She's visited the neighborhood too often already."

"That isn't the safest place for anyone, let alone a lady." Fletcher shook his head. "I don't understand why Reynolds doesn't want to pursue the case."

Henry had pondered the issue during the walk to Amelia's. "I think it comes down to the fact that he isn't willing to commit resources to the death of two orphans. Something else must occupy his mind." But what could be more important than children dying?

"Humph. If it turns into three, will he change his tune? Or will it take four before he decides action is needed?"

"Let us hope we don't have to find out." Henry frowned. "If only the records you found at the morgue of recent children's deaths could be tied to the mudlark murders."

"There might have been more than the additional three I discovered. Of course, it's impossible to know if they are related to the poisonings when the cause of death wasn't confirmed. Other than being orphans who died at a young age, we don't know anything. Still, it makes me wonder." Fletcher sighed. "Better records should be kept."

"I would agree, but postmortems cannot be performed on everyone. Given the stack of cases on Mr. Taylor's desk, I fear he is already overwhelmed." Henry glanced at the sergeant. "For now, we will have to assume it's just the two mudlarks that have been poisoned. Any suppositions as to why someone would do so?"

"A grudge of some sort?" The sergeant lifted one shoulder in a half-hearted shrug. "Perhaps they find them offensive for digging in the mud."

"Hmm. If that were the case, wouldn't the killer choose a simpler method than to dispose of them using poison? What else?" Henry prodded.

"Well, if you take their last meal into consideration, they had to have been at a restaurant or a middle-class house. No poor person would waste a meal like that on someone then kill them."

"True. Why feed them first?"

"Maybe the promise of a good meal was used to lure them to the place."

"Then why not offer it and not provide it? That would be cheaper."

"Right. That could mean expense isn't an issue. Perhaps they felt guilty about giving them the poison and providing a decent meal beforehand eased it," Fletcher suggested.

Henry nodded as he mulled over the idea. "Possibly. Or maybe the poison has a different effect with food. Mrs. Greystone suggested that possibility."

"Interesting—though I still can't think of a reason to poison them to begin with." Fletcher was quiet for a long moment. "I would be happy to do more to help with the investigation other than a visit to the morgue, even if it's not official."

"I appreciate that, and I might take your offer as soon as I determine a direction to pursue. While I'm relieved to have the stolen painting resolved, another case is waiting to take its place."

"As always," the sergeant agreed. "And we still have Mr. Spencer to find."

Henry shared a dark look with Fletcher as they crossed a road. "I am starting to believe that unless his body makes an appearance, he won't be found."

"That thought crossed my mind, as well. We received word from the constable in Shropshire who spoke with his mother and stepfather," Fletcher said with a heavy sigh. "Apparently, the mother is quite distraught over his continued disappearance. The stepfather...not so much."

Henry's interest was piqued. A direction, a lead, that was what they needed. "That's not a complete surprise, given the limited time they've been married. Were they aware of his suspected penchant for gambling or the lottery tickets he frequently purchased?"

"No," Fletcher replied with a wry expression. "The constable said the mother was shocked and suggested there had to be a mistake."

Henry smiled. "No mother likes to hear of their children's faults." He knew for a fact his own mother would defend him to the ends of the earth. "I wonder if that is true or if she doesn't want to admit to the problem?"

"Good question. Are you leaning toward his involvement in the lottery being at the heart of the matter, or shall I request that the constable look into his stepfather?"

Henry considered the options carefully, weighing the few clues they had along with the man's background. He didn't care to rely solely on instincts, even after his success with the stolen artwork. His father and grandfather might swear by them, but Henry couldn't forget he wasn't a true Field. His adoption meant he was a Field by happenstance. He needed to pursue all possibilities, regardless of supposed instincts, until they were ruled out by cold, hard facts.

But in this case, the stepfather seemed unlikely given that he lived some distance away and had no obvious motive.

"The lottery seems more likely," he said at last. "And it also seems probable that our previous idea of him realizing the numbers didn't add up and mentioning it to someone who took offense could be right, especially given Spencer's background in accounting. The warning I received at the wrong end of a knife upon leaving the pub confirms how much they take offense to anyone asking questions."

"Excellent *point*." Fletcher caught Henry's eye and winked. "No pun intended."

Henry shook his head at his friend's poor jest but had to smile.

"How do you suggest we proceed?" Fletcher asked.

How indeed, with such flimsy evidence? "Let's have another accountant take a look to see if he finds anything in the numbers that proves it's a scheme."

Fletcher smiled. "I like it. One of Spencer's colleagues or someone else?"

"Someone unrelated to the case and wise enough not to ruffle feathers with those running the lottery. We don't need another missing person on our hands."

"On that we agree. Why don't I see if that fellow we used a few months ago is still available?"

"Excellent." Henry paused to glance around, dismayed to see how quickly the end of the day was coming. "Thank you for your assistance, but I must go. There's something I want to see to before dark. I will meet you at the Yard first thing in the morning."

It didn't take him long to return to Puddle Dock. He stood near a street corner and studied the area, watching the mudlarks working in the fading light as he tried to envision what happened to first Nora and then Charlie. What—or who—had lured them away?

Once again he walked to where Constable Gibbons had traced Nora's steps then turned to look in the opposite direction to see if anything out of the ordinary caught his eye. Allowing his feet to lead the way, he walked away from the water, pausing to look at some of the buildings he passed.

It wouldn't have been buildings that beckoned the children since they would have seen them every day. It had to have been a person or a destination they had in mind. He changed his focus to watch the people passing by. All seemed intent on their business, though one or two did look at him strangely. Most appeared to fit in with the area with rough clothing suitable for the work offered near the docks.

For the mudlarks to have come to the killer's notice he had to have seen them, which suggested he lived or worked in the vicinity of the mudflats. Was the killer the same man Carl and Charlie had told him about, who offered the mudlarks training to become a servant?

Unfortunately, he couldn't see the logic or a connection between the deaths and the person offering training, even if it did strike him as odd. It wasn't as though there was a sudden shortage of servants in London.

He walked farther, passing over the next two streets where warehouses and businesses gave way to lodging houses, most in desperate need of repair. He continued on, feeling that those behind the tattered curtains and windowsills with peeling paint would have no interest in poisoning mudlarks, nor were they likely to have fed the children a fine meal or have had a crystal perfume bottle for Nora to take.

Another street, followed by another, eased into more affluent homes. Those who lived here seemed even less likely to have a reason to poison the mudlarks. Again he paused to study the area and considered how far it was to the mudflats.

Close enough in distance, but miles apart in other ways.

If someone had lured first Nora and then Charlie to a strange place—and perhaps others before them—they had apparently gone willingly. Nora had prepared for the meeting by dressing up, which made it clear she hadn't been snatched from the street.

That suggested a certain familiarity. Perhaps a stranger with an offer of something the mudlarks couldn't refuse. Considering their living conditions, any manner of items would have been appealing to the kids. Carl had mentioned Nora's hope to better herself, and training to become a maid would do that.

Henry sighed, deciding his current mission was pointless. Looking around the neighborhood served no purpose when he didn't know what he looked for.

The memory of the perfume bottle Nora had clutched in her hand surfaced again. He could easily imagine her running to escape whatever situation she'd found herself in and taking the bottle perhaps because she realized too late it had contained poison...or perhaps to provide a clue as to what happened.

If only he knew what she wanted him or her friends to know.

With a heavy sigh, Henry turned to walk to a nearby cab stand, at a loss as to what action to take next. Yet there could be no doubt of the urgency of the situation.

He didn't want another mudlark to die.

Twenty-Three

Amelia rose early the next morning, quickly washing and dressing in an older gown and even older boots, her thoughts on the mudlarks—especially Agnes and Pudge. They must be more worried and scared than ever now that another of their mudlarking family had died.

Poor Charlie. What could have happened to him? In her mind, there was no doubt he'd shared a fate similar to Nora's.

Though there was little she could do, she would at least venture to the mudflats to offer comfort and sympathy. While there, she would try to discover more about those who lived and worked in the area—and whether they might be a suspect or have witnessed anything unusual.

Someone had to know something. It was just a matter of finding it. If Henry wasn't permitted to work on the case, she would continue to do what she could to help.

Of course, she would take care while there, well remembering Henry's warnings.

Amelia quickly ate breakfast, settling for toast with jam and a bit of sausage. Mrs. Appleton was pleased to put together more sandwiches and biscuits for Amelia to take to the children, especially after she had told the cook of their gratefulness the previous time.

After leaving a message for her aunt who was still in her room, and reassuring Fernsby that yes, she would be careful, she departed with the basket of food.

She had purchased a tide guide just the other day, and so knew the tide should be going out. Hopefully she would find the mudlarks working. Perhaps Carl would be there, and she could further question him. As closely as he watched his workers, one would think he had seen something out of the ordinary.

The hansom ride passed quickly and she soon alighted, her gaze searching the river's edge for the mudlarks. Fog lingered along the water, adding an extra damp gloominess to the day. The children were already at work, scattered along the shore, most bent double as they scoured the mud for treasure.

Amelia was relieved to see Agnes and Pudge working beside each other. Thank goodness they had one another. Remembering to be on guard, Amelia surveyed the area. There was no sign of Carl, Captain Booth, or Captain Salem, but many other men were near the dock getting on with their day.

With a look of regret at her boots and the mud that stretched between her and the girls, she lifted her skirts and started toward them, hoping Fernsby would forgive her.

The girls straightened as she neared.

"Good morning to you," Amelia greeted them but didn't bother to force a smile when they were surely despondent after the events of the previous day.

"Mornin', ma'am." Agnes nodded, as did Pudge.

"Any finds so far today?"

Pudge reached into the bag on her shoulder and pulled forth a bit of twisted metal covered in mud to hold out for Amelia's inspection.

"What is it?"

"A bit of silver, we think. Jewelry maybe?" Pudge looked rather pleased with herself as she tried to scrape off more of the mud. "Hard to say until it's cleaned proper like."

"How exciting. That must mean it will be a good day," Amelia suggested.

"It often does," Agnes agreed with a nod.

"Let us hope so."

Amelia cleared her throat, loath to raise the subject of Charlie when the girls had found something to distract them from the awful news. "I...I was very sorry to hear about Charlie."

The girls shared a somber look. "Yeah, it's terrible."

"Did the inspector find who did it?" Pudge asked with a wary look.

"Not as of yet, but he is looking," Amelia reassured them. "I wondered if you might have heard any news." She glanced toward the other mudlarks. "Has anyone mentioned anything? Did Charlie tell someone where he was going or what he was doing?"

"We spoke to Sarah, but she didn't know anything. She said he'd been quiet of late. Since Nora's death, he's been keepin' to 'imself."

"He was very sad." Pudge sniffed. "We all were and now it's worse."

"And worried, I'm sure," Amelia suggested, taking in their concerned expressions.

"A bit," Agnes agreed. "Not knowin' what 'appened to them makes it hard."

"Sarah did say he was wearin' his good boots. She noticed when they lifted him out of the boat."

Just like Nora in her best dress. "Can you think of any reason he would have worn them?" Amelia asked. "Did he always wear them when he wasn't working?"

"Not that I saw." Agnes' brow furrowed as she looked at Pudge. "Didn't Judith say she saw that man the other day? The one who keeps tryin' to talk to us?"

"Talk to you about what?" Amelia asked, heart thumping at the thought of a true lead.

"Trainin' to be a servant." Pudge shook her head. "He's told some that they're lookin' for those willin' to learn."

"You don't believe that?" Amelia noted the skepticism in her expression.

"Hard to believe when others are better suited than the likes of us." Agnes scowled.

"How often have you seen him?" Amelia glanced around, wishing he would make an appearance so she could have a look at him for herself.

"Only a few times."

"Is there a particular hour of the day he comes?"

"Any time from mid-mornin' to mid-afternoon, dependin' on the tide."

The opportunity to see him made Amelia even more determined to remain there for a time. She didn't know if the man had anything to do with the mudlarks being poisoned, but his presence was odd enough to be of interest.

The girls were becoming restless, studying the ground as if anxious to return to their work—and probably equally anxious to think of something other than the unsettling murders of their friends as well as the possibility of experiencing a similar fate.

"I brought sandwiches for when you're hungry." Perhaps that would make them more willing to accept her presence.

"That's nice." Agnes' eyes lit up at the news.

"Tell me again what you look for. Maybe I can help." Amelia set the basket on a nearby rock and studied the ground, only seeing a mix of mud, sand, and pebbles. If she was going to linger, she might as well make herself useful rather than keep them from their work.

"Anything unusual. Straight or a perfect circle." Agnes squatted down, oblivious to the way the hem of her dress dipped in the mud. Then again, it was already filthy. "If somethin' catches yer eye, it's worth checkin'."

Amelia shifted to watch over her shoulder, fascinated when the girl poked her finger into the tiny pebbles and pulled forth a fishhook that had been invisible to Amelia.

Pudge took several steps before leaning down to reach into the mud and pulled out a pottery shard then tossed it over her shoulder.

"Don't you worry you'll end up finding the same one again?" Amelia asked.

Pudge shook her head. "We find 'em all the time. There are too many broken bits to pick up. Unless they're pretty, then I sometimes keep 'em."

Amelia spent the next hour looking over their shoulders, then doing some searching of her own while keeping an eye along the street for the man they'd mentioned. Her back and neck grew sore from bending over, and she knew she couldn't continue much longer without true discomfort from the unfamiliar work.

She didn't miss the curious looks the other mudlarks cast her way, nor the glares Carl sent toward her when he arrived to watch over his workers. She spoke with him briefly, but he didn't have anything helpful to share, nor did he seem inclined to talk.

They soon stopped for the sandwiches and a concern came to Amelia's mind. "Girls, if anyone you don't know offers you food, please don't take it."

Agnes looked at the sandwich in her hand and back at Amelia with a puzzled look.

"Yes, I realize you haven't known me for long, but I hope you have come to trust me," Amelia said awkwardly. "But I don't want anything to happen to either of you, or the other mudlarks. Nora and Charlie more than likely ate something that contained poison. Please don't eat anything given to you unless you're absolutely sure it's safe. Can you do that for me?"

The girls nodded, but their eager wolfing down of the offered sandwiches did not exactly bode well.

The three ate their sandwiches together after Amelia handed some out to the other mudlarks, along with the biscuits, and repeated her warning. Carl had disappeared once again, probably in search of his own luncheon. She talked to a few of the children but didn't learn anything more.

"Oh!" Pudge's quiet exclamation shortly after they returned to work immediately caught her notice.

"What is it?" Amelia asked as she quickly straightened, back protesting.

"Shhh," Agnes warned, continuing to search even as she eased closer to Pudge. "We don't want the others to know until we have a chance to search for more of whatever she found."

Amelia nodded and casually moved toward Pudge, anxious to see what she'd discovered.

Pudge held the item, rubbing it to remove more of the mud.

"A coin?" Amelia didn't recognize the size of it. Yet as Pudge kept rubbing, a glimmer of gold became visible. "A gold coin?" she whispered in amazement.

"Oh, that's wonderful." Agnes squatted next to her friend but didn't reach for it. "Is there more?" She glanced around, her excitement palpable despite her attempt to hide it.

"I don't see none." Pudge tapped the spot where she'd uncovered it then, using a little stick, dug deeper. Agnes did the same nearby.

Amelia was impressed by their casualness when they had to be excited by the find. "What will you do with it?"

"Sell it, o'course."

"How do you know who to sell it to and that they are giving you a fair price?"

"Well, Carl always offers to help us," Agnes said as she shared a look with Pudge. "But we have others who buy from us and another who buys coins."

"And doesn't cheat you?" Amelia had difficulty believing that. Any of the shops who dealt in such items in this area wouldn't hesitate to take advantage of a young girl.

"We don't know fer certain, but he seems better than most. Certainly better than givin' some of the money to Carl." Pudge shrugged. "Hard to know when we so rarely find the same things to sell."

"What if I offered assistance?" Amelia was no expert in such things, but couldn't she fetch them a fair price? "My neighborhood has several reputable pawnbrokers who might pay more than one near Blackfriars."

Both girls stared at her as if she'd suggested they jump from the bridge.

"I give you my word to be honest and find the best price possible. Captain Booth will vouch for me if that reassures you." Amelia stretched her shoulders, deciding she needed to stop bending over if she wanted to be able to walk this afternoon. "The two of you discuss it and let me know. I will be nearby for a while longer and intend to return tomorrow as well." What she would tell her aunt, she didn't know—yet she hated to leave until she had found some kind of clue. "Do let me know what you decide." With a smile at the two girls, Amelia lifted her skirts, though there was no longer a point since the hem was already heavy with mud, and made her way toward the street.

"Ma'am, wait!"

Amelia turned to see Pudge hurrying toward her.

"We would like yer help if ye can," the girl whispered.

"Of course." Amelia was ridiculously pleased by her trust. "I will do my best."

Pudge slipped her the coin and stepped back with a nod. "Thankee."

"I hope you find more before the tide comes in." Amelia clutched the coin tight, careful not to look at it as she knew Carl was watching them closely.

"Doubtful but y'never know." Pudge smiled and returned to Agnes, her step light.

Amelia continued to the street and found a place to watch for a time, leaning against a warehouse. Now that she wasn't moving, the cold November air eased beneath her cloak and made her all too aware of her damp feet and the wet spots on her gown. She wouldn't linger too long and risk catching a chill.

As subtly as possible she removed the coin from her glove to have a better look. The face of it had been worn nearly smooth and would take further scrubbing to identify the date it had been minted but given its rough edges, it had to be fairly old.

She tucked it back into her glove and allowed her gaze to sweep the area, arms folded across her chest to ward off the cold.

There was still no sign of Captain Booth or his barge. In fact, only one barge was tied to the dock. The rest must be delivering loads of one sort or another.

Carl had returned and paced near the edge of the mudflats as he watched his workers. Was something on his mind or was he merely anxious for them to find a valuable trinket? She supposed the man had bills to pay, just like everyone else.

She continued her observations, looking to where the street ran parallel to the river's edge before winding its way in the opposite direction. A man in a black suit with a bowler hat stood on the pavement, his focus on the mudlarks before he turned to watch Carl.

Her breath caught and she stiffened. Could that be the man the girls mentioned who spoke to them about training to become a servant?

She pushed away from the brick wall and started toward him, hoping to speak to him. As nicely dressed as he was, it seemed unlikely he could have anything to do with the mudlarks' deaths. But there was a chance he had witnessed something that could help with the investigation.

The man looked directly at her, and she realized he looked vaguely familiar though she couldn't say why. Had he been an associate of Matthew's? From this distance, she could only see he had blond hair and a beard, but few other details. She lifted her hand, to signal that she wished to speak with him, and started forward.

He watched her for a moment before turning to stride in the opposite direction.

She would have to hurry if she wanted to catch him. She did just that, dodging several workers carrying barrels and around a cart loaded with crates, only to find the man had disappeared. Her steps slowed as she searched the street to no avail.

How strange. It was almost as if he hadn't wanted to speak with her and that roused her suspicions even more. Why did she think she recognized him? Or was she simply mistaken, given that his appearance was rather nondescript?

Amelia slowly continued forward looking for him until suddenly the hair on the back of her neck rose. The sensation of someone watching her crawled over her, leaving gooseflesh in its wake.

She turned to search for whoever observed her without success. The knowledge that she was a well-dressed woman alone in a rough area came rushing back into her mind, something she'd almost forgotten during her time with Agnes and Pudge.

Suppressing a shiver, she started back the way she'd come, knowing she should return home, even as she hated to feel forced to do so by whoever it was that watched her.

Twenty-Four

Another day passed quickly as Henry and Fletcher continued their search for Spencer, making one final push to locate the man. They retraced his steps and re-questioned those who knew him, moving from the bank to his lodging to the lottery drawing offices with no success. Fletcher spoke with the accountant he trusted to assist in cases, who agreed to examine the numbers Spencer had more than likely seen and provide a report the following day.

If Spencer had discovered an 'error', who had he mentioned it to? Logic suggested that whoever it was had been high enough in the organization to eliminate him and end the potential trouble he might cause. Or perhaps he had pressed the issue without realizing the danger. Why had he been foolhardy enough to do so? Was he so naïve that he thought it simply an oversight in need of fixing?

Impossible to say, unless they found him. Henry had a good guess as to what the accountant would report and was already pondering their next step.

The weather took a turn for the worse as dusk dimmed the sky, a cold wind sending the temperature plummeting. Henry had spent much of the day outside and felt the chill in his bones. It would take some time to warm once he went home for the night.

But his work wasn't over yet.

He fought off a shiver and wrapped his muffler tighter about his neck. Working hours might be officially over, but now was his chance to return his focus to the mudlarks—not that they'd ever been far from his thoughts.

Once again, he returned to Blackfriars. Another conversation with Carl—one away from the mudflats and his workers—was in order. Speaking with him at his home might bring different answers, especially after the man had time to consider what had happened to Charlie, a death which had appeared to truly affect him.

Tomorrow, he and Fletcher would take a precious hour or two during the day to approach the case from the opposite end—the poison. The information Amelia had provided was helpful, but he needed to learn more as he knew very little about mushrooms.

How exactly did one procure poisonous fungi? Was it something a person with the proper knowledge could find on their own? Did it require special skills to process? Was it dried to strengthen it? Were there benefits to some types over others? Could such fungi be purchased from an apothecary?

The challenge would be to find an expert in the field, if there were such a person. But that task was for tomorrow.

The cabbie dropped him off on the closest street corner but advised he wouldn't wait. "Not a good area at this time of night, guv," he muttered as he'd flicked the reins of his horse and continued on his way in search of the next fare.

Henry hoped he could find another once he was done speaking with Carl, the area and the freezing air making the prospect of walking home unappealing.

It took several tries before he located the right address, but he soon knocked on the door of an apartment on the second floor of a shabby three-story building. Sounds coming from within the apartment suggested someone was home, and he held onto his patience as he waited for his knock to be answered.

A woman jerked open the door, wiping her hands on an apron that had seen better days. Her hair was pulled back into a severe knot at the nape of her neck, strands a mix of gray and blonde, her expression wary. "What is it?" Her brow furrowed.

"I would like to speak with Carl."

She eyed him up and down with a scowl. "What fer?"

"I have a few questions for him." Henry eased closer to place a foot in the doorway to prevent her from shutting the door in his face and took the opportunity to look into the small flat.

Faded curtains hung at the window, and the mismatched furniture had seen better days. A worn rug graced the floor, its swirled pattern of muted colors lending a warmth to the room. Bits and bobs covered the surfaces of several second-hand tables, perhaps treasures Carl had yet to sell. Some looked intriguing, and under different circumstances, he would've liked to have a closer look.

"Humph." The woman, who he assumed was Carl's wife, glanced over her shoulder. "Carl. Someone to see yer."

A muffled reply came from one of the rear rooms and soon Carl emerged, brows shooting up at the sight of Henry in the doorway.

"Workin' late this evenin', eh?" he asked, a wary look in his eyes as if fearful Henry's visit meant more bad news.

The man looked different without his pipe and cap, the tan line on his forehead testament to how much time he spent outdoors. He appeared younger and somehow more vulnerable in his shirtsleeves and out of his boots. His pale hair was thick, sticking straight up at the back as if happy to be free of the hat.

"I have a few questions for you. They won't take long." Henry glanced at the man's wife, preferring to speak with him in private, but he needn't have bothered. She had already turned toward the kitchen at the rear of the apartment.

"Any news on what happened to Charlie?" Carl asked. A hint of emotion crossed his face, coloring his tone. Perhaps he cared more for his charges than he let on.

"Not as of yet."

Carl shook his head as he led the way to two chairs with lumpy cushions in the front room. There was no fire in the hearth, but the apartment was fairly warm. No doubt the stove in the kitchen was burning while his wife made dinner, and that was enough to keep the place relatively warm. Henry welcomed the feeling.

"Can't hardly believe it. Two mudlarks gone in little more than a week. What's the world comin' to?" Carl gestured to a chair as he sank into one.

Henry wasn't certain if he referred to their deaths or the fact that he'd lost two workers. He decided against asking, uncertain if he'd like the answer.

"How did Charlie come to be part of your crew?"

"Nora brought him along one day. Said how he was on his own and wanted to try mudlarkin'."

"Do you know what happened to his parents?"

"Never asked. Questions 'bout the past tend to raise bad memories fer the kids." He smoothed his hands over his trousers, his knuckles gnarled.

"How old was the boy?"

"Hmm. Don't think he knew fer certain. I'd guess eight or nine. Small fer his age but most orphans are."

Lack of food, not to mention living in the city where the air was heavy with soot, didn't help. But that was another problem Henry couldn't solve.

"Did he speak of what happened to Nora?"

"Some. He seemed convinced that the man comin' around offerin' to train them fer servants had somethin' to do with her death. I told him to leave it be, but if it was true, he'd best keep his distance."

"How did he respond?"

Carl frowned as he looked at Henry. "How should I know?"

"Surely you knew him well enough to guess. Did he nod in agreement or did the suggestion make him angry?"

"Neither," Carl said at length. "I'm sure he carried resentment fer what happened to Nora." He sent Henry a glare. "He asked why more wasn't being done to find who poisoned her."

Excellent question. Henry kept the response to himself. The public either thought the police didn't do enough, or that they stuck their noses into affairs that didn't concern them. The court of public opinion was a fickle one. Henry rarely tried to sway it, hoping his actions spoke for themselves, but in this case, his hands were tied.

"Did you speak to the other mudlarks to see if he told them of any plans he had to look into the matter himself?"

"I did. If he meant to follow in Nora's steps, he kept it to 'imself."

Henry nodded even as he wondered whether the children would tell Carl if they did know. Given the man's gruff manner, Henry couldn't imagine them sharing a confidence. Perhaps it would be best if he spoke with them again himself. Amelia would be happy to help, but he refused to ask that of her when it would place her in danger.

"Did that widow lady discover any news?"

Alarm trickled through Henry. "Why do you ask?"

Carl shrugged. "She was at the mudflats for some time today, pokin' through the mud with Agnes and Pudge. Luckily, she kept her distance from my workers other than to offer them sandwiches. Can yer believe that?" He shook his head. "I hope she doesn't make a habit of wastin' their time with all her questions, else I'll have to have a few words wiv her. Don't need 'em more upset than they already are."

Anger stirred and Henry leveled him a look. "Mrs. Greystone has already proved helpful, which is more than I can say for you. I think the only way to calm the children at this point is to discover who killed Nora and Charlie and why. If doing so upsets them, it can't be helped." He wasn't about to curtail his efforts so the mudlarks could put the deaths from their minds. Not while they were in danger.

Carl's lips twisted, but he was wise enough not to disagree.

"Is there anything else you can tell me?" Henry prodded. It must be nearly time for dinner based on the scent of fried onions and meat coming from the kitchen, though it didn't smell particularly appealing. "Something that has come to mind since Charlie was found?"

"Nothin'." Carl shook his head and lifted his hands, palms up, as if he wished otherwise. "Charlie is—was a smart boy. If he su'pected the fancy man of bein' behind the trouble, it's worth lookin' into."

Henry stood. "We need more information about the man to do so. Let me know if you see him again."

"I'll try to strike up a conversation with him if I do."

"Take care. He could be dangerous." Despite his warning, Henry wasn't about to tell him not to when he was desperate for clues.

After thanking Carl for his time he departed, already pondering whether he could find time to speak to the mudlarks the next day. Who was this well-dressed man and how could he find him?

Henry blew out a breath as he stepped out of the building, leaving a wispy puff in the frosty air. His stomach rumbled, reminding him that his midday meal had been some time ago. He'd have to hurry home if he hoped to have dinner before his landlady stopped serving.

Henry walked briskly in the direction of the nearest cab stand, scowling as he noted how dark the street was even for this area. He'd only gone a short distance before the prickly sensation of someone watching him pushed away thoughts of dinner.

He glanced around, wondering if some desperate soul would be foolhardy enough to try to steal from him. The street was fairly deserted, as if everyone else had already found their way home for the evening. Unfortunately, he couldn't see much in the dark, light from windows only casting a faint glow that hardly reached the pavement.

The scuff of a shoe behind him had him spinning to face whoever approached. Only then did he realize another was coming from the opposite direction.

He couldn't see much more than a beefy form in a long coat before him. He raised his hands to defend himself but a blow he didn't see coming had already struck him in the stomach.

Henry grimaced at the pain but managed to knock his assailant in the jaw before turning to throw a punch in the direction of the second man, damping down the panic and focusing on fighting back. The blow grazed the man's chin, and he hesitated as if thinking twice about continuing the attack. Apparently he hadn't expected Henry to put up much of a fight.

He turned to face the first man a second too late and grimaced as another blow landed, this time in his ribs. The pain stole his breath even as anger took hold. He kept low and rammed his shoulder into the man then threw an elbow at the one behind him, his blood pounding.

"Get 'em," the first man called but the second one stayed out of reach when Henry snarled in response.

Before he could prepare, the two rushed him at once and Henry threw punches wildly, determined to give as good as he got despite being outnumbered. He was not going to die here as long as he could continue to fight.

A sharp prick stuck him in the side, halting Henry's movements. The sensation was all too familiar. "Ye best keep yer nose out of business that don't belong to ye," the first man warned.

"According to who?" Henry managed to breathe out, surprised this wasn't a simple theft.

"Stay off the mudflats," the man snarled before pushing Henry back. "You and the lady both."

The mention of Amelia shook him, and he lashed out at the man only to be shoved harder. Off balance, pain in his side burning, he stumbled back, striking the back of his head on the brick building behind him. Dazed, head spinning and nausea rising, Henry braced himself and lifted his fists before him even as he wondered how much longer he could put up a fight.

To his relief, the two men fled.

Henry slid down the wall and sank onto the pavement, his breathing shallow as he took stock of his injuries. He was clearly upsetting someone with the limited investigation he'd conducted. Somehow, that thought helped to ease the pain.

With a slow, careful breath and a hand on his ribs, he told himself to get up. *This was no place to linger.* He managed to push to his feet, bracing a hand against the wall as he willed his vision to clear.

His head ached but not as much as his side. Henry touched the back of his head where he'd hit the brick, and it came away damp, never a good sign. After rolling his shoulders to ease the stiffness already setting in, he started walking, hoping like hell that a cab would be at the stand.

The walk took longer than it should've, but his legs trembled with relief when he saw a driver huddled on the seat of a cab two streets away.

Though he couldn't say why, it was Amelia's address which spilled from his mouth. Of course, he needed to warn her to take care and let her know they were being watched—but he wouldn't deny how comforting the idea of her aiding him was.

The cabbie eyed him for a long moment before agreeing to take him to the address he'd given, so he must look a sight. God, but his head swam.

His landlady would be less than pleased if he returned to his apartment in such a state. No, no, he couldn't do that. Pain—pain in his side, pain in his head. Amelia's aunt was still there, he was fairly sure, so he needed to take care. He blinked, desperate to clear his head. Fernsby—Fernsby would help. Perhaps the butler could take him to the kitchen and ask Amelia to come downstairs? Amelia would lend aid.

The ride passed in a blur and soon he was explaining to an alarmed Fernsby what help he wanted. The butler led him to the kitchen, where both Mrs. Fernsby and Mrs. Appleton exclaimed over him while Fernsby went to fetch Amelia.

"You look a fright, Inspector. Terrible when you're accosted going about your business," Mrs. Fernsby said after she directed Mrs. Appleton to get a bowl of hot water and clean cloths. "What is the world coming to?"

The housekeeper helped him to remove his coat and jacket and only then did he realize his side was bleeding more than he'd thought.

Perhaps he shouldn't have come to Amelia's.

"My goodness!" Mrs. Fernsby exclaimed. "We should send for the doctor."

Henry nearly grimaced at the thought of stitches. "No—no need. A bandage should suffice." In truth, his side hurt more from the blow to his ribs than the cut.

Then a quiet gasp filled the room. "Henry!"

He looked up to meet her concerned gaze, thinking once again that he shouldn't have come...yet he couldn't deny relief that he had.

Twenty-Five

Amelia stared in disbelief at Henry's battered face, heart racing. Then she took in the rest of him—mud and blood and obvious pain. She'd never seen the always composed man in quite such disarray, not even after the altercation outside her home during the ravenkeeper's investigation.

"What on earth happened?" she asked as she rushed forward.

Between the beginning of a bruise on his jawline, a cut above his swollen brow, and the blood on his shirt, he looked frightful. He leaned back in the chair as if barely able to stay upright.

"Apparently my limited investigation of the mudlark murders has gained attention." He moved his jaw back and forth. Did it hurt to talk?

"Oh, dear." Amelia shook her head. "I suppose that's good and bad news. Let us see to your injuries, and then we'll discuss the details."

She didn't care to share too much in front of the servants as she didn't want to worry them. Fernsby was already concerned enough about her trips to Blackfriars.

Henry seemed to understand as he gave a single—careful—nod. "Thank you."

His slow movements worried her even more than the blood, not so different than the constable who'd been struck on the head on her front porch a few weeks ago.

"Did you hit your head?" Amelia asked, wondering what caused the dazed look in his eyes.

He touched the back of it, his fingers coming away red with blood. "On a brick wall. Not by choice."

Mrs. Fernsby handed Amelia a damp cloth. "I'll leave this to you and find some salve." She bustled away to where Mrs. Appleton tore strips of linen for bandages. "Looks as if we'll be needing several," she told the cook.

Amelia braced herself and tried to set aside her worry. Henry's wounds needed tending and hysteria wouldn't help. She stepped closer and moved aside his thick, dark hair to better see the wound. The lump was relatively large with a nasty split.

This injury seemed worse than the one he'd received during the last case, which she'd also tended. "You're making a habit of head injuries."

"Also not by choice," Henry mumbled.

"Madam, shall I send for the doctor?" Fernsby asked, brow wrinkled as he watched from the doorway, clearly prepared to fetch the physician himself.

"No—no need." Henry shifted in the chair. "It's nothing serious. Mostly aches and pains."

"Except for your head, and whatever is causing the blood staining your shirt," Mrs. Appleton added with a reprimanding look at their patient.

Amelia halted her effort to clean the bump on his head to look at his side, the blood on his shirt giving her pause. "Let us have a look."

"One of them caught me with a blade. Clearly, they were intent on making sure I listened." He lifted an arm to look at his side, though he still wore his shirt. "I-I don't think it's that deep." The hopeful tone in his voice only made her worry more.

Amelia pressed her lips tight to contain her emotions. The idea of Henry in danger made her tremble with upset. She considered him a friend after all they'd been through, and to think he'd been stabbed—which could've easily resulted in his death—terrified her.

Frustration took hold and she welcomed it, using its energy to say what must be said. "Since you haven't yet viewed it, I don't think we can accept your opinion."

His mouth curved almost imperceptibly at her high-handed tone.

She set the rag on the table and reached for his shirt. Though she had been married for six years, she couldn't dispel the nerves that fluttered through her as she worked the buttons. Now was not the time to act like a...well, like a maiden aunt, when an injury needed tending.

Mrs. Appleton joined her to help remove his shirt. Based on his stiff movements and grimaces, the injuries were hurting Henry more than he let on.

Amelia ignored his broad shoulders and strong chest with its light coating of dark hair. At least, she tried. Henry was much fitter than Matthew, and she couldn't help but make comparisons. It was not as though she saw many naked men.

Heat rose in her cheeks, and she could only hope the staff and Henry put it down to her concern. Such thoughts were quickly forgotten when they eased the shirt aside to reveal a two-inch slice between his ribs surrounded by drying blood.

"Oh, my." Amelia shared a worried look with Mrs. Appleton. "That should have stitches."

"A bandage will do," Henry argued as he attempted to twist to better see the injury then hissed with pain.

Amelia frowned. "We shall see once we clean it, but it will heal quicker if it's stitched."

Henry's lips twitched as if tempted to argue but he said nothing.

"What is this other cut?" she asked, noting a smaller wound not far from the deeper one. Though partially healed, it still looked sore.

"It's nothing."

Amelia had difficulty believing that. How often did he end up on the wrong end of a knife?

Much to her relief, Mrs. Appleton dampened another cloth and began to gently wipe the cut. While Amelia could tend the bump on Henry's head, she didn't think she could maintain her composure while doing the same to his side. That was a level of intimacy for which she wasn't prepared.

Returning to her previous task, she gently cleaned his scalp. "Some ice would help reduce the swelling." She glanced at Fernsby who dipped his head.

"Excellent idea, madam. We received a delivery just this morning."

Amelia glanced again at Henry's side where Mrs. Appleton had wiped away the drying and oozing blood. "Stitches?"

"It would be best," the cook said with a questioning look at Henry.

"There is no need." The determined glint in his eye hinted at a stubborn side to him she'd never witnessed.

"Very well," Amelia relented. "But if it's bleeding come morning, you should have it stitched."

Fernsby returned with the ice, and his wife carefully wrapped it in a cloth for Henry to hold on the bump.

Right. What else could she do to care for the man? "Have you eaten dinner?"

"Not as of yet." His stomach grumbled as if to confirm his reluctant admission. "But I've caused enough trouble."

"Nonsense. What do we have, Mrs. Appleton?" Amelia asked firmly.

"There's a bit of beef left from dinner," the cook said as she applied salve to the knife wound. "Will that do?"

She and Mrs. Fernsby wrapped bandages around Henry's ribs, covering the cut.

"Sounds delicious." Henry raised his arms to allow them to finish. "Thank you."

Amelia and Mrs. Fernsby helped Henry back into his shirt, the housekeeper tutting at the darkening bruises along his ribs visible below the wrap. "Might've broken a rib or two. You're going to be sore come morning," she declared.

"More than likely," Henry agreed. The way he moved so gingerly made it clear he already was.

"Don't we have some willow bark on hand?" Amelia asked Mrs. Appleton as the cook pulled out the beef and some bread. Amelia's father often prescribed the remedy for fever as well as aches and pains.

"Indeed, we do." Mrs. Appleton nodded. "I'll brew some."

"Thank you." Amelia turned to Henry, anxious to hear the details of what had happened. "Why don't we adjourn to the dining room, and I'll keep you company while you eat," she suggested.

"I don't want to impose," he protested. "I know you have a guest."

"Aunt Margaret is writing letters before she retires for the night, so you needn't worry."

Henry removed the wrapped ice from his head, shifted to the edge of the chair, and slowly stood. "If you are sure?"

"Of course."

Henry turned to the servants, looking at each one in turn. "Thank you for your assistance. I truly appreciate it."

"Take care of those injuries, Inspector," Mrs. Fernsby said with a smile. "Rest when you can, or I shall do those stitches myself."

"Yes, I will."

Amelia knew that to be a lie. If she were to guess, Henry would be more determined than ever to find who had killed the mudlarks.

She led the way up the stairs to the dining room then paused before the door of the study. "I'll only be a moment. Go ahead to the dining room."

Henry nodded, looking like he needed to sit down again. The fact that he didn't insist on waiting for her took her aback. Definitely a cracked rib or two.

Amelia strode into the study, pleased that enough light came from the corridor to show the way toward the glasses and whiskey decanter that still sat on the side table. While she thought the willow bark would do Henry good, a glass of whiskey would do the same.

She poured a generous portion and carried the glass to the dining room, anxious to hear what happened.

"This should help." She set the glass before him and took a nearby chair.

Henry took a sip followed by another and sighed, setting the glass on the gleaming table. "Thank you. I don't mean to make a habit of seeking refuge here when I'm injured." He looked away as if embarrassed, his expression warming her for reasons she wasn't prepared to examine.

"I'm pleased to offer any help I can. You know that." She cleared her throat, hoping her cheeks weren't as flushed as they felt. "Where were you attacked?"

"I had just stepped outside after conversing with Carl at his home. Certainly not the best neighborhood. I thought they intended to rob me. Instead, it was a warning."

"They?" Her heart thudded painfully at the insight that more than one person had attacked him.

Henry shared the story, though Amelia had to wonder how much he left out so as not to frighten her. He needn't have bothered. The entire situation shook her, especially what had happened to Henry and how likely another mudlark would die before they could discover who was behind it.

"You're obviously being watched," Amelia said. "At least the times you're near Blackfriars."

"As are you." His worried gaze held hers. "They mentioned you in their warning—that is why I came directly here. To warn you to take care. It's too dangerous for you to visit the mudflats again."

She'd known he was going to say as much and appreciated the genuine concern behind the statement. But she couldn't imagine leaving the mudlarks to fend for themselves while another one died. She knew Henry couldn't either.

"I will be careful." She couldn't promise more when the urge to return to Blackfriars tomorrow had already taken hold.

"Amelia, you must see you can't return," Henry continued even as he touched the back of his head with a wince.

The extent of his injuries gave her pause. Was he right? Was it dangerous even during the day? "I will certainly keep that in mind, but those children shouldn't be left on their own when someone is trying to murder them."

"No, but your life is valuable, too."

Was it? The question caught her breath. She realized it had been simmering below the surface for some time. *Did her life still hold value?*

She was no longer a mother. No longer a wife. What was her purpose in the world now that both of those roles had been taken from her?

The ache in her chest made it suddenly difficult to breathe. She was surprised her heart still beat, given everything she had endured. Lily and Matthew were gone, and she was still here.

Why?

On her stronger days, she was determined to keep moving forward until she found a new purpose, certain it would be revealed in time.

But in her weaker moments, she wasn't so sure there was any meaning to life. Certainly she'd been unfortunate to experience the losses she had. Fate wasn't always kind, but others had lived through worse.

She had tried to focus on the blessings in her life. That she was still here, when her daughter and husband weren't, mattered. Not to everyone, but to some. Her parents. Her staff. Maeve, and now maybe Henry. Maybe even Agnes and Pudge, if she could help to make sure no harm befell them.

Perhaps she was reaching for attachments that weren't there. Hoping for a tether to hold her to this world and give her existence meaning.

Amelia gave herself a mental shake. Now wasn't the time for such morose thoughts when Henry was watching her with eyes that held far too much sympathy and understanding. Did he guess at the level of despair she sometimes felt?

With a deep breath, she lifted her chin, trying to focus on this moment and the day that followed. She didn't have answers to the questions about life. She only knew that assisting with this investigation, just like the ravenkeeper's, provided a sense of purpose, however fleeting.

Of course, that wasn't the only reason she wanted to help. The mudlarks might be poor orphans, but they deserved justice as much as anyone else, including Matthew. She had done all she could to help find her husband's killer to no avail. Was it any wonder she wanted to find justice for the mudlarks?

"Amelia," Henry began when she didn't respond.

"I will be *very* careful, but please don't ask me not to help." A well of emotion rose in her throat and she didn't think she could say anything further on the matter without breaking down.

She needed a reason to keep going and to put one foot before the other. Hopefully he could understand and respect that. As long as she believed her efforts made a difference, she would do all she could.

Henry held her gaze and for the briefest moment, she thought he'd reach for her hand. Instead, he nodded. "Very well. I will hold you to that."

Twenty-Six

"Well, look at that. Apparently you picked a fight you couldn't win."

Henry glanced up from his desk to see Perdy saunter into the room. He returned to his work, not interested in anything the man had to say. His head pounded, and his side burned with every breath.

What precisely had possessed him to venture straight to Amelia's after the attack was something he was avoiding contemplating. Had he truly wanted to warn her, or had he been in search of sympathy? Either way, being with her had done much to help him recover his balance. Of course, having his wounds tended, along with a hot meal and a whiskey or two, had helped, as well.

The emotion swirling in her eyes as they'd spoken in the dining room was impossible to forget. He longed to ease the pain that had flashed across Amelia's face. She'd been through so much, and he wanted to protect her from further harm.

Damn if he didn't admire her courage and perseverance. Those qualities had no doubt served her well in the past few years. But would they protect her now?

"Why is it that you always seem to be on the losing end of things?" Perdy asked as he leaned a hip against Henry's desk.

Henry knew he looked a sight, the bruise on his jaw and the cut on his swollen brow the worst of his visible injuries. But it was the hidden ones that hurt the most.

With a sigh, Henry realized the other man wasn't leaving until he responded. "Some of us spend more time out of the office than in it and end up in the thick of things."

"Humph." Percy scowled. "Some of us use our intellect rather than brawn. I think your father and grandfather would agree with me."

Henry sat back in his chair, careful not to move too fast—his ribs wouldn't thank him for that. Though he knew that wasn't true, doubt about his recent efforts still rose. "I don't see how staring at case files helps solve them."

Before Perdy could do more than sputter, Henry heard his name.

"Field." Reynolds studied Henry's bruised face for a long moment. "My office. Now."

Perdy chortled. "In trouble again!"

Henry ignored him and followed Reynolds to take a seat before his desk.

Reynolds' lips twisted as he observed the careful way Henry moved. "Want to share what happened?"

Though tempted to refuse since it had nothing to do with his current cases, Henry decided honesty was best. "After work hours yesterday, I ventured to Blackfriars to question someone and ran into trouble."

"On what case?"

"None of ours. It was regarding the death of the two mudlarks." Henry knew resentment darkened his tone, but he couldn't help it. The case should be an official one.

"I thought I made it clear we would not be investigating those deaths."

"You did, but in all honesty, sir, the murders of those children are suspicious. Even you must admit that."

"I don't have to admit anything." Reynolds gave a frustrated sigh. "Field, you are a good detective, but you need to stay focused. Chasing down someone who killed two orphans is not a prudent use of your time."

"That is why I am looking into it after work hours." While not completely true, Henry didn't disclose that.

"Damnit, man, I can't dictate what you do with your own time but don't let it interfere with police business."

"Yes, sir." Henry started to rise only to realize the conversation wasn't over.

"And what was the reason for the altercation?" Reynolds asked as he studied Henry's brow and jaw.

"I was warned to keep away from the mudflats. At the end of a knife."

Reynolds' eyes narrowed behind his glasses even as a glint of interest—or was it anger?—gleamed. "Is that right?"

"Yes. It has me even more convinced that something foul is afoot. I worry another child will die soon if nothing is done—and the two we know about might only scratch the surface."

Based on his expression, Reynolds did not like that news. "I don't want to see children murdered any more than you do. I...suppose it would do no harm to look into it. But I am not opening an official investigation solely because you received a few punches."

Henry didn't bother to mention the knife had been more than a threat; his injury wouldn't much change Reynolds' mind. It was enough that the director recognized something concerning was at work.

For now, he'd take what he could get. "Thank you."

"Do you have any solid leads?" Reynolds asked.

"Not exactly." He paused to mentally run through the few he had. "Thus far, we have a barge captain who pays the mudlarks a penny for a kiss, a dredger who openly resents them, a man who runs a crew of mudlarks, and one we have yet to identify who has offered training as servants to a few of the children."

"We?"

Henry nearly groaned at the inadvertent slip. "I meant me. Of course, a few of the mudlarks are doing their best to help. Two of them found the first child, sir." Would Reynolds believe him? He wasn't about to tell the director that Fletcher and Amelia were assisting with the investigation.

"I hardly think involving children is wise."

"No, but they were witnesses, and they have a vested interest in the outcome. They're the ones digging in the mud while someone is preying on them."

"Terrible." The director looked even less happy. "Have you looked into the poison?"

Henry chose his words carefully to avoid revealing Amelia's efforts. "Enough to know it's made from a type of fungi. Both children ate fine meals before they died, more than likely dosed with the mushrooms."

"From a restaurant?" Reynolds asked curiously, leaning forward.

"Doubtful when they couldn't afford such a meal. I tend to think they were at someone's home. Perhaps the man who is offering the training to become a servant?" None of it added up, that was the frustration.

"Why offer a meal only to poison it?" Reynolds mused as he stared across the office. "Seems like a waste."

"Perhaps to mask the taste of the poison? Or to see how it's affected by food? An experiment of some kind?" Henry shook his head as he pondered the questions that had surfaced since Nora's death. Amelia's idea of testing the dosage made some sense, but he had yet to find a motive.

"An odd experiment to conduct. And to what end?"

"A misguided attempt to clean up the streets by removing orphans?" Henry shook his head. "I can think of far worse problems in the city if that is the goal." He started to shrug but thought better of it when his side protested. "No logical ideas have come to mind."

"All the more reason you should focus on your assigned cases instead." Reynolds propped his elbows on the desk. "What of the missing man? Any luck?"

"Very little. We continue to trace the money angle of the lottery tickets, but with each day that passes and no sign of him, I fear the worst."

"Keep me apprised of your efforts." Reynolds glanced at the piles of papers on his desk, suggesting the meeting was over.

"Yes, sir." Henry pushed to his feet, careful not to jostle his ribs.

"Field?"

Henry glanced at the Director.

"I can see that more than your face was hurt, I'm no fool. Take care that you don't injure yourself further."

"Yes, sir." Inspectors weren't allowed to carry weapons, otherwise it might've been a fairer fight, and he wouldn't be quite so miserable, but nothing could be done about that.

Venturing to speak to Carl at night hadn't been the wisest course of action, yet what choice did he have when forced to investigate an 'unofficial' case on his own time?

Perhaps Fletcher wouldn't mind accompanying him when he returned to the area. The thought of the sergeant was reassuring, but it didn't alleviate his worry for Amelia—and would make it harder to lie to Reynolds and keep Fletcher's involvement out of this. Blast.

The sooner he solved the case and found the killer, the better.

With that in mind, he quickly finished the notes he'd been working on and departed Scotland Yard, putting on his hat with care, only to nearly run into Fletcher.

The sergeant's eyes widened as he took in Henry's face. "What does the other man look like?" His mouth gaped, eyes lighting with interest. "Tell me you had it out with Perdy."

"No, to the last question." Henry managed a smile, amused by the thought. "And the other two probably don't look as bad as I do." He had enough pride to reveal that he'd been outnumbered.

"Then we should probably be happy you're still upright and walking."

Henry touched his side. "I suppose so."

"How hurt are you?" Fletcher asked as he looked him up and down.

"Sore, but I managed to avoid stitches."

Fletcher shook his head. "I suppose that's good news given your dislike of needles."

"Indeed." Henry filled him in on the events of the previous evening as they walked toward the accountant's office.

"Sounds as if you're making more progress than you realized," Fletcher kept his stride even with Henry, despite his slower-than-normal pace.

"I only wish I knew which part struck a chord."

"Surely it was your conversation with Carl."

"Doubtful. He has no motive to poison the mudlarks since they earn him money. Nor would he have access to provide the type of meal the two victims ate prior to taking the poison. Trust me, I smelled his kitchen."

"True. But someone in the area has seen you." Fletcher paused to allow a man to move past them, then again walked at Henry's side.

Henry nodded, uncomfortable with the way the injuries on his face were attracting the notice of people on the street. "That's rather surprising given how rarely I'm there."

"And at the wrong time apparently." Fletcher studied the wounds again. "Or the right time, depending on how one looks at it and where this leads. I assume Reynolds saw you." At Henry's nod, he asked, "What did he say?"

"He's not particularly pleased that I have been looking into the murders when they're not an official case, but agrees they're suspicious. He went so far as to say that if I wanted to continue to do so, even during daylight hours, he wouldn't stop me as long as it didn't interfere with my official cases."

"So you have unofficial permission," Fletcher offered with a wry look.

"Something like that."

"Well then, I assume that extends to me." The sergeant straightened his shoulders. "What would you like me to do first?"

Henry breathed a careful sigh of relief to have the man's help and support.

Twenty-Seven

"We can't forget our missing person," Henry advised Fletcher as they continued toward the accountant's office. "Reynolds is pressing me on that case. Let us see what this accountant of yours has to say after reviewing the information we provided. Afterward, we'll pay a visit to the lottery office, followed by the mudflats. Tomorrow, I intend to take the train to speak with Spencer's mother and stepfather."

While he was anxious to speak with the man's parents, the idea of riding on a train given the state of his ribs was less than appealing. Then again, neither was walking. His body hurt no matter what he did.

"Excellent plan," Fletcher said.

"It might also be wise to put out word among the dredgers to advise us if they find a body that fits Spencer's general description." He didn't like the thought, but they had to cover all options, since it had been so long since the man went missing.

"I can do that." Fletcher nodded. "Though they tend to be interested only if there's a reward."

Henry considered the idea. "Perhaps we will come across a dredger or two during our visit to the mudflats, and we can mention it then." Speaking with Tobias Watson again seemed like a good idea, if he could find the man, and he had yet to question Captain Salem. So much to do...

"All right." Fletcher held his gaze. "Just be sure not to venture there alone again, especially after dark."

Though Henry was loath to admit it, Fletcher was right. "That would probably be wise."

They discussed the details of their plans as they walked, the pace slower than Henry would've liked. He considered taking a cab but that wouldn't be any less painful than walking given the traffic and the cobbled streets that made one feel every rut.

The accountant, Mr. Thompson, greeted them with a reserved nod as they entered his office, his gaze lingering on Henry's injured face.

Henry didn't bother to explain and got directly to the point. "What did you find?"

"There is a concern with the numbers." The slim and tidy man reached for a sheet of paper at his elbow and turned it toward them so they could see for themselves. "The first is the total followed by a line for expenses, but the details given for those are vague. If one considers the average cost to run a drawing of this sort, including printing costs, perhaps some advertising, security for the selling of tickets, and basic overhead expenses for a small office and hiring out rooms in a pub, the expenses are far too high."

"How difficult was it to come to this conclusion?" Henry asked, curiosity and excitement rising. This had to be a lead. "Would it be logical for someone with an accounting background to see the numbers are misleading?"

"Any accountant worth his salt could easily do so by taking the average number of tickets sold for the last three drawings and comparing that to the prize money and expenses."

"It's a scam aimed at the lower and middle class." The thought obviously didn't sit well with Fletcher. "Those who can't use education to assist them."

"I would say so," Mr. Thompson agreed. "Whoever is behind it seems to be pocketing a large percentage of ticket sales."

"Thank you, Mr. Thompson." Henry stood, having learned exactly what he'd hoped to. "We appreciate the information. Send the department a bill for your time."

"It's my pleasure." The accountant smiled. "I look forward to reading of an arrest thanks to my contribution in the paper."

Henry didn't confirm or deny the likelihood of that. He'd rather the papers stayed out of police business. However, in this case it might be wise to share the news with a reporter or two if an arrest was made—to warn the public to be vigilant about such schemes.

A half-hour later, he and Fletcher arrived at the lottery office, only to stare at the empty building with dismay.

"I'll be." Fletcher peered into the dark space, using a hand to shield the glare. "Completely empty. It's as if they were never there."

Henry backed up to look over the building. "Are you certain this is the proper address?"

"Without a doubt. It was a bustling place when I last visited. They'd even moved in a printing press."

"Not an easy feat." Henry sighed, frustration simmering. "Let's speak with the nearby businesses to see if they can tell us anything."

They split up, making their way down each side of the street. The owner next door told Henry the lottery men had cleared out overnight without warning. He wasn't sure who would take over the office or if it would stand empty for a time. Another man provided them with the name and address of the building owner who had leased the space to the lottery office not long ago.

Henry and Fletcher agreed to meet later for lunch, and the sergeant departed to speak with the building owner. Henry continued to question a few other businesses to see if they knew anything. One man who worked across the street said he wasn't surprised by their sudden disappearance.

"Never got a straight answer when you asked any of them a question," he advised darkly. "Always seemed a little suspicious to me. You know, I wouldn't be surprised if they used false names."

That only deepened Henry's worry over what fate had befallen Spencer. Hopefully Fletcher would have better luck with the building owner.

The time for luncheon soon arrived and Henry found Fletcher already waiting at the pub with a pint in hand. Henry placed his order at the bar and joined him, relieved to rest his feet but dismayed by how tired he was.

Fletcher sent him a sympathetic look. "You appear rather peaked. How are you faring?"

Henry touched the bump on the back of his head and drew a slow breath, wishing he had more of the willow bark tea Amelia had provided—or the whiskey. "Could be better. My head aches and my ribs hurt like the devil."

"I suppose it's preferable to the alternative. I'm relieved you're not laying on Taylor's slab."

Henry's chest tightened at the sergeant's words even though his friend didn't look at him as he spoke. The fact that he had said them was enough.

Henry waited until Fletcher met his gaze and then smiled. "Thank you."

Fletcher nodded and took a big bite of his meat pie, clearly done with the topic.

The remark made Henry consider who would mourn him if the attack the previous evening had ended badly. How terrible to be like Spencer and disappear, only to have so few people raise the alarm. Even the two mudlarks had received more attention from those around them than Spencer.

The thought had Henry vowing to visit his parents again soon, as well as Amelia, grateful for the opportunity to come to know her better. If not for the mudlark murders, he wasn't sure when he would have managed to speak with her again after Maeve left. He'd taken her husband's files home but had yet to study them. He must do so soon and hoped to find a clue he'd overlooked.

The remainder of lunch passed in either companionable silence or conversation on inconsequential things. Soon they were on their way to Blackfriars, and Henry couldn't deny a certain relief to have Fletcher at his side when they arrived.

"What should I be on the watch for?" Fletcher asked as he glanced around.

Henry wished he knew. "Anything. Anything and anyone that looks out of place." That was the most he could offer.

Fletcher nodded.

Perhaps the man's experience in the Navy would prove helpful yet again. Nothing like someone knowledgeable around a dock to know if anything was out of place.

Carl stood some distance away and nodded at Henry. He was the first person Henry wanted to speak to. Anger took hold, even though he didn't think Carl had anything to do with the attack—yet part of him couldn't deny the connection. Someone had to have told the men to watch for him, and it could have easily been Carl. No matter that Carl hadn't known he was coming to his home last evening; nor had anyone else.

THE MUDLARK MURDERS

"Mr. Jeffries," Henry greeted the man as he approached.

The other man dipped his head. "Inspector." Carl's eyes narrowed as he took in Henry's appearance. "What happened to yer face?"

"You don't know?" His blank look said he didn't, but it was still worth asking.

"How would I?"

Henry didn't intend to share the details. He'd already told the story more times than he cared to. "Suffice to say that someone in the area doesn't like my inquiries into the mudlarks' deaths."

Carl processed that information with a puzzled look. "They came fer ye after leavin' my place?" His obvious confusion didn't appear feigned.

"Two of them," Fletcher supplied, leveling Carl a glare that suggested he considered him a suspect.

Carl held up his hands, palms out. "I had nothin' to do with it. Why would I? Sure I don't like the coppers stickin' their nose in our business, but I don't like my mudlarks dyin' either."

"Sentimental sort, eh?" Fletcher glanced at Henry, making it abundantly clear he had reservations about the man.

"Apparently." Henry suspected Carl's gruffness hid a soft spot. Of course, that didn't keep him from taking advantage of his young workers.

Henry glanced at the foreshore where a handful of mudlarks squatted in the mud, scouring the ground for treasures. A new one was working whom he didn't recognize. Apparently Carl hadn't wasted time finding a replacement. Of course, losing two of his workers must've put a dent in his meager profits.

He returned his attention to Carl. "You don't have any idea who it might've been?"

"None." The man openly studied Fletcher. "No wonder yer brought reinforcements."

Henry didn't bother describing the men as he never got a good look at them. The little he could share matched half the men in the area. "Have you seen Captain Salem of late?"

"Do yer suspect him?" Carl appeared surprised. "Hard to imagine the man settin' upon yer."

"I didn't say he did," Henry countered, ignoring the tweak of agony in his ribs. "I merely wish to speak with him."

"Humph." Carl scowled. "Seems as if yer mood is rather foul after what happened last evenin'."

"It is," Henry agreed, allowing a little of the pain and irritation to seep into his voice. "I don't appreciate being threatened by two strangers on my way home from questioning...you." Though tempted to call Carl a suspect, he resisted the urge. He preferred to have the man's cooperation so he would be willing to share anything of interest.

"Well, Salem just returned. That's him over there." Carl gestured in the direction of the dock where Henry saw a man coiling a rope on the deck of a barge.

"Thank you." Henry turned in that direction with Fletcher and made his way toward the man.

"Carl seems mean enough to hurt the mudlarks," Fletcher commented as they walked.

"It wouldn't surprise me if he cuffed one or two, but I don't think he would've bothered to kill them."

"True. No reason for him to go to such an effort, meals and mushrooms and the like."

"Exactly. I have yet to speak with Salem, but Mrs. Greystone took a strong dislike to him."

"Ah yes, the coin-for-a-kiss man." Fletcher shook his head in disgust. "I suppose it takes all kinds, but still..."

"Still." Henry knew exactly what he wanted to say to the man but first, he had a few questions. "Captain Salem?"

The older man straightened, moving slowly as if in pain—something to which Henry could relate.

Salem looked between Henry and Fletcher, seeming to take their measure. "Yes?"

"Inspector Field and Sergeant Fletcher from Scotland Yard. How's business?" Henry asked with a glance at the boat. Shards and dust of red brick sprinkled the deck, hinting at his last load.

"Good enough." The man shook his head. "Though we were a man short to unload." He placed a hand on his lower back. "I'm getting too old for such nonsense, but I had another load waiting and couldn't risk losing it."

"Tough business," Fletcher said as he looked over the barge. "How big is she?"

"Hundred and twenty tons with a wooden hull," Salem supplied. "Six sails handled by two men."

"Amazing what they can haul." Appreciation glinted in Fletcher's eyes.

Salem smiled with obvious pride. "Indeed, it is. Always a joy to watch her go. She's not always fast, but she's dependable and as steady as the rain."

"How fast can she go when empty?"

"Twelve knots."

Fletcher nodded. "That is impressive."

"Captain," Henry began, hating to interrupt but his side protesting at standing so long. "I have a few questions for you about the mudlarks who died."

Salem's expression sobered. "That Charlie always had a smile. Do ye know what happened to him?"

"He was poisoned, just like Nora." Henry watched for his reaction.

"Terrible thing. Who would poison children? To what end?" the captain demanded.

"That's what we're trying to discover. There has been mention of a stranger in the area, a man dressed in a nice suit. Have you seen him?"

He shook his head. "Impossible to say. There're many people in the area, I don't pay them any mind."

"This one was seen speaking to the mudlarks several times. You seem to have a keen interest in them," Henry pointed out.

Salem shrugged. "Sure I speak to them once or twice a week." His gaze shifted past Henry's shoulder. "Carl is here more often. If anyone has seen the stranger, it would be him."

"We need everyone's help to ensure another mudlark doesn't die."

Salem gaped in shock, revealing discolored teeth. "You expect another to die?"

"It's happened twice. Perhaps more. We have every reason to believe it could happen again." Henry withdrew his notebook. "Can you tell us where you were on the evenings they were killed?"

"At home as one should be." His outrage was palpable.

"You know both dates of the murders just like that, without a reminder?" It was hard not to be suspicious of such an instant alibi.

The captain scowled. "I'm home every night."

"Is there anyone who can verify that?"

"My wife. She'd have my head if I wasn't."

"Is she aware of your penchant for providing a penny in exchange for a kiss to the mudlarks?" Henry asked, trying and almost failing to keep his voice level.

The captain scowled. "She...she knows I often give them a penny."

"A word of advice, Captain Salem." Henry sent the older man a pointed look. "Your habit of paying for kisses from children would be frowned upon if revealed to the general public. While I applaud your attempt to aid them, your method of doing so is questionable."

"It's not anyone's business," the man protested.

Henry had no intention of arguing. "Given the children's age and vulnerability, I would hate to see what the ladies at the local church might do if they discovered your...habit."

The man's lips twisted as he considered what Henry had said. Revulsion stirred in Henry's gut; the fact that the man had to even think about it demonstrated the depths of his depravity.

Fletcher leaned close in a surprisingly sympathetic manner. "Trust me, you don't want the church ladies in your business."

"No, I don't. Especially when my wife is one of 'em."

"That isn't to say the mudlarks or any other orphans don't appreciate a kind word and a penny," Henry added, hoping to get his point across.

Salem looked anything but pleased as he reluctantly nodded.

Movement caught Henry's attention in the near distance, and he turned to see Carl waving at him. The man pointed to someone on the street dressed in a suit—one who fit the general description of the man Carl and Charlie had mentioned.

The stranger looked between Carl and Henry then spun on his heel and strode in the opposite direction.

"Stop him," Henry yelled at Fletcher and ran, pressing a hand to his aching side, his ribs and head making him feel every painful step.

Fletcher raced past him, allowing Henry to slow his pace, more than relieved the sergeant had accompanied him.

Now to catch the man and hopefully shed some light on the mudlark murders.

Twenty-Eight

"Care to explain what is going on?" Aunt Margaret sent Amelia a pointed look when she joined her in the drawing room that afternoon.

Amelia frowned at the accusatory tone, taken aback by the question. "Good afternoon, Aunt Margaret. I hope the day finds you well." What better way to remind her aunt of good manners than to use them?

She had yet to speak with her houseguest today, having her customary breakfast in the kitchen followed by spending the remainder of the morning in her laboratory to continue the fungi experiments, some of which were inspired by Elizabeth Drake's lecture. Unfortunately, she hadn't discovered anything insightful.

In truth, Amelia had needed time alone to process her conversation with Henry from the previous evening, along with the danger he'd faced. That had frightened her as much as the mudlark deaths.

Given her circling thoughts, she'd requested a light luncheon in her sitting room after finishing her work, preferring to avoid another stilted meal with her aunt. Despite Amelia's numerous attempts to draw out the cause for her unsettled behavior, the older woman had yet to admit anything was wrong, which was maddening.

Aunt Margaret had adjusted the chair in the drawing room more times than Amelia could count, insisting it was either too close or too far from the window. Yesterday at luncheon, she had complained the bread was too soft and tore when she spread butter on it. She had declined Amelia's suggestion of taking a drive and another of going to an art gallery. She didn't want to do anything but didn't seem happy staying in. And yet her aunt had never acted this way before on previous visits, often taking too much of Amelia's time with her suggestions for various outings and activities.

Amelia was losing patience, especially when she wanted to focus on helping the mudlarks. Though the urge to rush to the mudflats had nearly overwhelmed her when she woke that morning, Henry was right—she had to take care. Neither Nora nor Charlie had died while working. Since she couldn't follow the children home to watch over them, going to the mudflats would have been an attempt to make herself feel better rather than truly protecting them.

"Yes, yes, good day to you too." Her aunt dismissed the greeting with a disgruntled frown. "Don't pretend you didn't have a *guest* last night."

Amelia drew a calming breath. She didn't care for Aunt Margaret's suspicions or the guilt that filled her. She didn't have to answer to anyone, she reminded herself. She was a grown woman who had a family of her own. Who'd *had* a family of her own. Her heart pinched at the thought that the latter was no longer true.

"A man was here last night," Aunt Margaret continued. "I heard him speaking. Given the fact that you chose not to introduce me or advise me of his presence, and you have been avoiding me since, I must assume you are hiding something."

Though Amelia presumed her aunt was merely being protective, she did not appreciate her demeanor. This was her house and her life. As much as she loved her aunt, Amelia wouldn't allow her to take out her frustration in such manner.

While Amelia would've preferred not to tell her aunt what was happening, she would not lie. She was doing nothing wrong. Unconventional, yes, but not wrong.

"I would be happy to explain exactly who he is and why he was here, if you would care to listen without judgement." Amelia wanted to make it clear that she did not appreciate the unspoken accusation.

Aunt Margaret shifted to the edge of her chair, chin lifted, and made the accusation plain. "Have you taken a lover?"

Amelia gasped. "No, but if I had, it would be none of your business. What on earth has got into you?" Her aunt had never acted this way before.

Yet, even as the words came out, an idea arose. Perhaps her aunt was the one who'd taken a lover. If so, it must have ended badly.

"I'm not the one entertaining gentleman callers late in the evening."

"I will share the reason for his visit if you return the favor and explain your obvious unhappiness." Amelia waited to see if her aunt would accept the challenge.

As expected, Aunt Margaret stiffened in surprise. "Wh-Whatever do you mean?"

"You have been miserable since your arrival. Will you tell me what is wrong?"

"I have no idea of what you're speaking."

Amelia sighed. "As you wish." She waited a moment longer to see if she would change her mind, but her aunt remained silent. It seemed clear she was trying to fool not only Amelia, but herself into believing all was well. She could only hope her aunt would talk when she was ready. "My guest last evening was Inspector Henry Field."

Her aunt's expression shifted to a curious one. "Is he not the one who investigated Matthew's death?"

"Yes, and he still is, although no new clues have arisen in quite some time. However, we came to better know one another when he was looking into the murder of the ravenkeeper at the Tower of London."

"You wrote an article about the man, didn't you? I remember reading it."

"That's right. During the interview, I met his daughter." Amelia bit her lip, not mentioning that Maeve was nearly the same age Lily would've been, had she lived. "She sought me out after the murder and stayed with me while Inspector Field solved the case." No need to mention the danger that had involved.

"Why was he here last night?"

"He is investigating the death of two mudlarks."

"What does that have to do with you?"

"The first body was discovered while I was interviewing a barge captain. I'm the one who sent for Inspector Field."

Aunt Margaret's eyes narrowed once again. "Are you...somehow aiding him with the investigation? Is that why you've made all those trips to Blackfriars?"

"In part, although I am still working on the article." In truth, she could finish it with what she had, but chose not to share that. "Unfortunately, Henry was injured last night after questioning one of the suspects."

"Henry? You are on a first name basis? What did—did he expect you to aid him?" Her aunt looked astounded, though Amelia didn't know about which part.

She hesitated, wondering how much to say. She would rather the details didn't find their way to her parents until she was ready to share them herself, and she had Henry's privacy to think of too. "I am happy to help in whatever way I can."

"Amelia! You can't think to run about London investigating crimes. That's far too dangerous." The concern on her aunt's face was a reminder of the risk—not that Amelia needed it after what had happened to Henry.

"I realize that." She held her aunt's gaze, wanting her to understand the stakes. "But someone is cold-bloodedly poisoning children. Given my knowledge of chemistry, I am doing what I can to help." She didn't mention that Henry had come to warn her or that she'd tended his injuries...without his shirt. There were some things her aunt didn't need to know. "Yes," she continued, "I've made several trips to visit the mudlarks with the hope they will come to trust me and share more of what they know. Someone might have seen something that could help and asking more questions is the only way to know."

"That is a job for the police," Aunt Margaret insisted, looking so much like Amelia's mother that Amelia nearly relented.

"They have yet to open an official investigation. Henry is working on the case in his spare time, which he has little of—and I am taking care, I promise you. I only go during the day and remain near the shore where the mudlarks are. But something has to be done before another child is killed." Had she revealed more of her upset than she'd intended? She didn't share that somehow, saving the mudlarks might help to make up for her failure to protect Lily from the illness that had claimed her.

Clearly her aunt wasn't the only one with secrets.

Her aunt's lips pressed tight, her disapproval clear. "I still think it's too dangerous. But I couldn't live with myself if something happened to you while I am here. If you go again, I insist on going with you."

"That's not necessary," she said hastily as alarm filled her chest. She wanted to give Pudge the money from selling her coin and couldn't imagine doing so with her aunt at her side. "I don't think you would enjoy it—"

"I'm not there for enjoyment but to offer added protection."

Amelia sighed. Was there any point in arguing? "In fact, I am planning to go shortly."

Aunt Margaret stood. "Allow me to get my things. I will be ready in but a moment."

"Very well." Amelia hated to think what her aunt would report to her parents, but it couldn't be helped. "You can see for yourself what the area is like. I appreciate your concern and know there is safety in numbers."

Perhaps her aunt needed to find a purpose as well. Thinking of others rather than oneself often lifted one's spirit. Amelia was proof of that.

"Indeed." Aunt Margaret turned to go then looked back. "But please know that if I find it too dangerous, we will be having this discussion again."

Amelia nodded. This might well be one of her last visits to the mudflats until the murderer was caught.

Twenty-Nine

Henry grimaced with each step as he chased the fleeing man, watching as he shoved people out of his way as he went and glancing over his shoulder at his pursuers, though Henry himself wasn't much of a threat.

But the man hadn't got far, and Fletcher was nearly upon him.

Henry kept moving, his gait uneven but he refused to remain behind, unwilling to give up on the first true lead they'd had. Surely the man's attempt to escape meant he was connected to the case?

Blowing out a painful breath of relief, Henry tried not to grin as Fletcher caught the man, grabbing his arm to drag him to a halt.

"Release me at once!" The stranger struggled breathlessly against Fletcher's hold.

"Not until you answer a few questions." Fletcher continued to restrain him until Henry joined them.

"Who are you?" the man frowned as he looked between Henry and Fletcher.

"Scotland Yard, Inspector Field and Sergeant Fletcher," Henry supplied even as he nodded at Fletcher to release him.

The man took a step back as if tempted to recommence his headlong run. "I've done nothing wrong."

"Then you won't mind answering a few questions." Henry pulled out his notebook, ignoring the curious stares of passersby. "Your name?"

The man huffed, clearly unhappy. He tugged on the bottom of his jacket to straighten his clothing. "Bernard Allard."

He had pale hair clipped short, blue eyes, and a well-groomed beard. He appeared fairly affluent from the cut of his wool suit to his polished shoes, much different than most men in the area. No wonder he had stood out.

"Why did you run?" That action alone was enough to make Henry suspicious, even as he tried to catch his breath and ignore the agony in his side. From the look on his face, Fletcher had the same question.

"Wouldn't you if two men began to chase you in this area of the city?"

Henry nearly scoffed. Perhaps that's what he should've done last evening instead of standing his ground. Then he wouldn't be nursing an aching head and sore ribs. "You must've noted that one of us is in uniform." He gestured toward Fletcher.

"I suppose I didn't notice. You run at me, I run away."

Henry found that difficult to believe. "What were you doing near the mudflats?"

"I walk frequently. For my health," Mr. Allard added, casting a glare at Henry that made his disdain of the question clear. "I often walk to the river and many other places as well."

"We are investigating the death of two mudlarks. Do you know anything about them?"

"No. Why should I?"

"You were seen speaking to the children on several occasions." Henry tried to balance his tone, removing the accusatory edge but keeping firm in his directness. This had to be a lead, didn't it?

"I was merely being friendly. I like to hear of any special objects they've discovered." He shrugged. "I consider myself a bit of a history *aficionado* and find the items interesting."

"Did you speak to Nora?" Henry asked.

"Is she a mudlark?" His furrowed brow spoke of confusion...but could have been feigned.

"She was, yes." Henry wasn't sure what to think of the man. "Brown hair and eyes. Approximately nine years of age."

Mr. Allard shrugged. "That describes several of them."

Henry clenched his jaw, frustrated it was true. "Do you live or work in the area?"

"I live a few streets from here. On Richmond Street."

Henry wrote down the address he provided. "Did you offer training to the mudlarks for them to become household servants of some sort?"

"What?" Allard stared at Henry as if he'd lost his mind. "No—mudlarks as servants? Whatever for?"

The line of questioning didn't seem to be getting them anywhere, but Henry didn't allow that to deter him. "What is your occupation?"

The man hesitated, his gaze shifting to the side as if to consider his answer. Though only brief, it still made Henry wonder. Was the man seeking for a believable lie? "I provide financial services for several wealthy individuals."

"Your business address?"

"I work from home."

"Where were you on Tuesday evening?"

"At home, I'm sure, as I am most evenings."

Henry's frustration mounted. The man's answers weren't leading anywhere. "Is there anyone who can vouch for that?"

"My wife and our maid, I suppose." He frowned. "Surely—you're not suggesting I'm a suspect?" He looked shocked at the thought, the inflection in his voice making it clear he thought the idea ridiculous.

"We are questioning everyone involved with the mudlarks in any way," Henry advised, noting he didn't wear a wedding ring, though not all married men did. "I'm sure you understand."

"Yes, that's part of our job." Fletcher's scowl suggested he didn't care for the man's attitude. Neither did Henry, but sadly dislike was no reason to arrest people, or else Perdy would no longer be roaming the streets.

"Clearly you're not doing it well or the killer would be caught by now." The man straightened his hat. "And I had nothing to do with any murders."

"And I'm sure if you were guilty, you would immediately admit as much," Fletcher said with a growl.

Mr. Allard cast him an angry glare, then looked at Henry. "If we're done here, I would like to be on my way."

Henry glanced at Fletcher to see if he had any other questions. Fletcher shook his head.

"We might need to verify the information or require additional details in the coming days," Henry warned.

"If you must. Though it seems you should spend your time speaking with those who might have something to do with the matter instead of innocent citizens walking about."

With that, Mr. Allard turned on his heel and strode away.

"That was less than helpful, but we have no reason to detain him." Henry sighed as he tucked the notebook back inside his pocket. "I had hope that he would either know more or confess," he said, only half joking.

"Why is it that such things rarely happen?" Fletcher asked with a hint of a smile.

"We can still imagine such an outcome, can't we?" Henry glanced once more toward the quickly disappearing Mr. Allard. "What did you think?"

"Hard to say. The moment he ran, I thought we had our man...but he seemed genuine in his answers."

"Mostly." The slight hesitation and vagueness regarding his occupation still bothered Henry. "We will verify his whereabouts with the wife and maid tomorrow to make certain his statements are truthful."

"Good idea." His friend shook his head. "Frustrating, but someone has to know something. It's only a matter of finding them."

Henry agreed. It sounded simple yet was anything but.

They made their way back to the mudflats, only to find Amelia speaking with Carl, along with an older woman who bore a faint resemblance. The visiting aunt, he presumed.

"Good afternoon," Henry greeted them, barely able to hold back his frustration at Amelia's presence after their discussion of the risk—and with another woman, endangering them both. While it didn't come as a surprise, it still upset him that she'd chosen to come and brought her aunt along.

"Henry. Sergeant Fletcher." Amelia nodded at them both, a hint of a blush rising in her cheeks as if aware of his disapproval. "This is my aunt, Miss Margaret Baldwin, who as you know is visiting for a time."

Henry forced his attention to the other woman who returned his look with a curious one of her own. "It is a pleasure to meet you."

"Carl told us you pursued the stranger they've seen several times. Did you catch him?" Amelia asked after pleasantries were exchanged, hope lighting her eyes.

"Yes."

"What did he have to say fer himself?" Carl asked with a frown.

"He insists he knows nothing of the murders, that he has spoken with a few of the mudlarks on occasion but only to inquire what they have found. Claims he has an interest in history."

Carl muttered something under his breath that wasn't fit for present company. Henry sent him a warning look, and the man wisely cut off his words with a scowl.

"You don't think he is the one who spoke to the children about training to become a servant?" Amelia asked.

"He denied it," Fletcher answered. "There's always the chance he lied."

"Shouldn't ye have experience decidin' that?" Carl chuckled as if he found the idea amusing.

It would be easier if people just didn't lie, Henry wanted to answer, but he held back. His doubt and reluctance to follow any hunch without sufficient proof was something he frequently battled. Would he have better instincts if he'd been born a Field rather than being one by accident?

"Are you certain he was the one you saw before?" Henry asked.

Carl reached in his pocket for his pipe and clenched it in his teeth. "Not fer sure, I suppose."

Henry nearly groaned with frustration. This crime was impossible! "We will verify his story as we do with all those we question. As we have done so with you."

No matter how many times he told himself that eliminating a potential suspect was progress, it didn't feel like it, especially today. He need only look at the mudlarks along the riverbank to feel a sense of urgency.

"I have no doubt Inspector Field will determine the truth," Amelia said with a reprimanding look at Carl. "Though it's surprising how little help you've been able to provide. You must pay closer attention, Mr. Jeffries."

"Yes, ma'am." Carl gave her a sheepish look.

"Who will you question next?" Amelia asked when she turned to Henry.

He was warmed by her staunch support. "I had hoped to speak with Watson again, but it doesn't look as though he's here. Perhaps having a word with Agnes and Pudge would be helpful." Henry searched the mudlarks for them, pleased to see them nearby.

"I will come with you," Amelia declared. "I need to speak with them as well." She looked at her aunt. "If you would wait here with Sergeant Fletcher, I won't be long. I wouldn't want you to have to navigate the mud and Fernsby should only have to clean one pair of boots."

Before her aunt could respond, Amelia led the way toward Agnes and Pudge, leaving Henry to follow.

He felt the weight of her aunt's gaze as they walked toward the girls but did his best to ignore it. What she thought of him and his association with Amelia wasn't his concern, though he hoped it didn't cause any issue for Amelia with her family.

Amelia slowed her pace to allow Henry to catch up, studying his expression. "How are you faring? Sore, I imagine."

"A bit, but I will soon recover." He saw no point in mentioning how much he hurt. "I was surprised to see you here today after what we discussed last evening."

"You can't think I would stay away," she countered with a slight lift of her chin. "And I did not promise to. But I do intend to be careful, which is one of the reasons my aunt joined me. Or rather, insisted on joining me."

Her exasperation, perhaps with himself or her aunt or both, had him smiling. "Good. I am pleased I'm not the only one concerned for your safety. Besides, I now have unofficial approval to continue the investigation, so I will be in the area more often as well."

"Oh, that's good news! Though I don't care for the unofficial part."

"Nor do I," he murmured as they reached the mudlarks.

"How is the search today, girls?" Amelia asked after greeting them.

Agnes shared a few of the things they'd found, though they hardly seemed worth picking up to Henry.

"I have good news," Amelia said with a smile as she withdrew a small black velvet satchel closed with a string from her pocket and handed it to Pudge.

Henry frowned, very curious as he watched the girl slowly take it as if afraid to look inside.

"Ye already sold the coin?" the girl whispered.

"I did. I think I got a fair price for it."

The girl wiped off her free hand before undoing the string. She peered inside and gasped but didn't withdraw the contents. Though Henry couldn't see inside, he could guess based on their expressions.

"Can I see?" Agnes asked.

Pudge handed her the pouch so she might see for herself. Agnes' excitement matched her friend's, and the two girls shared a look that spoke volumes, as they so often did.

Henry thought it wise not to pull out the money for everyone to see, lest they were robbed later by some desperate person who'd seen them waving it about.

"This is more than we hoped. Much more. However can we thank ye?" Pudge asked in a low voice.

"That's not necessary. I was happy to do it. If I can assist with any of your other finds, you need only let me know." Amelia turned to

Henry, her bright smile scattering his thoughts. "Now then, Inspector Field has a few questions for you."

"Did you see the man who was just here?" Henry asked. "The one we chased."

"No." Agnes glanced around as if hoping for the chance. "We were workin', I suppose."

Disappointed, Henry nodded. This Mr. Allard could still have something to do with the situation, even if Carl was now less than certain. He hadn't been able to provide much of a description of the man to begin with. Perhaps all men in black suits looked alike to him.

"Have you heard anything more from the other mudlarks?" He watched the other children who remained focused on their search, no doubt because Carl was nearby. "Have any of them been approached about the servant training?"

Both girls shook their heads to his disappointment.

"Be sure to send word if you learn anything," he advised. "The constable who patrols the area knows how to reach me."

He and Amelia said their goodbyes and started toward the others.

"Now you're helping to sell their finds?" He shouldn't have been surprised by her thoughtfulness, yet he was.

"They found a gold coin that looked quite valuable. A friend of my late husband's specializes in such things, and he was happy to buy it."

The mention of Mr. Greystone sobered Henry, not that the man was ever far from his thoughts while he had yet to solve his murder. "Who might that be?" he asked gently, having spoken to most of his friends and associates more than once over the past year.

"Benjamin Norris." She glanced at him, holding her skirts to avoid the worst of the mud. "Do you remember him?"

Henry searched his mental notes and nodded. "His shop is near where Mr. Greystone's was."

"That's right."

He hadn't spoken to the man in some time. Perhaps it would be worthwhile to call on him again. At this point, staying in touch with those who'd known Mr. Greystone was the only way he could think of to shake loose a clue.

Matthew Greystone deserved justice and Amelia deserved closure. Precisely how to provide that remained to be seen—but perhaps together they could give both justice and closure to the mudlarks before another of them was killed. That had to be enough for now.

Thirty

The following morning Amelia settled in the drawing room to finalize her article for the magazine when a headline in the news sheet Fernsby had left on her desk caught her eye.

The article in *The Standard* shared that further unrest in Egypt near the Suez Canal had resulted in the death of five British soldiers. The reporter demanded that action be taken to ensure the safety of those protecting England's interests abroad.

While she was proud of her country for many reasons, she had concerns about its expansion into every corner of the globe. Just because the government considered themselves 'kind rulers' didn't mean they knew better than the local ones who'd preceded them.

Of course, her opinion didn't matter since she was a woman, another topic that rankled.

Still, progress shouldn't mean the suppression of other countries' cultures and beliefs. Who was England to insist their way of life was better when so many problems remained at home?

One need only venture to the East End to know numerous people required help in London, not to mention the rest of the country. How could the government attempt to solve problems on other continents when they couldn't prevent issues such as hunger and poverty on their own streets?

The article went on to suggest that silencing those abroad attempting to speak out against the Crown was the surest method of protecting Britain's interests.

By the time she finished reading, Amelia was too upset to focus on anything else. She couldn't help but wonder if those in the government shared the same opinion, even if the idea was preposterous.

"What has you frowning so?" Aunt Margaret asked as she entered the drawing room.

Amelia handed her the article, pacing the room while her aunt read it. Weak sunlight shone in the window but did little to improve her mood.

"Can you believe the audacity of the journalist?" Amelia asked when her aunt looked up at last. "It's as if he suggests eliminating leaders in other countries who don't agree with England."

Her aunt shook her head, clearly concerned. "The events there are one of the reasons I decided to come to London rather than travel. This is shocking. Do you think people agree, given that the editor placed the article on the front page?"

"If so, that is even more distressing. Or perhaps they're trying to sway the public—I realize unrest of any sort sells news sheets, but spreading such an idea is foolhardy."

"It is," her aunt agreed. "The next thing we'll read about is the death of a political leader in some foreign land." She folded the paper and set it aside with a disgruntled look. "Let us speak of something more pleasant."

Amelia sighed, hoping to shrug off her upset. "Do you have plans for the day?"

"No." Aunt Margaret smoothed her skirts as if doing so would also smooth her nerves. "Please do not tell me you intend to return to Blackfriars."

"I suppose not when there would be no point, though I do wish there was some way to help."

"Those poor children. To watch them digging through the mud in an effort to provide food and shelter for themselves was heartbreaking. To think most have no real home or family to watch over them..." The older woman shook her head. "Would it be possible to aid them in some way? Perhaps send food or clothing?"

"That is a tremendous idea." Excitement took hold. This might be just the purpose her aunt needed. "I have taken them sandwiches twice, and they were gone in an instant. But perhaps aiding them on a larger scale would be possible. I am sure there is a church in the area."

"I will do some research on the topic to see what I can discover." The thoughtful look on her face had Amelia hiding a smile. "Does Inspector Field have any idea how the children were poisoned?"

"Not as of yet." Amelia hesitated to share the details—not when her aunt was already scandalized at the mere action of going to the mudflats.

Fernsby entered the room, a silver tray in his hand, saving her from saying more. His insistence on formalities amused Amelia. "A message for you, Mrs. Greystone."

"Thank you."

The unfamiliar script on the envelope caught her interest. Aware of her aunt watching closely, she opened it to scan the contents. Her breath caught, both flattered and surprised.

"What is it?" her aunt asked.

"Mrs. Elizabeth Drake, a chemist I admire, has invited me to call on her." Excitement trickled through her at the unexpected invitation. How the lady had come to know her name was curious, especially given the cool reception she'd received when she had attempted to speak with the lady at her lecture.

"Oh?" Her aunt's tone suggested it wasn't particularly interesting, let alone shocking.

"I recently attended her lecture at South Kensington Museum. It was fascinating. In fact, my latest series of experiments are based on what I learned."

The look on her aunt's face suggested that was less than riveting information, but Amelia couldn't suppress her excitement. To be recognized by someone so accomplished in the field was amazing; to have it be Mrs. Drake, whom she greatly admired, truly thrilled her.

"She is someone I have followed for several years," Amelia explained. "The progress she's made in chemistry is astounding, especially because she's a woman."

"I can only imagine a number of men grimacing as we speak," her aunt said with a smile.

"How true." Amelia read the message again, unable to comprehend what was behind the unexpected invitation. "She requests I come to her home tomorrow afternoon for tea." She rose and walked to her desk, anxious to pen an acceptance.

"How lovely," her aunt said as she picked up her embroidery.

Yes, Amelia thought with a smile as she penned a reply. It was indeed.

"Who?" The older gentleman who had answered the door at the house on Richmond Street stared at Henry in bewilderment.

Henry frowned, taking a moment to consult his notebook to make certain he had the correct name and address.

"Mr. Bernard Allard." He already knew he hadn't got either one wrong.

"There's no one here by that name."

Henry's stomach plummeted. "Are you certain?"

"Quite. What is this about?"

Henry shook his head, realizing he'd been lied to. *Damn*. No logical reason existed for the man to have done so—except that he was guilty of something. Whether it had to do with the mudlark murders remained to be seen, as Carl hadn't been certain if Mr. Allard was the same man he'd seen before or not.

Still, Henry felt like a fool for falling for the man's story and so easily accepting what he had been told.

There could be other reasons the man had run and then lied when Fletcher caught him, but Henry had to think it was related to the mudlarks. How unfortunate his hunch had come too late. As his grandfather always said, there was no such thing as a coincidence.

"You've never heard of the man?" Henry asked, reluctant to relinquish his only tie to the potential suspect.

"No."

"He's a few years older than me and my height, pale hair and blue eyes. Nicely dressed..." Henry searched his memory, but no distinguishing characteristics came to mind.

"As if that doesn't describe half the men in England." The man shook his head and started to shut the door, clearly done with the conversation.

"Wait." Henry put a hand out to stop the man from closing the door, but realized there was no point. What else was there to say? "Never mind." He dipped his head. "Thank you for your time."

The man grunted in acknowledgement then shut the door, but Henry remained looking around the neighborhood as if he could conjure this Allard, or whatever his name was, with his thoughts. The address had come easily to the man. That had to mean he was likely familiar with the area.

But as Henry studied the surrounding houses, he realized that didn't make it any more likely that he could find him. This Allard, if that was his real name, might simply know someone who lived on the street.

All he could do was advise Carl and the others near the mudflats to watch for the man and alert a constable if he was seen. He would tell Constable Gibbons about him as well so he could watch for him on his regular patrol.

With a scowl, Henry walked down the steps, frustration mounting. While he'd had no reason to restrain the man, now he wished he had.

After a glance at the nearby houses, debating whether it would be worthwhile to inquire at any of them, he decided it would only be a waste of precious time.

The case was becoming more maddening by the minute. He sighed deeply, only to regret it when his ribs protested. His injuries had yet to improve, though he knew better than to expect that in one day—yet still, he cursed the pain.

Fletcher's response to the news when they met for luncheon was much the same as Henry's. "Why that...scamp." His angry expression was at odds with the rather tame word. At Henry's questioning look, the sergeant shrugged. "Mrs. Fletcher's been after me to clean up my language. You would think she forgot I was in the Navy all those years."

Henry hid his amusement. One day, he hoped to meet Mrs. Fletcher. She must be quite the woman to rein in her husband.

"I tend to think our mystery man will turn up again," Henry advised, though he couldn't say why. That gut of his again, though he still wouldn't rely solely on it. "We will warn the mudlarks and Carl to watch for him."

"Before or after another child turns up dead?" Fletcher asked with a disgruntled look.

Henry had no answer. All they could do was continue the investigation and press forward until a new lead arose.

Thirty-One

"Amelia Greystone, to see Elizabeth Drake." She handed her card to the butler at Mrs. Drake's home the following afternoon. She hoped her excitement wasn't too obvious, but she had hardly slept the previous night in anticipation of the meeting.

"Of course." The man held the door wide, then gestured toward a nearby reception room. "A moment, if you please."

Amelia stepped inside, pleased not to linger in the cold as she noted the fine décor. The small room was done up in green and gold, tasteful but not extravagant. The large house with its high ceilings generous foyer appeared elegant and well-maintained, a nod to the lady's success. Was there still a Mr. Drake?

She couldn't deny how flattered she was to have come to Mrs. Drake's attention, though she couldn't begin to guess how it had come to pass. After so many years of being torn between being proud of her interest in chemistry versus hiding it, she was honored by the invitation. Few women were in the field and Mrs. Drake was the only one she even vaguely knew personally.

Before she could consider taking a seat in one of the lovely brocade-covered chairs with clawed feet, the butler returned. "Mrs. Drake will see you now."

Amelia frowned at the oddly worded statement. She was there at the woman's invitation, after all—of course the lady would see her.

Shaking off the thought, she followed the servant to a large drawing room, surprised to find it empty. Odd when she'd been invited to tea.

"Mrs. Drake will join you shortly." The butler departed.

After a few minutes with her host still absent, Amelia strolled around the room, admiring the fine furnishings, though the room was sparsely furnished compared to the current trend of filling a drawing room with as many items as possible to show one's wealth. No personal preferences could be gleaned from the room, as much of the décor included items easily found in other homes. A claw-footed, wide-backed set of chairs, a settee in brown and gold paisley, a polished writing desk along one wall, and several tables with only a few well-placed knickknacks. All of it tasteful and of excellent quality.

Amelia was disappointed. She would have liked to learn more about the brilliant woman before meeting her. As she studied an intricately carved box on a small table, a rustling sound caught her notice.

She turned to see Mrs. Drake enter the room, dressed in a green-striped gown with a high collar and long, tight sleeves. The no-nonsense style, with no ruffles or flounces, had an almost masculine appearance.

"Mrs. Greystone, how kind of you to come." A polite if cool smile graced the woman's lips.

A flutter of satisfaction filled Amelia. "The pleasure is mine. I appreciate the invitation."

The lady continued into the room, studying Amelia as she came to stand before her. "It is so rare to meet another woman interested in science."

"How true. I enjoyed your recent lecture at South Kensington Museum."

"Oh?" The vague look on the older woman's face suggested she didn't remember seeing Amelia there. Then again, there had been a number of people at the lecture. "I'm pleased to hear that." She gestured toward a chair. "Please have a seat."

"Thank you." Amelia perched on the chair and adjusted her skirts as curiosity overcame her. "May I ask how you came to hear of me and my interests?"

"A mutual acquaintance, but that hardly matters." She sat as well, waving a hand in dismissal of her guest's question. "Tell me what fueled your interest in chemistry."

Amelia hesitated at the direct question. She'd expected to exchange pleasantries before a discussion about chemistry ensued. Then again, she already had the impression that Mrs. Drake had little time for what she deemed unimportant. Clearly that included social niceties.

"My father is an apothecary in a village north of London. My interest started at a young age as I often accompanied him to his shop."

"How interesting. A family endeavor."

"You could say that. What of you?"

Mrs. Drake gave another one of those polite smiles. "I had an interest from a young age as well."

Amelia hoped to learn more, but perhaps that would eventually follow. They had only just met for the second time, after all. "Your knowledge of organic materials is impressive. The idea of compounds from biological sources being used to aid humankind is truly exciting."

"I find it so as well."

"I dabble in toxicology, myself," Amelia said, feeling as though she was confessing rather than conversing, "and have a laboratory in my attic."

"Toxicology? Fascinating. What in particular draws you to that field?"

Amelia had the strangest sensation she was being interviewed for a position for which she hadn't applied...and there was still no sign of tea.

She shook off the odd feeling and reminded herself that she was conversing with a fellow female chemist, something she'd only imagined. If the conversation didn't progress as she'd expected, that was understandable. This was new ground, perhaps for both of them.

She cleared her throat and collected her thoughts. "As much as my father is focused on remedies that improve peoples' ails and lessen their symptoms, I suppose I became curious about actually curing illness instead of treating it."

"Ah, yes. Understandable. I admit to having the same curiosity."

Amelia's breath caught. Never had she imagined having this conversation, let alone that they might find common ground. "Isn't it fascinating how some poisonous substances can also be used for good if used in the proper dosage?"

"True." Mrs. Drake sat forward in her chair. "I find myself intrigued by where the difference lies. The line *between* good and bad, one might say."

"It is a precarious question, is it not?" Amelia's father had dismissed it when she asked his opinion. His focus was solely on aiding people. But what if a slightly different remedy, previously considered harmful, could actually cure them? He had refused to consider the notion, insisting the risk was too great, much to her frustration.

Amelia felt certain that pushing the boundaries of what was previously believed was where discoveries could be made, much as Mrs. Drake had mentioned after her lecture.

"Quite. One need only look at the poppy, feverfew, or comfrey to start. The list is a long one." Mrs. Drake narrowed her gaze. "Tell me, Mrs. Greystone, have you ever gone too far with this question?"

Amelia blinked, the excitement in the other woman's expression taking her aback. Nor was she precisely sure what she meant. "I...I don't know that I have. I suppose it is often an indistinct area."

"It is. But that is where true advances are made." The fervor in the woman's eyes had Amelia watching her more closely.

"Have you made discoveries with those particular plants?" Amelia asked.

"Most certainly. I won't bore you with the details but suffice it to say that developments are emerging as we speak."

"In any particular area?" To learn of them before they were announced intrigued her.

"I am not at liberty to say as of yet. But soon." The satisfied look upon Mrs. Drake's face spoke volumes. "Tell me more about your laboratory."

Amelia shared a few details but didn't mention her recent experiments since the ones she'd conducted on fungi hadn't produced any significant results. Discovering a better method of cleaning soot from bricks had eased Yvette's workload, but Mrs. Drake wouldn't care about such a mundane experiment. Nor would she want to hear of the amusing ones she and Maeve had done together, even if they'd brought a smile to the young girl's face. It was difficult exactly to know what to say; how to impress without boasting, how to share mundanities without boring.

"I understand you've worked with the police on occasion," Mrs. Drake said, not quite but almost an interruption.

Amelia stiffened in surprise, hardly able to believe her host knew of that. Perhaps Henry had told others at Scotland Yard of when she had tested the meat found in the ravenkeeper's pocket and discovered arsenic, or perhaps that she'd found the fungi in the perfume bottle.

She could only think that Mrs. Drake must also be somehow connected with the police and work with them on occasion. How thrilling, to find another connection with this fine woman.

"Yes, I have." Amelia only wished she could be of more help with the mudlark deaths. "It is rewarding to have what has been a hobby of mine to be of assistance in an official capacity."

"I'm sure. Do you work with them on a regular basis?"

"Only a few times, thus far." The question made Amelia realize how much she wished she could do more. Her longing to feel worthy kept her from disclosing the full truth.

She might have used her skills and knowledge in chemistry only twice for the police but had assisted in other ways with Warder Pritchard's case and now the mudlark murders. Yet the truth was that her assistance had never been requested through official channels, only through Henry, and that did not feel as though it were something she should share.

She lifted her chin, reminding herself that since he was a member of the department, one might say she had been officially asked to lend assistance.

"Fascinating." Mrs. Drake lifted a brow. "One hears rumors, as I'm sure you can appreciate. Tell me, do you find them as inept as some say?"

Amelia did her best to hide her sparking irritation, protectiveness of Henry tempting her to make a quick retort. "No, not at all."

Though it was on the tip of her tongue to mention that Henry had recently been recognized for helping to save the Queen, she held back. After all, men like Inspector Perdy also represented the department. It was indeed a mixed bag.

"Hmm." Mrs. Drake's lips tightened. "I suppose everyone has a differing opinion based on their experience."

"Have you?" At the woman's questioning look, Amelia added, "Had experience with the police, I mean?"

"No, I have not, though I do work with a few members of the government."

"Oh? In what capacity?" Amelia's fascination was surely evident in her expression.

"Alas, I cannot discuss the details. I'm sure you understand."

Amelia nodded, though she was disappointed. It almost seemed as if Mrs. Drake wanted to learn more about Amelia than she was willing to share in return. "Are there any other new experiments you're presently working on?"

To her surprise, the woman shared two related to her work with organic compounds.

Amelia was intrigued. The woman might not be especially adept at social niceties—tea had still not yet been served—but the conversation compensated for it.

"Perhaps you might like to join me in my laboratory one day soon," Mrs. Drake suggested.

"I would enjoy that." Amelia hoped she didn't sound as excited as she felt. It wouldn't do to appear overeager—but to spend time in a laboratory with her heroine? *Be still her heart.*

"I shall send a message when an appropriate experiment arises."

"Where is your lab?" Amelia imagined it to be a large space, something more formal where other chemists worked at her direction, much different than her modest one.

"I have several. It's best to keep some experiments separate, of course."

Several labs? Amelia was nearly breathless at the thought. She hoped Mrs. Drake made good on her offer as Amelia longed to see one.

"Thank you for coming by this afternoon." Mrs. Drake rose, a not-so-subtle signal that the meeting was over.

Amelia reached for her reticule and stood, mouth parched but soul sated with their conversation. "I appreciate the invitation and hope to speak with you again soon."

"Indeed. I look forward to deepening our acquaintance, Mrs. Greystone."

"As do I." With that Amelia took her leave, doing her best to maintain her composure as she returned to the waiting hansom cab. The afternoon had been amazing. She settled on the seat, proud of herself for not revealing any disgracefully uncouth outward signs of her joy.

Only once the cab was several streets away did she allow herself to grin and press a hand to her heart, thrilled by her new acquaintance and the chance to have a friendship with someone who shared her interests.

Thirty-Two

"Should've known that was comin'." Carl scowled and scuffed the toe of his muddy boot on the pavement as Henry told him Mr. 'Allard' had lied. "Just when I thought ye were makin' progress and all. But it's my fault fer not payin' closer attention. Men in suits tend to look alike as far as I'm concerned."

His genuine upset reassured Henry. Perhaps he didn't have anything to do with the men who'd attacked Henry, which confirmed what Henry believed. If all of this was an act and Carl was somehow connected to the murders, the man's time would be better spent on the stage in Drury Lane rather than the mudflats.

"Each piece of information we discover is progress," Fletcher reassured him before Henry could—a good thing as he didn't think he would've sounded nearly as convincing.

"You'll tell the mudlarks to stay on the lookout?" Henry asked. The children had departed for the day while the men had been talking since the tide was coming in and the light was fading.

"Sure, sure. I'll tell 'em."

Henry saw Captain Booth striding across the dock and nudged Fletcher. "Let us have a word with the captain."

They bid Carl farewell and hurried to catch the man before he disappeared.

"Captain Booth," Henry called, pleased when the man turned and strode forward to join them.

"Gentlemen." Captain Booth nodded as he looked between them, his gaze lingering on Henry's bruised face. "How's the investigation coming?"

"Slower than we'd hoped." Henry glanced toward the river, wishing it could reveal what had happened to the children since it had surely witnessed it. "A man has been seen talking to the mudlarks on several occasions. We caught up with him yesterday—"

"After he attempted to flee," Fletcher added.

Henry nodded. "The fact that he ran was concerning. But unfortunately, he provided us with a false address. Perhaps even a false name."

"Ah." The captain's brows rose. "That sounds suspicious. And now you don't know where to find him."

"Not at the moment," Henry reluctantly confirmed. "We're asking those in the area to be on the lookout for him." He gave Booth a brief description.

"Of course. I try to look around when I'm here but haven't noticed anyone unusual. I will be more vigilant from now on."

"We appreciate that. Send word if you do."

The man nodded. "Is Mrs. Greystone still involved in the case?"

"More than I'd like," Henry admitted.

"She's a clever one." Captain Booth grinned.

Henry frowned, not appreciating the man's obvious admiration for Amelia. His own protectiveness of her was only due to his worry because she continued to place herself in danger, or so he told himself. Regardless of what he advised her, she would keep doing so.

He had to admit that he appreciated her help, given the limited time he could spend on the investigation. She had ingratiated herself with the mudlarks, at least with Agnes and Pudge, and had somehow garnered the respect of Carl, and that was a positive he couldn't overlook. There was a chance they'd tell her things they wouldn't mention to him. The smallest detail often led to a break in a case.

"Yes, she is very clever," Henry agreed, at last, casting the captain a warning look to suggest he didn't overstep his bounds.

A knowing look gleamed in the man's eyes, but he kept his easy smile. "I will keep watch over her as well, if I see her."

"It's unfortunate she was here when Nora was found." Henry detested the fact as it was the only reason she was involved. Otherwise, she would be safe. Then again, her presence was also the reason he was there, and that he'd had so many excuses to see her these last few days.

"It is." Booth looked remorseful for that at least, though it was hardly his fault. "I hope the villain is soon found, though I still don't understand why someone would want to poison a mudlark. They don't harm anyone."

"No, which makes it all the more worrisome." Henry had yet to piece together the details to make sense of the whole situation, and it was frustrating to be so foiled.

"I will ask the other barge captains to keep a close eye on the area and the mudlarks and be sure to send word if anything is out of the usual." With that, Booth departed.

Henry glanced around one last time, but the serene scene with the river flowing in the dusky light, the hint of fog rising from the water, and the bridge in the background looked peaceful. He could only hope it remained that way.

"What do you have, Field?" Reynolds tapped his fingers on his desk as if impatient. "Any news on your cases?"

Henry had just returned to the Yard with Fletcher after leaving the mudflats when Reynolds waved him over. He'd expected the Director to have left for the day by now and hoped to follow suit. He was hurting and tired, and ready to rest.

He would've preferred not to provide an update on the missing man or the mudlark murders since neither was going well. The press frequently criticized the Criminal Investigation Department and referred to them as the 'defective department,' something Reynolds, along with every other member, detested.

Though Henry had seen success on a couple of cases of late, that never seemed to outweigh the constant criticism or his own doubt. Yet there was no point in stating anything but the truth.

"We confirmed with an accountant that the numbers on the lottery tickets don't work. It's clearly a scheme to part people with their money, and we wonder if Spencer realized that and told the wrong person. However, when we returned to the lottery ticket office to confront them, we found it cleared out. Fletcher went to the pubs where tickets were sold, but they don't know anything about their whereabouts and haven't seen any of those involved in the drawings for the last few days."

"You think Spencer met with foul play," Reynolds suggested.

"Based on what we know, yes. It seems likely."

"And the mudlark deaths?"

"We spoke with a potential suspect yesterday only to learn today that he provided a false address and probably a false name." Henry wished he would've brought Allard in and held him until they could verify what he'd told them—but knew he would've been in trouble if he had. One simply could not go around arresting people based on a knowing sensation.

The exasperated look his supervisor sent him had Henry bracing for a lecture. "That's unfortunate," the Director said.

Henry frowned, waiting to hear what he should've done differently on both cases. Reynolds couldn't possibly be any more frustrated than he was.

"However, another situation has arisen that requires our attention." The Director shuffled the papers on his desk, the restless movement unusual for the normally composed man.

"What might that be, sir?" Henry had the distinct feeling he wouldn't like whatever it was.

Reynolds studied the top paper then drew a deep breath. "Have you read the news of late? There have been several articles that mention unrest abroad."

"I saw those." Henry's stomach clenched, wondering why that would concern the Director—or himself.

The other man looked past Henry as if to make certain no one listened. "Close the door."

Henry stilled in surprise. Rarely had he heard or seen that occur. When Reynolds lifted a brow, he did as requested then sat to listen, curiosity and a sense of dread taking hold in equal measure.

"This matter requires our immediate attention and must be kept confidential. The Home Secretary has heard whispers of a plot in the Home Office tied to the unrest. Someone is planning to eliminate leaders of countries stirring trouble for the English rulers who have taken over."

Henry waited but Reynolds didn't offer further information, leaving him confused. "What does that have to do with our department?"

"Normally, nothing. You no doubt remember the Counter Revolutionary Secret Service Department, formed to fight the threat of Fenian terrorism, was disbanded several years ago. But there are some who have continued in a similar vein without formal approval or directives."

"Because they consider the problems those local rulers are causing to be a form of terrorism?" Henry asked. His father had been suspicious of the organization, believing they were *too* secretive, and had been relieved when they were disbanded. Henry tended to agree.

"Yes, but not everyone thinks the same. Certainly not enough to commit murder. These would more than likely be subtle assassinations. An illness of some sort perhaps, one that's unlikely to catch the attention of the press but would still eliminate the perceived problem."

"How concerning." Subtle assassinations...such as poison? He caught his breath as Amelia's idea of testing dosages on the mudlarks came to mind.

"The Home Secretary no longer knows who to trust and has asked for our help to determine who is involved."

"How?"

"I have been given two names to investigate, to start." Reynolds heaved a beleaguered sigh. "We must rely on our usual methods. Observation, asking questions, seeing what surfaces." He handed Henry a slip of paper.

Reginald Davies and Stephen Barnes. Both men were familiar to Henry, he'd met them once or twice. Both came from powerful, influential families. He could already see why this might end badly.

"Do you have any specific orders?" Henry asked.

"The plan is in the early stages from what we know. We are to proceed boldly. Question each man to gain their reaction. Use your instincts if needed and gather as many facts as you can. Start by speaking with them at their offices at Whitehall. The Home Secretary is more concerned with halting the plan before someone dies than making arrests."

Henry nodded. This was not going to be a task to relish.

"Think on a plan, and we will meet come morning to confirm it."

"Yes, sir." Henry rose. It was unlikely he'd be getting any sleep that night.

Thirty-Three

Henry arrived at Scotland Yard the next morning after the restless night he'd expected. The Director's request to investigate the two powerful men still seemed outlandish when the supposed plot sounded like something out of a mystery novel.

International intrigue, poison, assassinations...

And yet...he couldn't set aside the tie to what Amelia had mentioned about the poisoning of the mudlarks. An experiment, someone testing. Even if a voice in the back of his mind suggested they could be connected, he had doubts. Serious doubts.

He needed proof to believe it and had no plan to mention the idea to the Director until he had it. Reynolds might want him to follow his instincts, but he was reluctant to trust them. Better that he questioned the men, as well as those who worked with them, to gather information. Whether they would answer his inquiries remained to be seen but given their status, it seemed doubtful. Questioning the nobility or their families was fraught with difficulty and could easily result in a career-ending encounter. The Director wouldn't be able to save him if that occurred.

Henry had made some notes of potential questions the previous evening and wanted to review them again before he met with Reynolds. He greeted a few other inspectors then settled at his desk and took out his notes, working on them for half an hour before their appointment.

The meeting was brief. Unfortunately, the Director hadn't changed his mind about their course of action. Henry was to proceed with due haste to Whitehall. He left Reynolds' office with his stomach churning at the idea of marching into Whitehall with his notebook and questions. At least Perdy hadn't made an appearance yet that morning.

Though anxious as he was to uncover a plot for murder, he was equally reluctant to stir a hornet's nest. Perhaps it wouldn't be as difficult as he thought, but given the vague nature of the supposed plot, he had to keep his questions vague as well. Somehow, he expected to be laughed at before being asked to leave.

He shook his head, unable to believe this was going to go well.

"Field?"

Henry looked up to see Johnson approach with his hand held out.

"Message for you." The sergeant returned to his post at the front desk.

Henry opened the paper, the masculine scrawl unfamiliar. He glanced at the bottom, alarmed to see Captain Booth's signature. An entirely new level of worry descended as he read the hasty message.

Agnes and Pudge are missing.

Amelia finished breakfast in the warm kitchen, wondering if she could convince her aunt to venture to a museum or art gallery or somewhere else later in the day. Though it was cold, there wasn't any wind and the woman needed to leave the house—with a destination other than the mudflats.

Aunt Margaret's mood remained improved, but she still hadn't shared what was wrong. Maybe if they did something together, she'd be more inclined to talk. If not, Amelia would ply her with wine at dinner until she lowered her guard.

Amelia walked upstairs in time to see Fernsby close the door, a slip of paper in hand.

"A message was just delivered for you, madam." The butler glanced about in search of the silver tray, but Amelia took the paper from him with a smile.

"Thank you." She opened it quickly, spotting Captain Booth's signature before his other words chilled her.

Agnes and Pudge are missing.

"Oh, no." She pressed a hand to her mouth, thoughts swirling as panic took hold.

"Two more are missing?" The astonishment in Fletcher's voice pinched Henry's heart.

He pressed his fingers to his chest and rubbed the ache there at the thought of Agnes and Pudge in danger. The pain in his sore ribs was nothing in comparison. The idea of any of the children in danger terrified him, especially after what had already happened to Nora and Charlie...and who knew how many others.

"What's our plan?" Fletcher asked in a gruff tone as they left Scotland Yard, the cold, damp air greeting them.

Henry ground his teeth as frustration took hold. "I just met with Reynolds and unfortunately there's another matter I must look into."

"Something more important than two missing children?" Fletcher's astonishment only frustrated Henry more.

The sergeant wasn't saying anything Henry had already thought, yet what could he do? "A pressing situation at Whitehall requires immediate investigation. I'm to question a few individuals there now."

Fletcher shook his head. "See what happens when you save the queen? They expect you to delve into other areas of the government."

Under other circumstances, Henry would've chuckled. Instead, he merely met Fletcher's gaze. "Luckily, you are still free to make a trip to Blackfriars to see what occurred." Reynolds might not be pleased to hear Fletcher was helping with the mudlark murders, but that was a worry for another day.

"Excellent." Fletcher gave a decisive nod. "What do you suggest?"

As Henry considered, they continued along the busy walkway toward Whitehall, carriages, coaches, and riders already slowing traffic on the street.

His thoughts were in turmoil, but they had to do something. "Find Booth to discover what he knows—Carl as well. Send Constable Gibbons to where the girls live." He pounded his gloved fist into his opposite hand, wishing he could go with Fletcher. "Somehow we need to find Allard or whatever his name might be. He is our best lead. I feel certain he is involved with—"

Henry broke off, steps slowing at the sight before him. As if he had conjured the man with his mere thoughts, Mr. Allard stood a stone's throw down the street speaking heatedly with another man.

Fletcher followed Henry's gaze then glanced back at Henry in disbelief. "Isn't that..."

"I do believe it is." Henry fought the urge to run to catch the man and shake him until he told them whether he had anything to do with Agnes and Pudge's disappearance.

But he had lied once, and they had to assume he'd do so again. He was hiding something—perhaps something dangerous. They needed to take care.

Arresting Allard for providing false information might not solve anything. At this point, they had no evidence of any other crime. Henry studied the other man Mr. Allard spoke to, a terrible sense of knowing spreading through him when he recognized Reginald Davies, one of the men he was to question.

As they watched, Mr. Allard shook his head and stalked away, clearly angered by the conversation.

If there was any chance of Mr. Allard leading them to the girls, they had to take it.

"Follow Allard. Be sure he doesn't see you," Henry ordered. "We need to know if he has anything to do with the mudlarks' disappearance."

"Very well. And you?"

"I will see where the other end of this trail leads." He watched as Davies stalked toward Whitehall, wondering if it might be possible to take care of two problems at once.

Fletcher offered a grim smile. "Efficient as always. I'll send word if I discover anything of interest." He kept his focus on their suspect, watching as the man dodged a carriage to cross the street.

Henry touched his arm before his friend took more than a step. "Take care. He might very well be capable of murder. For all we know, this all involves more than children."

"And you as well." Then the sergeant was gone, disappearing as he crossed the crowded street.

Henry blew out a breath and tried to gather his thoughts. He assumed Booth had alerted Amelia as well and wanted to send her a message as quickly as possible to ensure she didn't attempt to take matters into her own hands. Unfortunately, duty called; Amelia would have to wait until after he had a word with Davies. He'd have to trust that she wouldn't do anything foolish.

Thirty-Four

Amelia paced the drawing room, unable to sit still. She spun to stride back to her writing desk, where the message from Captain Booth sat, and read it again, wishing it revealed more.

The fact that Agnes and Pudge were both missing was terrifying, yet how could she aid in finding them? She had already sent a message to Scotland Yard for Henry, and one for Fletcher as well, hoping they'd respond. She could do no more there.

Though tempted to return to the mudflats, that wouldn't help. The girls weren't there, that was the problem. Yet time was of the essence, considering what had happened to Charlie and Nora. The thought of how frightened the two girls must be had her pressing a hand to her mouth as a sob threatened to escape.

"Amelia? What is it?" Aunt Margaret asked as she entered the drawing room and saw her expression.

Amelia attempted to compose herself. "Two...two of the mudlarks have gone missing. Agnes and Pudge."

"Oh, no." Her aunt continued forward, eyes dark with concern. "What can we do? Should we attempt to search for them?"

"I would if I had any idea where to look." Amelia shook her head. "I can only guess they were trying to do their part to discover who killed their friends."

"But they're only children."

"Yes." Images of her own Lily flashed through her mind—of her laughing and playing, and then of her lying so still in her bed, face pale and thin. She drew a shuddering breath. Amelia handed her aunt Captain Booth's message. "This is all I know."

"Unbelievable." Aunt Margaret's concern was touching. "Surely we can do something."

"I've sent a message to Inspector Field to advise him of the situation." Amelia bit her lip as an idea came to mind. An undertaking she should've attempted previously, if her insecurities hadn't kept her from doing so.

"I will call on Mrs. Drake to ask if she is familiar with the fungi I found in the perfume bottle the first mudlark had. As a chemist, she might know something that could help. Perhaps she knows where it can be purchased, or how it's processed—anything that would provide a clue."

"Shall I accompany you?" her aunt asked.

"If you could remain here in case Henry sends word, I would be grateful."

Her aunt reluctantly nodded. "If you're sure."

"Thank you." Relief filled her lungs, helping them loosen. She didn't want anything to happen to her aunt and keeping her home was the best way to ensure that. "I won't be long. Hopefully by the time I return, we will know more."

She hurried out to request Fernsby to send for a hansom cab, then went upstairs to gather her things. Soon she was waiting impatiently in the front entrance, wondering if she should walk to a cab stand instead.

"Here it is," Fernsby said as he opened the door. "Please take care, madam."

"I will," Amelia called over her shoulder as she hurried down the steps and gave the driver Mrs. Drake's address before sitting back, clutching her reticule as if her life depended upon it, needing to hold tight to something.

With a steadying breath, she attempted to gather her emotions as the cab navigated the busy streets of the city, at last turning the corner from Carey Street onto Richmond Street.

Somehow, she didn't think Mrs. Drake would appreciate an emotional request that involved attempting to save orphans' lives. The woman was a scientist through and through, from what little Amelia knew. She couldn't claim the same herself, especially when children were involved.

She had a fragile hold on her upset by the time she knocked on Mrs. Drake's door and asked to see the lady, telling the butler it concerned an urgent matter. He advised her to wait, which proved a difficult task.

By the time he returned to escort her to a sitting room where Mrs. Drake waited, Amelia's hands were trembling. She held tight to her reticule with the hope the chemist wouldn't take notice.

"Mrs. Greystone, what an unplanned surprise." The woman's furrowed brow suggested it wasn't necessarily a pleasant one.

"Thank you for seeing me." Amelia attempted a polite smile.

"I confess that this isn't a particularly good time. I'm rather busy at the moment."

"I won't take much of your time." She would not be rushed. This was too important. "I have come upon a puzzling situation, and I was hoping you could help."

"Oh? What might that be?" Mrs. Drake's lips pursed, hinting at her impatience.

"It's regarding fungi."

The lady's eyes widened in response before she smoothed her expression—which was only natural when the topic was unusual.

"Fungi? I don't understand." Mrs. Drake studied her as if she were a specimen on a slide.

"Nor do I. But it seems a certain poisonous fungi is being used for nefarious purposes." Should she have said murder instead?

"Nefarious is an interesting term."

"But apt in this situation. Fungi has been used to kill several innocent children." While she knew of only two for certain, it could've been more—and there were two more missing. Agnes and Pudge. They had trusted her.

Impatience darkened the woman's eyes rather than sympathy. "How unfortunate, though I don't see how I can be of assistance. Now if you'll excuse me—"

"Your expertise in organic chemistry could prove helpful," Amelia plowed forward, hoping flattery would help. "Given your vast knowledge in the field, you are probably familiar with various fungi and how they could be used to kill someone."

"Mrs. Greystone, as you surely know, many mushrooms are poisonous. Children, indeed anyone, should avoid eating any that aren't known to be safe." She walked to the doorway and gestured to the opening for Amelia to go. "Now as I have said, I really can't spare more time."

Amelia ignored her and walked farther into the room, refusing to be dismissed. The woman had to know more, though why she wasn't willing to share that knowledge, Amelia did not know.

A stubborn streak Amelia hadn't realized she possessed took hold as she tapped a gloved finger on her chin, thoughts racing. "It's the strangest thing," she began.

Mrs. Drake snorted coldly. "Fungi are known to be unusual. There is much we have yet to understand about them."

"Yes, but the two victims were given the poison with food and wine." Amelia turned to hold the woman's gaze, hoping she appealed to her sense of curiosity since she didn't seem to have any empathy. "Aren't there some mushrooms that have an adverse effect when consumed with alcohol?"

Mrs. Drake's expression tightened. "I believe there are."

"Ink cap, isn't it? Do you know anyone who would be truly knowledgeable about them?"

Mrs. Drake stiffened, as if outraged Amelia had asked for someone else's expertise. "I might be of some help but not for several days. I am in the midst of a series of experiments that are of vital importance. I am sorry, but I really cannot visit with you any longer."

Disappointment rushed through Amelia. How disheartening to realize her heroine wasn't quite who she thought she was. Anyone who couldn't be bothered to save a child's life had no place in Amelia's world. "Well. I am sorry you think such things would take priority over a child's life. I won't trouble you again."

With a glare Amelia turned to go, only to hear an odd cry coming from the hallway. It almost sounded like a muffled scream. A questioning look at Mrs. Drake revealed her hostess was less than pleased by the noise.

"No need to concern yourself," the woman assured her even as the sound of a door slamming echoed through the house. "One of the maids is prone to dramatics."

"I see." But Amelia didn't. It was clear that something was amiss as Mrs. Drake looked most uncomfortable.

"Perhaps she saw a mouse. Now, as I said, I really must go." The pointed look the chemist gave her would've sent the Amelia of old scurrying to the door.

But the Amelia who had protected a child from murderers before wasn't so easily intimidated. Instead she studied her host, still puzzled by the sound...but other than ask to see the maid, or search the house, she didn't know how to find out what caused it.

"If anything comes to mind regarding the fungi, I would appreciate you letting me know." Amelia tried to think of something else she might say to keep the conversation going—but what, when Mrs. Drake clearly wanted her to leave?

"Of course." Mrs. Drake gestured again to the doorway. "I'm pleased you stopped by."

"Thank you for your time." Amelia walked slowly toward the stairs. The sounds she'd heard bothered her, enough to send chills down her spine. A voice in her head demanded action, but she had no idea what that would be.

She took her time as she made her way to the front door, listening carefully to no avail. She smiled politely at the butler when he held open the door. No further sounds reached her as she exited the home.

Amelia sighed as she walked toward the waiting hansom cab. The visit had been fruitless, yet she didn't regret it. There were so few options to pursue, and she'd taken the only one that had come to mind. So what should she do now?

"Where to, ma'am?" the hansom cab driver asked.

Amelia hesitated, then decided to return home to see if Henry had sent word. "My residence, please."

After a glance back at the house, she stepped into the cab, disappointment weighing like a burden on her shoulders. While she appreciated that Mrs. Drake had pressing business to attend to, how could hearing about children dying not appeal to her sense of humanity?

Clearly Amelia had been wrong about her, she decided as the cab rolled forward. But she wouldn't give up. There had to be someone else who could provide information on the fungi and—

"Hey!" The driver called out in alarm as the cab jerked to a halt. The door rattled, startling Amelia, before it opened to reveal a disheveled young girl standing there.

Amelia gasped, unable to make sense of the situation. "Agnes? How on earth—"

"Ma'am." Her chest heaved, eyes wide with fear. "I heard yer voice and knew I had to do somethin' before ye left. We've been so scared, not knowin' what to do."

A terrible realization dawned. "You've been in Mrs. Drake's house?"

Agnes nodded, her panic clear.

Amelia reached for the girl's arm and pulled her into the cab. "Tell me everything."

"There's no time." Agnes sank onto the bench beside her. "Pudge is still in there." Her face crumpled.

"Agnes." Amelia wrapped her arms around the girl and held her tight as a dreadful thought took hold. She leaned back to look into her eyes as her pulse raced. "Have you had anything to eat or drink since going to Mrs. Drake's?"

"No, and she's awful angry about us refusin' her fancy food." Amelia said a silent prayer as Agnes continued, "We remembered what ye said. How we shouldn't take food from strangers after what happened to Nora and Charlie."

Thank goodness. The relief coursing through Amelia weakened her limbs. "That is very good news."

"How are we gunna free Pudge? She's so scared. I feel terrible fer leavin' her." The girl's lower lip trembled as tears threatened.

"She won't be there for long." Amelia refused to allow it. Part of her was tempted to march inside and demand the girl's release—but if what she now feared was true, Mrs. Drake was capable of appalling deeds and wouldn't be above physical violence.

The thought had Amelia's heart racing even faster, but fear did not change the fact that she refused to allow Pudge to be hurt. She would do all in her power to save the girl, regardless of the consequences.

An image of Lily filled her mind, along with the terrible helplessness of being unable to protect her from the illness that had taken her away. She would've traded her own life for her daughter's, but that had not been an option. Guilt for not having saved her was something that still weighed on her.

A burden she could never escape. Irrational, perhaps, but there all the same.

Perhaps today—right now—she could make a difference. Doing so wouldn't bring back Lily, but rather lend aid to another girl in honor of her own daughter.

How she wished Henry were there. But he wasn't—not yet anyway.

"Where exactly is Pudge?" Amelia asked.

"Upstairs, all the way up, second door on the left. I was in the room next door and when the maid brung food, I stuffed a bit of cloth in the door latch so as it wouldn't shut proper when she locked it again."

"How very clever of you, Agnes. Well done." The girl's resourcefulness amazed her. Surely Amelia could follow her example. With that thought firmly in mind, she drew a deep breath. "I need you to be strong for a little while longer. Can you do that?"

The girl nodded, though she still looked frightened.

"I need you to take the cab to Scotland Yard and ask to speak with Inspector Field. Tell them it's urgent and that a life is at stake." The worry of someone like Inspector Perdy dismissing Agnes swept over her. "Do whatever it takes to make someone listen to you. Don't leave until they do. They must send help, preferably Inspector Field, to this house on Richmond Street."

Agnes glanced out the cab window toward the house, though it was no longer in view, and her chin lifted a notch. "I can do that."

"Good. Pudge is counting on both of us."

Amelia had her repeat the house address twice to make sure she remembered it, and then reached for the door only to feel Agnes's small hand grip her arm.

"What are ye goin' to do, ma'am?"

Amelia forced a smile. "I'm going back inside to find Pudge. I'm not leaving without her."

The girl gasped. "But that lady is mean—she won't let 'er go!"

"She won't have a choice." Amelia patted the girl's hand. "Now, there's not a moment to waste. I will see you soon."

"Take care," Agnes called out as Amelia shut the door behind her.

"Driver, take the girl to Scotland Yard." She reached into her reticule to pay him and included a hefty tip. "As fast as you can. The matter is urgent."

"Sure enough, madam." The driver flicked the reins, leaving Amelia on the pavement, feeling very much alone.

A glance about revealed no obvious source of help. Why was it that a constable was so rarely nearby when one needed him?

Gathering her courage, she turned toward the house, hoping Mrs. Drake wasn't yet aware of Agnes's escape. Though Amelia had no weapon to defend herself, she knew the truth and prayed that it, along with her wits, would be enough.

Thirty-Five

The corridor inside Whitehall teemed with people, all of whom ignored Henry. Clerks with papers rushed past, along with several recognizable faces. Henry continued forward, moving down the hall to look inside every open door with the hope of finding Reginald Davies.

The man's name had been bandied about by the press of late as he was the second son of an earl and already showed promise of a bright future in the government. He was young and handsome with enough charisma, not to mention an influential father, to make those around him want to believe every word that passed his lips. For some reason, that alone made Henry wary. To Henry's mind, the man's words were vague and his manner secretive.

Seeing him speaking with their only suspect for the mudlark murders confirmed Henry's suspicions. Though reluctant, Henry went with his instincts and continued farther into the depths of Whitehall to find the man.

At last, he came to an open doorway and saw Mr. Davies standing behind a desk, staring out a window. Before he had time to fully consider what he might say, Henry had knocked on the door and stepped inside, hat in hand. "Mr. Davies?"

The man turned to look at Henry with no sign of recognition. Given that he'd shaken Henry's hand shortly after he'd helped to save the Queen a few weeks ago, it made Henry like him even less. "Yes?"

"Excuse the interruption." Henry forced himself to be polite. There would be hell to pay if nothing came of his inquiry, and good manners might help ease the damage. "I am with Scotland Yard, Inspector Henry Field. I wanted to ask a few questions about the conversation you just had outside with a gentleman."

Mr. Davies frowned as his gaze took in Henry's bruised face. "What gentleman?"

Henry masked his frustration. "Bernard Allard, though that might not be his real name."

"You must have mistaken me for someone else." Davies' bored look of dismissal set Henry's teeth on edge. He'd shown little reaction to Allard's name, but Henry refused to be deterred.

"You were speaking with him less than five minutes ago," he persisted.

"As I said, you're mistaken." The glare Davies sent him would've withered a lesser man.

But not Henry. Especially not today. "I see. I'll just step outside and find one of the several other men who witnessed your conversation with the hope it aids your memory."

Henry turned to the door, though he had no idea if anyone else had seen the two men talking. Would he be able to find Fletcher in time to—

"Wait."

Henry turned back with a raised brow.

"I believe...yes, I remember now. What is it that you want to know?"

"His name, to start." Henry retrieved his notebook to make it clear this was only the beginning of the conversation.

"Bernard Marlowe," the man answered reluctantly.

"And your relationship?"

"None."

Henry searched for patience but found little. "How do you know him?" he asked, rephrasing the question.

"An acquaintance of an acquaintance." Mr. Davies waved a hand as if the matter was of little importance. "Nothing more."

"You had a rather lengthy conversation. What was the nature of it?"

"What possible business is it of yours?" Arrogance was visible in every inch of his demeanor, which did nothing to endear the man to Henry.

"I am investigating two murders and two missing persons." He didn't mention they were children. "Mr. Marlowe, if that is his real name, is a potential suspect."

If he hadn't been watching closely, he wouldn't have seen the slight tightening of Davies' expression before he masked it. "You can't think I know anything about murder."

"I'm sure you can understand that my suspicions are roused more with each minute that passes, and that you don't answer my question."

Mr. Davies scoffed as he turned aside. "You police must be desperate for information if you're wasting time speaking with me."

"And I ask you again, what was the nature of your conversation?" Henry knew losing his temper wouldn't serve any purpose, but that didn't keep it from flaring.

The man heaved a beleaguered sigh with a noble roll of the eyes. "Marlowe was to deliver something to me but failed to do so. I expressed my displeasure, and he has promised to rectify the situation."

"And what was that?"

"I'm afraid that's as much as I can tell you. Government business, you know." Mr. Davies folded his arms across his chest. "Now, unless you intend to arrest me for something, I must ask you to leave. I, unlike you, have important matters to attend to." He gestured toward his desk where several papers rested.

Frustration simmered in Henry. "Do you have his address?"

"I don't. Sorry." Clearly, he wasn't.

Henry flipped his notebook shut. "I am sure I will be speaking with you again soon. Thank you for your time, sir." He took his leave, shifting his shoulders to dispel the tension.

If not for Fletcher pursuing the newly named Marlowe, Henry would've planted himself in Davies' office until he learned something helpful. But given who his father was, Henry needed to tread carefully. He could already hear Reynolds warning him to avoid offending the nobility unless absolutely necessary.

He exited Whitehall and headed toward Scotland Yard, anxious to hear from Fletcher, though he supposed it would be at least an hour before he returned. It had been a foolish thought he'd had—in truth, he couldn't quite make a connection between Davies and the mudlark murders.

His steps slowed. *Or could he?*

The memory of the papers on Mr. Davies' desk filled his mind. One of them had been a news sheet, the paper folded to reveal a headline...something about better control in the Empire's colonies, much like the article Reynolds mentioned.

This helped confirm his suspicions, much like seeing Marlowe and Davies together. He still needed proof, irrefutable evidence that tied everything together.

But first, he had to find Agnes and Pudge. The image of the girls had him grimacing. *Were they still alive?* He could imagine how much their disappearance bothered Amelia.

Surely she wouldn't do anything rash.

Henry shook his head as he increased his pace. Captain Booth's message had said so little that he hoped she wouldn't place herself in danger. He'd send a message, asking her to stay away from the mudflats, just in case. Surely given everything that had happened, she would heed his request.

He opened the door to Scotland Yard only to be assaulted by the sound of angry voices renting the air.

Sergeant Johnson was out from behind his desk and Inspector Perdy was there as well, along with a constable. They all appeared to be in a tussle with another person, though Henry couldn't tell precisely what was happening.

"Release me!" a young voice shouted.

"I told you that you can't stay here." Perdy shook the arm of whoever he held, and Henry caught a glimpse of a child.

"Perdy, what is this about?" he demanded.

The other inspector turned toward Henry, his face red with temper. "Field, this is your doing—we can't have the likes of her coming in here and disrupting things."

"Inspector Field!" The girl tugged free of Perdy's grip and rushed toward him.

"Agnes?" He could hardly believe his eyes. "Are you all right?" He placed a comforting arm over her shoulders and glared at the other men.

"Yes." She glanced over her shoulder as if worried they might stop her from speaking with him. "I told 'em I had to see ye. Ye have to come, ye must come now!"

"What is it? Where's Pudge?" There was no sign of the other girl.

"It's Mrs. Greystone. She's savin' Pudge." She tugged on his arm to make certain he was listening. "They're both in terrible danger."

His heart dropped to his feet. "Where?"

Thirty-Six

The front door of Mrs. Drake's home somehow looked more formidable and less welcoming than before. Amelia drew a shaky breath, mouth dry at the thought of the monumental task before her.

Wanting to save Pudge was one thing. Actually doing it was quite another, especially given the fact that she had no idea how to go about it.

Amelia couldn't imagine what was going on inside Elizabeth Drake's home, but knowing Agnes, and Pudge still, had been held inside was all she needed to know.

Did she dare confront Mrs. Drake with what she knew and demand Pudge's release? She tended to think the woman would only deny it and insist she leave. Her servants could easily force Amelia out the door.

Did she ask to speak with Mrs. Drake again to continue her previous questions about fungi and make herself a nuisance until Henry arrived? That option sounded more appealing, but would that save Pudge from harm? What if Pudge gave in to hunger and ate what had been put before her? What if Agnes didn't reach Scotland Yard or Henry wasn't there? It could be hours before he returned, and Agnes could give him the message.

Her stomach clenched at the realization that she needed to be prepared to free Pudge herself if help did not arrive. While she didn't know if she was capable of the task, she knew she had to try.

Besides, there was no time to attempt anything else, not even send a message home to her aunt. If Pudge was to be saved, Amelia had to act now. She glanced about one last time for anyone who might aid her to no avail.

With a lift of her chin, she raised her fist to knock on the door only to pause. This was no time for good manners. There was no need to alert Mrs. Drake or the staff to her presence unless forced to. Heaven forbid she find herself locked in with Pudge.

Though it went against her upbringing which insisted on polite behavior at all times, Amelia tested the door latch, thrilled when it clicked open. She pushed the door to peek in, expecting to see the butler or another rush forward in protest.

Silence had never sounded so sweet. The entrance was empty.

Amelia slipped inside and closed the door behind her. As quietly as possible she hurried to the stairs, alarmed when the first step creaked. She paused but heard no footsteps or calls. With a hand pressed to her heart in an attempt to calm its rapid beat, she continued upward, hoping none of the other stairs announced her passage.

At the landing she paused to listen, but still the house was quiet. Going up another flight meant taking the risk of being visible to anyone in the drawing room. She briefly closed her eyes, holding the image of a frightened Pudge in mind. That was enough to have her moving forward even as she cursed the rustling sound the fabric of her gown made.

The drawing room appeared empty from what she could see. She turned to go up the next flight only to gasp at the sight of an elegant, narrow table in the hallway with a collection of crystal perfume bottles on a lace doily. They closely resembled the one Nora had held. Why hadn't she noticed those during her first visit?

Full of regret, she continued up the stairs as the sound of voices echoed through the house. She paused to determine where they came from, relieved it was from somewhere below her.

Had she shut the front door behind her?

Dear heavens, she hoped so. She would make a terrible burglar. One by one, she climbed the stairs, resisting the urge to run when that would surely make too much noise.

She reached the next landing where the bedrooms would be. Most of the doors were closed and all remained quiet. The house was even larger than she'd realized. With another steadying breath, she continued upward, repeating in her mind 'second door on the left' over and over.

Another creak of the stairs had her grimacing, but she was close now and hurried up the rest. The corridor was dark with only a small window at the far end to allow in daylight. She moved to the second door on the left and pressed her ear to the panel to listen but heard nothing.

With a gloved hand, she grasped the doorknob, beyond relieved when it turned in her hand. She slowly opened it, the darkness inside the room causing her to blink as her eyes adjusted.

"Pudge?" she whispered.

The girl didn't answer. Amelia stepped forward, at last able to see the dim outline of furnishings in the room.

It was empty.

Panic took hold. *Now what?* She hadn't prepared for this particular scenario.

She moved back into the corridor and studied the other closed doors. Perhaps Agnes's directions had been from the servants' stairs at the rear of the house. Of course. That made sense—it would be on the right.

Moving as quickly and quietly as possible, she moved down the hallway, crossed to the opposite side, and turned the knob but found it was locked.

Drat.

Amelia bent to examine the knob, feeling for a lock only to realize it required a key. She'd once read a mystery novel where a woman picked a lock with a hairpin, but she had doubt as to whether that was anything more than fiction. She glanced around in search of anything helpful, then caught sight of a shadow on the doorframe above her.

She stretched upward and plucked a skeleton key from the ledge, praying it opened the door. With shaking fingers, she tried inserting the key first one way and then the other, nerves getting the better of her.

The feel of the key turning the lock weakened her knees and Amelia quickly opened the door. "Pudge?" she whispered.

The room was bright compared to the dim hallway, a shuttered window allowing in cracks of daylight. It appeared to be a servant's bedroom with only a narrow bed, chair, table, and—

A small form raced forward to grip Amelia's waist as if her life depended on it. Pudge trembled in her embrace as Amelia said another silent prayer of gratitude.

"Thank goodness. Are you well?" she whispered as she eased back to look at the girl.

"I-I can't...believe ye're...here," Pudge said between shuddering breaths. Then she buried her face against Amelia's gown.

Amelia smoothed her hair with one hand and held her tightly with the other with the hope of calming the young mudlark. "Agnes found me. Now then, let us get you out of here."

In truth, Amelia could hardly believe she'd not only made it this far but managed to find Pudge. However, the most difficult task lay ahead—escaping with the girl in tow.

Amelia bent to look her in the eye and mouthed the words, "We need to be very quiet."

Pudge was clearly terrified. Tears streaked her cheeks, eyes wild and face pinched with fear.

"Are you ready?" whispered Amelia.

The girl continued to tremble but nodded.

Amelia forced a smile. "You are very brave." She reached for Pudge's hand and held it firmly to bolster them both and turned toward the door.

She peeked out to look up and down the corridor, deciding it best to leave the way she came as it was familiar. Besides, the backstairs would lead to the kitchen where servants would be. If only she knew which way Agnes had escaped.

Keeping with her decision, Amelia moved slowly but steadily and took care with each step to be as quiet as possible. The sound of Pudge's shaky breaths filled the silence. She tightened her grip on the girl's hand and looked back to offer another encouraging smile as she held a finger to her lips to remind her to be quiet.

Pudge's face crumpled, and Amelia paused to hold her once again. Though she wanted to promise her all would be well, she held back, far from certain of it.

Hadn't she whispered such words to Lily to no avail?

She might have failed then, but she wouldn't now. After a pat on the girl's back, she turned and started forward again, pulling Pudge along behind her.

As they reached the landing, she paused to listen but only heard faint sounds far below. She started down the stairs, remembering to avoid the one that squeaked and guiding Pudge to do the same.

One floor managed. Two more to go.

They were halfway down the next flight when a commanding voice from above them sounded. "Where do you think you're going?"

Amelia stiffened and glanced upward to see an angry Elizabeth Drake at the top of the stairs. "Run," she whispered and sped down the next few stairs gripping tightly to Pudge's hand, only to draw to another halt at the sight of a man standing below them.

A familiar man...

Recognition came too late.

"You," she glared. "You are the one who was at the mudflats." She glanced at Pudge. "Offering to train the children as servants."

How had she forgotten the man who'd acted as both an assistant and guard to Mrs. Drake during her lecture?

He offered a menacing smile before his gaze shifted to his employer, clearly waiting for her direction.

"Let us have a civilized conversation in the drawing room." Mrs. Drake started down the stairs, but Amelia remained where she was.

"I am leaving with the girl." Amelia was pleased at how confident she sounded when she was far from feeling it. She descended the stairs, breath shuddering, Pudge's hand still in hers. The girl whimpered, but Amelia kept moving, her legs trembling. They had to keep moving.

"Release her." Mrs. Drake's voice came from directly behind her, closer than Amelia would've liked.

Amelia ignored her and hurried down to the next landing near the drawing room.

"Mrs. Greystone!"

Mrs. Drake's commanding tone didn't pause Amelia's progress but the man who rushed up the steps and blocked their path did. She stepped around him, only to have him grab her arm—Amelia jerked free and pushed Pudge behind her, keeping hold of the girl's hand.

"You have no right to detain us!"

The man grabbed Amelia's arm again, his grip painfully tight this time. "You aren't going anywhere."

She tugged on her arm to no avail—then stomped on his foot and gained her freedom, managing several steps before he caught her again, this time holding both of her arms.

"You fool," Mrs. Drake berated him as she reached them. "You need only control the girl to control her." She took Pudge by the hand, forcing her to release Amelia's grasp and dragging the girl into the drawing room.

Amelia twisted free, sending the man another glare for good measure. He only smiled in return but didn't try to grab her again.

A glance toward the stairs where freedom beckoned had her cursing under her breath. *They'd been so close.* But she wasn't leaving without Pudge.

With her stomach clenched in knots and her entire body shaking, she followed Mrs. Drake into the drawing room.

Thirty-Seven

Henry left Agnes in the care of Sergeant Johnson with strict instructions to get her something to eat and not to let her out of his sight, not for even a moment. He requested additional constables and a police wagon be sent to the address she'd given him and prepared to leave.

Perdy watched with a scowl upon his face, still refusing to believe anything the girl had said, arguing there was no case involving mudlarks or their murders.

Henry ignored him, called for Constable Stephens with whom he'd worked before to join him, and hailed a passing hansom cab. Anyone was better than Perdy.

"This is an emergency," he told the driver after providing the address. "Make haste."

The ride felt endless as he gave Constable Stephens a brief summary of recent events.

"Poisoning children?" Stephens looked appalled. "Why would anyone do such a thing?"

"That is the piece of the puzzle we need to confirm." Henry's growing suspicion seemed too bizarre to consider. The bits and bobs together made an odd sort of sense, but he needed proof.

Agnes had told him the man who offered servant training had returned to the mudflats that morning. Few were around except her and

Pudge, and they had decided the only way to discover what happened to Nora and Charlie was to go with the man. They thought to find out where he was taking them, then escape to give the information to Carl or Henry.

But nothing had gone as planned.

Once they had arrived at the house they tried to flee, but the man caught them and forced them inside. They'd been locked in a room and eventually offered a meal but neither had eaten or drank anything because Amelia had warned them not to.

She had already saved them with that simple advice. *Did she realize that?*

Traffic came to a snarled halt, along with the cab, amid shouts and much swearing.

Henry growled as he glanced about to see a coach had cut off a carriage and now neither was moving as the drivers argued about who was to blame, blocking the street in the process.

"Go around," he called up to the cab driver. "We must hurry!"

Stephens stared at him in surprise. "I don't think I've ever heard you raise your voice."

"Mrs. Greystone and another child are in danger." He could barely stomach the thought. "There isn't a moment to lose."

After some maneuvering and more swearing, the cab driver managed to move around the mess and continued on their way, the horses moving at a fast clip.

Hardly able to sit still, Henry watched the passing scenery. The Richmond Street address Agnes had provided must be near the false address Marlowe had given and was also within a mile of the mudflats. Perhaps the pieces of the puzzle were coming together after all, and it might not be long before the picture was complete.

But first came Amelia and Pudge's safety. All else fell in comparison to that single priority.

"We must gain entrance," Henry advised Stephens. "I have no doubt Mrs. Greystone and a young girl are being held inside against their will."

"Yes, sir." Stephens looked less than confident at the prospect of doing so.

"No doubt servants will attempt to stop us," Henry warned. "Do not let them. We are the law."

Stephens straightened. "You may count on me."

Despite the constable's declaration, Henry wished Fletcher was at his side. He needed a seasoned professional rather than a young man untried with the bounds of his authority.

"I will gain entrance through the front," Henry continued. "You enter through the servants' door. Advise them you are on official business and don't let anyone halt you. Just keep moving forward until you find me. Every room must be searched, you understand?"

"Very well." The constable's expression turned fierce.

Good, Henry thought. They would both need to be unstoppable in the coming minutes.

The cab slowed as they approached the house, allowing Henry to study it. The neighborhood was affluent and the house equally so. A residence that size would have numerous servants, and they would more than likely be loyal to whoever paid their wages.

Hopefully, they would also be intimidated by the arrival of the police.

Henry hopped out and paid the driver, promising him a hefty tip if he waited.

"I'll be here as long as ye need me," the cabbie advised with a tip of his hat.

"Ready?" Henry asked Stephens.

"Undoubtably." The constable tugged on the bottom of his jacket as he studied the house. "Where do you think the servants' entrance is?"

The question gave Henry pause. The young constable was even more inexperienced than he'd realized. "More than likely over there." He pointed toward the steps.

Henry led the way, but movement from the corner of his eye halted him. He turned, shocked to see Fletcher hurrying toward him from the edge of the property. "Fletcher?"

"How did you know where I was?" The sergeant's confused expression was almost comical.

"Agnes gave me the address." Henry didn't bother to explain the whole story, there wasn't time. "You followed the suspect here?" he asked as he started forward again.

"Yes, I waited a short time, but he's still inside. I was just leaving to send word to you. How did Agnes know of this house?" Then awareness dawned. "This is where she and Pudge were?"

"Pudge is still in there, along with Mrs. Greystone."

"Damn!" Fletcher grimaced. "Oh, blast, don't tell the missus. So Allard, or whatever his name might be, is involved." He nodded. "Just as we thought. What's our plan?"

Henry returned his focus to the residence, praying both Pudge and Amelia were unhurt. "Assist them to safety and arrest those involved."

"Very well. Are you ready, young man?" Fletcher asked Stephens.

The constable nodded but looked rather nervous.

The situation weighed heavily on Henry's shoulders, but he couldn't imagine allowing anyone to take his place. No one was more vested in seeing Amelia and Pudge to safety than he was.

He turned to Stephens. "It's imperative that you gain entrance however necessary. Search each floor for Mrs. Greystone and the girl. Don't let anyone stop you and then find us," he repeated.

Stephens glanced at Fletcher, seeming reassured by the sergeant's presence. That made two of them. "I won't, sir."

"Fletcher and I will enter through the front, and we'll meet inside."

They strode forward with Stephens hurrying around the side of the house.

Henry knocked on the door then immediately tried the knob but found it locked, causing impatience to simmer inside him. "Police," he shouted. "Open up."

Each second that passed without a response felt like an eternity.

"Shall we—" Fletcher began when the door swung open.

"Yes?" The butler who had appeared seemed rather frazzled.

"Inspector Field. Step aside."

"I cannot allow you in," the servant stated.

"Step aside," Henry repeated. "It is not a request but an order."

Fletcher cleverly placed a foot in the doorway, making their intention clear.

The servant lifted his nose imperiously. "The lady of the house is otherwise engaged at the moment and cannot speak with you."

"I insist." Henry shared a look with Fletcher who dipped his head to signal his readiness, shifting to turn his shoulder to the door.

"I cannot—"

Henry moved forward with Fletcher directly beside him, sending the butler stumbling back. "Where are they?"

"You must not—"

"Never mind, we'll find them ourselves," Henry snapped as they moved toward the stairs, leaving the servant sputtering.

Voices sounded from the rear of the house, and he hoped that meant Stephens had gained entrance as well. But he wouldn't relax until he saw both Amelia and Pudge.

The realization of what Amelia had done—coming here when she had to have known the girls were in danger—weakened his knees. He wanted to praise and berate her in equal measure, and perhaps hold her as well; at least until his knees stopped shaking and he could reassure himself she was safe.

He pushed aside his thoughts as he reached the landing, glancing around in search of their target. The murmur of someone talking drew his notice, and he and Fletcher followed an unfamiliar feminine voice into the drawing room.

"I told you—"

Their arrival cut off the woman's heated words.

"Henry!" Amelia's startled cry was music to his ears.

"Amelia." His gaze held on her, beyond relieved to see she appeared well, as did Pudge, though fear was etched in the girl's face. No wonder—her arm was being gripped by the unfamiliar woman.

"What is the meaning of this?" the woman demanded, glaring at him.

"That is what I want to know," Henry advised as he eased toward Amelia. "Why are you holding these ladies against their will?"

"What?" A trill of laughter tinkled in the air, sounding much like broken glass. The determination in the woman's narrow face despite being confronted by authorities was concerning. "What tales have been shared with you, sir?" She lifted a brow. "Your name?"

"Inspector Field and Sergeant Fletcher of Scotland Yard. And you are?"

The woman didn't look familiar. She was several years his senior, well-dressed, confident, and did not seem like the type to take in orphans out of the goodness of her heart.

"Elizabeth Drake." She said the name with pride, clearly expecting him to recognize it.

He glanced at Amelia as he searched his memory. "Ah...the chemist." He'd heard of her. Now everything made more sense.

Amelia nodded, chest heaving, eyes frantic. "Her assistant is the one who was seen speaking to the children. He's here somewhere."

"I see." Henry glanced behind them, then returned his focus to the older woman. "Care to explain, Mrs. Drake, why you've been poisoning mudlarks?" He kept his tone even and matter-of-fact.

The woman scoffed as she shook her head, still holding the girl. "Clearly you've been misinformed. I am working closely with the government on a special project of national importance."

"Is that right? Does it involve poisoning people using fungi?"

Pudge let out a whimper at his words, and Amelia sent the girl a comforting look.

Shock rippled across Mrs. Drake's face, sending satisfaction through Henry's chest.

"You have no right to barge in here." She tightened her hold on Pudge. "You must leave. Now."

"You are under arrest for the murder of innocent children." Henry had no doubt evidence would be found in the place to prove it.

"Henry!" Amelia called, looking past his shoulder.

He turned as Fletcher made a strange sound. The large man fell to his knees, eyes wide with disbelief, before he toppled forward to lie motionless on the floor.

"No!" Amelia's cry matched his own and Henry stilled at the sight of the man who'd struck Fletcher—the same man the sergeant had followed here.

The man's grim smile and the chill in his blue eyes were concerning, but the pistol in his hand caused fear to creep along Henry's skin, along with Fletcher's still form on the carpet.

Did he yet live?

"Bernard Marlowe, I presume." Henry did his best to keep his composure but worry for his friend shook him.

Marlowe's eyes narrowed at Henry's use of what had to be his true name, though he neither confirmed nor denied it.

"This is my assistant." Mrs. Drake sent the man a nod of approval. "Mrs. Greystone has already had the pleasure of making his acquaintance."

Mr. Marlowe pointed the pistol at Henry. "To the attic, madam?"

"Yes, that would be helpful," Mrs. Drake agreed. "I intend to finish my conversation with Mrs. Greystone."

The tables had turned far too quickly, Henry thought, worry coursing through him. He had no intention of leaving Amelia and Pudge in the woman's company, though the pistol suggested he wouldn't be given much of a choice.

He met Amelia's gaze, heart hammering at the fear in her eyes. He wanted to reassure her, but how? Stephens had yet to make an appearance. Henry couldn't hear him, so had no idea whether he'd been halted by the servants or might yet arrive. The idea of the inexperienced constable saving the day was impossible to consider.

It was up to Henry.

"What exactly is your plan?" Henry asked Mrs. Drake, ignoring the man and the weapon. "Poisoning leaders abroad who don't agree with the policies of the British government?" He lifted a brow, remembering the headline of the news sheet he'd seen on Davies' desk as well as what Reynolds had mentioned. "Those in Egypt, perhaps?"

The slight widening of Mrs. Drake's eyes suggested he had struck near the truth.

"Was this the suggestion of Reginald Davies or did you approach him with the scheme?" He took a casual step closer to the woman, determined to free Pudge and hoping the conversation would distract Mrs. Drake.

"I don't know what you're talking about." Mrs. Drake's look of disdain was almost convincing—except for the hint of fear in her eyes.

"Did Mrs. Greystone mention that she already determined that you have been testing the dosage and how it works with food and alcohol?"

Mrs. Drake's attention shifted to Amelia.

"She is far too modest about her skills in the laboratory," Henry continued in a calm voice even as he glanced at Fletcher, hoping to see the man stirring. The man hadn't moved an inch.

"You know nothing. Both of you are only guessing," the woman protested. "You have no proof."

"Mrs. Greystone surmised that the children were given wine which changes the effect of some poisons." He looked to Amelia. "Which fungi was it?"

"Ink cap." The words came out in a squeak, and she cleared her throat. "The addition of alcohol increases the toxicity."

"How clever you are, Mrs. Greystone," Mrs. Drake said grudgingly. "More than I would have guessed."

Amelia appeared less than flattered by the compliment. He didn't blame her.

The woman's assistant still held the pistol with a steady hand and seemingly unending patience, much to Henry's dismay.

"Marlowe, please take the inspector to the attic, and then return for his associate." She tipped her head toward Fletcher. "Or should I say, the associate's body."

"Of course, madam." The man took a step toward Henry.

Henry held up a hand to delay him, doubtful it would do any good. "How long has the experiment been underway?"

"Longer than you know."

"How many children have you murdered?" Amelia asked, voice fraught with emotion.

"Oh, please. No one even realized they were gone. Orphans serve no purpose." Mrs. Drake shrugged, seeming to easily dismiss the wrongness of her actions. "We did them a favor by ending their miserable lives, as well as the residents of London. Sometimes the poison *is* the remedy. Fewer mouths to feed leaves more for those of us who serve a purpose."

Amelia's mouth dropped open in horror. "They are children—innocent and defenseless—"

"Certain sacrifices must be made if we as a country want to move forward."

The fervor in the woman's voice disturbed Henry at a bone-deep level. She wasn't the only one who espoused such radical and ridiculous notions.

"Already, the sun never sets on the Empire," Mrs. Drake continued, "but our work is far from complete. The entire world will be ours with the help of science and the discoveries being made."

"No." Amelia took another step forward, her previous fear seeming to fall away. "Science should better the world. Help solve its problems. Starting at home."

"We are doing exactly that if you would but get out of our way. Advances come at a cost, and we must be willing to pay those." Mrs.

Drake glanced at the girl whose arm she still held with disdain. "Thus far, the price has been modest."

"You murdered Nora and Charlie. How many others?" Henry demanded as he shifted closer to Marlowe but kept his focus on the chemist. He would leave Pudge to Amelia to save and do what he could to disarm Marlowe.

Mrs. Drake glanced between them, clearly frustrated they didn't agree with her obvious insanity. "It hardly matters. A few more tries," she nodded as she looked at first Henry, then Amelia, and finally Fletcher, "with the three of you to finalize the dosage for adults, we will be ready. We don't need willing subjects. Unconscious ones will do."

She turned to Marlowe as if done talking.

Her words proved that she had truly lost touch with reality if she believed murdering two members of the police and an upstanding widow would be overlooked the same way the mudlark murders had been.

But Henry did not need to say that. Pudge let out an enraged scream, the high-pitched sound surprising them all. The girl kicked the woman on the shin. "That's fer Nora." She did it again. "That's fer Charlie." Then she shoved Mrs. Drake, causing her to stumble back. "And fer scarin' me and Agnes."

Before the girl had completed her tirade, Henry rushed to Marlowe and pushed the pistol upward. The gun went off, the sound startling Henry as he didn't know what—or who—the bullet might have struck.

To his relief, Stephens ran into the room at the sound of the shot and quickly joined Henry to subdue the struggling man. Fletcher stirred and managed to trip Marlowe and put him off balance. Henry wrenched the gun from the man's grasp and stuffed it in his own pocket. He and Stephens took the now unarmed man to the ground, then Henry placed a knee on Marlowe's back to hold him down.

"Well done," he muttered to Stephens as the constable jerked the man's hands behind him to snap handcuffs on his wrists.

"Sorry for the delay." Stephens huffed as he gripped Marlowe to ensure he remained in place. "The butler was more of a problem than I anticipated."

Henry stood to see Amelia holding a crying Pudge, and Mrs. Drake fleeing through the doorway. "Hold!" he called as he chased after her, catching her arm before she reached the stairs.

"You fool!" She attempted to jerk free. "You are ruining everything."

"On the contrary." Henry pulled her, still struggling, back into the room, relieved to see Fletcher now standing with a hand on the back of his head. "Are you all right?"

"Mostly." Fletcher shook his head. "Caught me by surprise. I suppose we'll have matching bumps." The sergeant drew cuffs from his pocket and handed them to Henry to secure Mrs. Drake.

"Mrs. Greystone," the woman pleaded, panic in her voice. "Amelia—surely you see that science must prevail at all costs."

"No, it shouldn't." Amelia shook her head. "I hope one day you see the error of your ways." She turned her back on the woman to speak low to Pudge.

The sound of voices and footsteps on the stairs reached Henry, and several constables filled the room. Stephens directed two of them to take the prisoners downstairs then turned to Henry. "What's next, sir?"

"Search the house for evidence of poisonous fungi—but for God's sake don't touch it."

"You heard him." Stephens sounded downright commanding as he strode out of the room with the remaining constables following him. "We'll search from top to bottom."

"We may have created a monster," Fletcher advised as he watched Stephens go.

"I have no doubt you will rein him in if necessary." Henry sent him a questioning look. "Will you be all right?"

"My pride is hurt worse than my head. And that's saying something." Fletcher grimaced. "I should've been on the watch for him, but with everything going on, I let down my guard."

"As did I." Henry pointed to a chair. "Rest for a moment before we join the search."

Fletcher complied, indicating just how much his head must hurt. Henry knew that sort of pain all too well.

Henry moved to Amelia and Pudge, placing a hand on the girl's shoulder. "Miss Pudge, you were a tremendous help today. And very brave. Agnes as well."

She smiled, wiping her eyes with the back of one hand. "That lady made me so mad."

"You weren't the only one." Amelia rubbed a hand along the girl's shoulder. "Well done, Pudge."

"Thank ye. I can't wait to tell Agnes what 'appened."

"Soon," Henry promised then studied Amelia. "You were quite the hero today, too."

She frowned. "I should've realized Mrs. Drake could have been behind it all along. I attended her lecture recently and have so admired her. It's disappointing to realize she isn't who I thought."

"Indeed. To think she was using her knowledge for such a terrible purpose. Still, I am grateful for your help." He held her gaze, aware of the others in the room, but knowing he had to speak. "And...and very relieved you weren't hurt."

"As am I." She smiled, twin spots of delicate pink appearing on her cheeks.

"Would you be able to escort Pudge to the Yard where Agnes awaits her?" he asked.

"Of course. I will also send word to Captain Booth to let him know the girls are safe." She glanced toward the doorway. "I am assuming you will be here for some time yet."

"Yes, I believe so."

"She has more than one laboratory, so if you don't find what you're looking for here, you might check the others."

"Thank you." There was so much more he wanted to say, but this was neither the time nor the place. "I...I will speak with you soon."

With one last look he departed with Fletcher at his side, pushing aside the rush of emotions that threatened. Those would have to wait as well. For now, it was enough to know that they'd once again solved the mystery. They could rest easy knowing the mudlarks were now safe.

Epilogue

Two weeks later...

Henry knocked on Amelia's door, anticipation coursing through him. The invitation to dine with her had pleased him more than it should, giving him something to look forward to after the difficulty of the last few weeks. The evening was cold but clear, stars faint in the inky black sky.

He'd spoken with her a few times since the arrest of Elizabeth Drake and Bernard Marlowe, wanting to keep her abreast of events, but those conversations had been far too brief as far as he was concerned.

No need to be excited, he reminded himself. Her aunt might still be visiting and could very well join them.

How he hoped not.

He wanted at least a few minutes of Amelia' company to himself. There was much he had to tell her.

"Inspector Field." Fernsby's warm welcome as he opened the door had Henry smiling in return. "Good to see you, sir."

"And you, Fernsby. I hope the day finds you and your good wife well."

"Indeed, thank you." He took Henry's things and nodded toward the stairs. "Mrs. Greystone is in the drawing room."

"Thank you." Henry forced himself not to take the stairs two at a time but still felt breathless by the time he passed through the doorway.

A fire blazed in the hearth and lamplight cast a cozy glow about the inviting room. He sighed with appreciation at the sight but quickly sought Amelia.

"Good evening," Henry said, then halted, surprised to see her wearing a purple gown with black lace. It was an astonishing sight; he'd never seen her in anything except black or gray since the day he'd come to tell her of her husband's death.

"Henry." She quickly stood to greet him, her joyous smile somehow settling his world. "I'm so pleased you could come."

"Thank you for the invitation." He dipped his head then glanced about. "Will Miss Baldwin be joining us this evening?"

"No, she has departed to a townhouse of her own."

"Oh?" He wasn't entirely clear if that was good or bad news.

Amelia moved to the sideboard to pour them drinks without even asking. The act hinted at a level of familiarity that he welcomed. She brought them back and handed him a whiskey before returning to her seat.

"Yes, she has become a member of a church near Blackfriars and met some new friends. The ladies have banded together, deciding something must be done to help the mudlarks and other orphans in the area. They have found food and shelter for the children, all of them, and offered them a chance for schooling as well." Amelia leaned forward as if to impart a secret. "Carl is indignant. And Mrs. Salem is one of the members, which should put an end to her husband's antics."

"Isn't that something." Henry marveled at the news, though the woman before him was a greater marvel still.

"I knew something was bothering her. Though she has yet to share any details, I believe it has helped her to find a purpose. She has done exactly that." Amelia's happiness added to his own.

"Does that include Agnes and Pudge?"

"Of course. They were the first to accept the offer. I have visited them and the others, and they seem to be adjusting to their new circumstances quite well."

"I'm sure they have." Henry nodded, more than pleased at the thought. Finally, the children would be cared for properly, as they deserved—as children.

"My editor has agreed for me to do an article on the mudlarks to shed light on their plight. He has even agreed to make a donation toward their education."

"How generous."

"Henry, I must ask. What has become of Reginald Davies?"

He shook his head, irritation bubbling in his stomach at the man's name. "Very little, I'm afraid. He has been removed from his position in government, but no charges have been filed."

"Not a surprise, given who his father is. But at least he's been stopped."

For now. But Henry didn't say that out loud. This time together was too precious to only talk of criminals.

The conversation continued until dinner was announced. The meal of roast beef with potatoes, carrots, and gravy, was one of his favorites, and he savored each bite. Dare he hope she had remembered his favorite, trifle, for dessert?

He treasured each time he made Amelia laugh. Once the dinner plates were cleared, he leaned back in his chair, nervous to ask his next question. "I wondered if you would like to join me for dinner at my mother and father's home in the coming weeks. Perhaps even for Christmas, if...if you don't have other plans."

Genuine regret touched her features. "That is a very kind invitation. However, I'm taking the train to spend the week at my parents' home."

"How nice that will be." He forced a smile though his chest filled with disappointment. "Perhaps another time."

"When?" She lifted a brow expectantly.

He hesitated, surprised by the forward question. "They are anxious to meet you. Would before you depart for the holiday be acceptable?" Goodness, was that far too eager? "Or after would be fine, too. Whatever is convenient for you."

"I don't leave until five days before Christmas and am at your disposal until then. I'm visiting Maeve before I return home."

"Good. That will be very special." With a quiet breath in an attempt to calm his excitement, Henry nodded. "I will see what is possible and let you know."

"Perfect."

Then Fernsby arrived with a trifle. Life didn't get much better than this.

"Henry, I would like to ask you something."

"Oh?" Given the pensive look on her face, he wasn't certain what to expect.

"Mrs. Drake said she heard of my interest in chemistry from someone, and since she also knew I had worked with Scotland Yard, I thought it must've been you."

He shook his head. "No, it wasn't. Director Reynolds knew of your involvement in the ravenkeeper case, of course. I also told him of your assistance with the poisoning of the mudlarks but only after her arrest.

I'm not certain who else knows, other than Fletcher of course, but he wouldn't have mentioned it to anyone."

"Interesting." Yet the news seemed to unsettle her, though he didn't know why.

"Is anything amiss?"

"No, no, it's fine. I was just curious." She shook her head as if to dismiss the question.

"I hesitate to mention it, but Elizabeth Drake has a concerning connection to London's criminal underworld." Henry fingered the stem of his wine glass as he pondered the link. He didn't want to frighten her with the information but rather warn her.

"Oh?"

"We are still sorting through the details, but from what we know thus far, she knows one or two of the more concerning criminals in the city." He watched Amelia, wondering at her thoughts about the information. "I assume her nefarious plan has been halted with her arrest, but that relationship makes one wonder."

"Indeed, it does." Her eyes narrowed as she considered the news.

"Amelia, I can't thank you enough for all you did to help save the mudlarks and solve the mystery." He raised his glass with a nod to her, she lifted hers, and they both took a sip.

"I only wish I put the facts together sooner."

He nodded with a wry smile. "I hate to admit how often I feel the same."

"What will be your next case?" she asked.

"I already have several. Unfortunately, the missing man we were searching for has been declared dead and shifted to a murder investigation."

Henry hadn't intended to share anything of the case, but Amelia's interest proved irresistible, and he found himself sharing a few details.

He didn't know exactly how it would proceed but was anxious to find justice for Spencer—for all those touched by crime who entered his life.

"I know it might sound odd, but I do enjoy hearing about your cases." Amelia led the way back to the drawing room. "And if there is ever a time when I can lend assistance, I would be happy to do so."

"I just might take you up on your offer." He smiled, his feelings mixed. While he appreciated all she'd done to help solve the previous cases, he hesitated to put her at risk again. How could he ask more of her or consider deepening their friendship until he discovered who had killed her husband—and why?

Solving Matthew Greystone's murder—the reason he'd come to know this intelligent, attractive lady to begin with—was once again his top priority.

Look for the third book in The Field & Greystone Series, The Gravesend Murder.

The past proves deadly when a witness to a case gone cold is murdered—a chilling message meant to silence those involved...

Summoned to Gravesend, Scotland Yard Inspector Henry Field is shocked to discover the body of a man he interviewed only days earlier. The brutal timing suggests his inquiries into the cold case that has haunted him for well over a year struck a nerve. But with more questions than clues, the investigation threatens to once again grind to a halt.

Widow Amelia Greystone's quiet life is upended by murder for a third time, this one striking dangerously close to home. A mysterious clue hidden in her late husband's desk compels her to investigate—a decision that forces her to confront the possibility that she didn't know her husband at all, and their life together was a lie.

As Amelia and Henry's paths intertwine, a second body is found, dragging them deep into the shadows of London's underworld. There, the lines between loyalty and betrayal blur, and the answers they seek may cost more than they're prepared to lose.

Dark secrets, surprising twists, and a relentless killer collide in this gripping historical mystery.

Order your copy of The Gravesend Murder today!

Author's Notes

I hope you enjoyed reading *The Mudlark Murders*. As with the first book, *The Ravenkeeper's Daughter*, this one was also inspired by newspaper articles my sister sent regarding the history of mudlarking and another about the sailing barges. I look forward to seeing what she sends me next.

The Thames Sailing Barge Match, held each summer, is the world's second-oldest sailing competition and helps to preserve a British tradition. Only a couple dozen of the hefty barges remain, though there used to be thousands. Henry Dodd, known as London's Golden Dustman, truly did begin this tradition.

Ice was delivered daily to those who requested it by leaving a small sign in the window. The ice-man chiseled off a block for customers to use to keep perishable food cold. Much of the ice came from Norway, though lakes and ponds in England also provided it if the temperatures were cold enough. It was stored in deep wells in the city which kept it frozen even in summer months.

Punch magazine did indeed refer to the Criminal Investigation Unit as the "defective department" in the 1880's.

In December 1867, the Counter Revolutionary Secret Service Department was specially formed to help fight against the threat of Fenian terrorism but was disbanded the following year. I took liberties with the department in this book, but its secretive practices were considered highly suspicious by some within the government.

Forgive my less-than-scientific explanation, but ink cap mushrooms, also sometimes called tippler's bane, are named for the black ooze they develop, which resembles ink. They contain mycotoxin coprine that is converted to a poisonous form when consumed with alcohol.

Thank you for reading *The Mudlark Murders*. Please look for *The Gravesend Murder*, the third book in the Field & Greystone series.

Other Books by Lana Williams

The Field & Greystone Series

The Ravenkeeper's Daughter, Book 1
The Mudlark Murders, Book 2
The Gravesend Murder, Book 3

The Mayfair Literary League

A Matter of Convenience, Book 1
A Pretend Betrothal, Book 2
A Mistaken Identity, Book 3
A Simple Favor, Book 4
A Christmastide Kiss, Book 5
A Perilous Desire, Book 6
A Sweet Obsession, Book 7
The Wallflower Wager, a novella connected to The Mayfair Literary League and the Revenge of the Wallflowers series

A Secret Seduction, Book 8

The Wicked Widows Collection

To Bargain with a Rogue, a novella

The Duke's Lost Treasures

Once Upon a Duke's Wish, Book 1
A Kiss from the Marquess, Book 2
If Not for the Duke, Book 3

The Seven Curses of London Series

Trusting the Wolfe, a Novella, Book .5
Loving the Hawke, Book I
Charming the Scholar, Book II
Rescuing the Earl, Book III
Dancing Under the Mistletoe, a Novella, Book IV
Tempting the Scoundrel, a Novella, Book V
Romancing the Rogue, A Regency Prequel
Falling For the Viscount, Book VI
Daring the Duke, Book VII
Wishing Upon A Christmas Star, a Novella, Book VIII
Ruby's Gamble, a Novella

Gambling for the Governess, Book IX
Redeeming the Lady, Book X
Enchanting the Duke, Book XI

The Seven Curses of London Boxset (Books 1-3)

The Secret Trilogy

Unraveling Secrets, Book I
Passionate Secrets, Book II
Shattered Secrets, Book III

The Secret Trilogy Boxset (Books 1-3)

The Rogue Chronicles

Romancing the Rogue, Book 1
A Rogue's Reputation, a Novella, Book 2
A Rogue No More, Book 3
A Rogue to the Rescue, Book 4
A Rogue and Some Mistletoe, a Novella, Book 5
To Dare A Rogue, Book 6
A Rogue Meets His Match, Book 7
The Rogue's Autumn Bride, Book 8
A Rogue's Christmas Kiss, a Novella, Book 9
A Rogue's Redemption, a short story, Book 10

A Match Made in the Highlands, a Novella

Falling for A Knight Series

A Knight's Christmas Wish, Novella, Book .5
A Knight's Quest, Book 1 (Also available in Audio)
A Knight's Temptation, Book 2 (Also available in Audio)
A Knight's Captive, Book 3 (Also available in Audio)

The Vengeance Trilogy

A Vow To Keep, Book I
A Knight's Kiss, Novella, Book 1.5
Trust In Me, Book II
Believe In Me, Book III

Contemporary Romances

Yours for the Weekend, a Novella

If you enjoyed this story, I invite you to sign up to my newsletter to find out when the next one is released. I'd be honored if you'd consider writing a review!

About the Author

Lana Williams is a USA Today Bestselling Author with over 50 historical fiction novels filled with mystery, romance, adventure, and sometimes, a pinch of paranormal to stir things up. Her latest venture is with historical mysteries.

She spends her days in Victorian, Regency, and Medieval times, depending on her mood and current deadline. Lana calls the Rocky Mountains of Colorado home where she lives with her husband and a spoiled rescue dog named Sadie. Connect with her at https://lanawilliams.net/.

Printed in Dunstable, United Kingdom